Memories of You

Elin Kind

Contents

Chapter One

I didn't want to think. I didn't want to feel. I didn't want to get off the bus. None of it. Thinking and feeling only meant pain, and I was so sick of that.

Fresh, humid air reached my nose as I stepped on the concrete outside, long-buried memories flooding back to me. I bit my lip to stop it from shaking and brushed my fingers against the pendant around my neck, engraved simply with *J & S*. It had been an entire year since I was last home. An entire year since I lost my twin brother.

James had always been my rock, the one with me through thick and thin. With him gone, the only family I had left was my dad. I loved him, but our relationship was strained at the best of times.

I kept my head down as I walked down the road, passing the *Welcome to Waterbury, WA* sign at the end of the bus station. The strap of my bag dug into my shoulder, and my hair fell over my face to create a sweaty but necessary barrier between me and the world.

A few minutes later, I stopped outside my childhood home. Everything looked just like I remembered it. The tan siding on the Cape Cod-style property was peeling, the grass needed to be mowed, and the pots by the front door all held long since dead plants. The hills weren't quite able to cover the view of Mount St. Helens in the background, the white and gray tips peeking over the tree line.

The rose bushes that lined the path up to the steps were the only things that seemed looked after. Mrs. Johnson, our neighbor across the street, always took care of them. With a quick glance over my shoulder revealed her watching me from her window. I gave a brief wave, then turned around and dragged my feet up the old wooden steps, not in the mood for a conversation about flowers, the weather, or anything deeper.

The key was in the same spot as always, under the plant pot at the top of the steps. The knot in my chest tightened and my nausea grew stronger as I swung the front door open. My bag fell to the hardwood floor with a thud, the familiar stench of alcohol hitting me like a punch to the stomach with the first inhale.

"Dad?" I croaked out into the silent and desolate house, then cleared my throat to try again. "Dad, are you home?" My voice echoed down the corridor as I pulled my shoes off.

The small hallway had several doorways leading to different parts of the house. To my left was the kitchen, small but practical. Just like the outside siding, the cabinet doors could use a fresh coat of paint, and the curtains in the window were the same ones my mom had put up when we moved in over twelve years ago. My dad and James didn't notice things like that. I never pointed it out because I didn't want to cause more pain, but staring at them day in and out growing up was hard.

It wasn't so much that my mom wasn't here anymore—I'd gotten used to that a long time ago. No, it was the little things that hurt. The fabric she'd bought from the store downtown to sew into the curtains, the vase on the dining-room table that used to hold fresh flowers but now only held fake ones, the scratches on the kitchen counter she would create because she never used a chopping board. The things that give life to a house. A life she left without even a look back.

James had been that life after she left—the only thing holding Dad and me together. But now? I wasn't even sure I could hold myself together, let alone Dad. But I had to try. I owed that to James.

I wiped my clammy palms on my jean shorts and trudged to my right towards the living room. The curtains were all shut, only a small amount of light shining in from the top. The TV was on, producing a gentle glow across the room that was just enough to spot a figure on the couch.

There he was. Ladies and gentlemen, David Harris. Fast asleep—passed out—on the old leather couch, beer cans littering the floor and the seat beside him. He wore his greasy work clothes, and by the looks of the leather couch, it wasn't the first time he'd forgotten to change when he got home. The stink of alcohol hung in the room, almost like smog.

"Dad, it's me. I'm home." I crinkled my nose and composed myself before I stepped over to him to nudge him. He grunted and barely opened his eyes enough to take me in. Glazed and distant, the acrid smell of his breath forced me to take a step back, promptly bringing up more terrible memories that fought for control with a burning in my throat.

"Stella, you're home!" He yawned, making his face wrinkle. His black hair was speckled with silver strands around his forehead, and the stubble he'd once sported looked more like an unkempt attempt at a beard. "When did you get here? I was about to come and pick you up." He rubbed his hands over his face as he tried to wake himself up. His foot kicked the beer bottles on the floor and he gave me an apologetic smile as he picked them up.

"I got in early. I tried texting you, but you must have been asleep."

"Yeah, sorry. I was catching a few more hours of sleep before work." He avoided my gaze as he spoke, a telltale sign he was lying.

"How is work?" I asked, trying to fish for information while not pushing so hard he would clam up.

"Oh, work is work. My boss has been hounding me more than usual lately."

Yeah, because you don't show up when you're meant to.

Dad had been an alcoholic most of my life. It started before Mom left and was probably one reason she'd had enough. The ups and downs in their marriage usually transpired at the same time as his worst episodes. He'd been pretty good before James died, but now he wasn't even the shell of the man he could be. He was a walking zombie. Drinking more than working, sleeping more than eating. He needed someone to help him, yet I didn't even know where to start.

"What about you?" he asked, breaking into the thoughts clawing at my raw insides. "How long are you staying?"

I reluctantly sat down beside him, breathing through my mouth. "Just over two weeks. My boss is on maternity leave, so they don't need me for a while."

I'd moved to Los Angeles straight after high school, needing to get out of this town. For the three years I had been there, I've worked as a personal assistant at a small business in the outskirts. It wasn't very exciting work, but it paid the bills while I decided what to do next. Well, that was until James passed away. After that, I just existed. Barely.

"Oh, good. I've missed having you around. The house is so quiet these days." His eyes turned red, and he tilted his head to the floor and cleared his throat. Glancing at his watch, he began to stand. "I should head to work."

"Okay," I said, rubbing a hand across my arm as a chill ran over my skin. "Do you want anything to eat before you go?"

He looked at the clock on the wall, steadying himself on the couch as he finished standing up too quickly. "You know I would love that," he mumbled, "but I'm late for my shift. Grab whatever you want from the kitchen." He gestured at his clothes, covered in engine grease. "I should go find something clean to wear."

"When are you off next? I was hoping to talk to you about..." My voice caught in my throat and I wasn't able to finish the sentence. My chest squeezed like a truck had parked right on top of it.

We'd put off James's memorial since he passed. We either weren't ready or were pretending it wasn't real. But that needed to stop, and with the anniversary quickly coming up, James deserved to be laid to rest. It was the last thing I could do for him.

"I've got Thursday and Tuesday off, so we can talk then," Dad replied, his tone strained and eyes once again averted. As he got to the door, he stopped and looked back at me. "I am happy you're home." He walked back to kiss me on the forehead before leaving the room.

"Bye, Dad," I whispered when he was gone, tears burning behind my eyes and my body so tight it might snap at any point. To force myself to relax, I slumped back on the sofa, finding it hard to take a decent breath.

We'd always skirted around the topic, never really getting anywhere. But this time, I wouldn't let that happen. The plan was for Dad to come with me when I returned to LA. We could both start a new life there, away from the painful memories scattered in this town. It was the only way I could see him surviving this. The only way I was surviving this.

A few minutes later, Dad headed out the door. He offered a quick beep on the horn to say bye before his car rumbled down the street. Silence filled the house. Once upon a time, music would have been playing from my brother's bedroom at the top of the stairs. His friends might have been up there with him, talking about soccer or girls; whatever teenage boys did.

The silence was deafening.

When the stench of old beer bottles burned so strongly in my nose that I was close to gagging, I jumped up. I tidied the chaos of the living room, opening all the windows to let a fresh breeze dance through the house for probably the first time in a long while. I could finally take the breath I had been trying to since walking inside. My lungs filled with the warm summer air, and I left the room in a much more tolerable state than I'd found it.

My stomach growled. I couldn't recall the last time I had eaten something. I headed to the fridge, tipping my head back with a grunt. The shelves were empty except for some very expired eggs, a carton of old takeout, and an opened six-pack of beer. I checked the rest of the kitchen, but all I found were a few old cans of tuna in the cupboard, along with some expired Top Ramen.

Even though I just wanted to go up to my room and hide from the world, I walked back out into the hallway and pulled my shoes on. Food wouldn't magically solve all my problems, but neither would starving. As I was leaving, I spotted my old bike through the open garage door and walked over to it. It had seen better days; the tires were flat and the chain dry and rusty, but if I got it working again, it would be quicker than walking forty minutes there and back.

After I found a pump hidden in one of the storage units, I got to work on the tires. My search for any type of grease or oil came up short. Hopefully, the bike would work well enough to get to the store and back. I flung my foot over the bike and tested the pedals, the clunky chain groaning with each stroke. It wasn't jumping out of place, and that was good enough for me.

The breeze played in my wavy brown hair as I made my way down the street. The nape of my neck was still slightly sweaty from my furious cleaning. I caught a few neighbors watching me from their driveways as I went past, but I ignored them as best I could. If Mrs. Johnson knew I was back, so would everyone else at this point. She loved to gossip almost as much as she loved her plants. I wished they would all leave me alone and pretend like nothing had happened. It was what I'd been trying to do since the accident. I buried my head so deep in the sand I could barely breathe.

Some people called it denial. I called it coping.

I spotted the store in the distance and picked up speed—the chain clunking louder with each pedal stroke. The quicker in and out I could be, the better. There were enough familiar faces in the store that I kept my gaze down. I dashed between the aisles, praying no one would come up to me. The few times someone looked like they might, I turned on my heel and walked the other way, worried I would scream in the face of the next person who looked at me.

But I wouldn't break down here, not in front of everyone.

"Stella, is that you?" a silky voice asked from behind me.

I tried to keep walking in fear of what reaction might come out of me, but the voice called out again. With knots in my stomach, I slowed my steps.

"Just breathe," I told myself before turning around.

"Oh my god, it is! How are you?" Kasey Southwell, the cheerleading captain in high school, walked up to me. She rested her basket on the floor before continuing to move closer for a hug—something I most definitely didn't want, but wasn't able to avoid. Her golden-blonde ponytail swung high on her head, and she looked ready for the beach in tiny cutoff shorts and a blue polka-dot bikini top. I hugged her back, holding the basket between us as a makeshift shield.

"Hi, Kasey," I muttered, taking a few steps back and hoping she would let me leave without a conversation. She didn't.

"Oh, I was so sorry to hear about your brother. I couldn't believe it!" She put her hand over her mouth as her eyebrows shot up. "He was such a great guy."

I held back a sarcastic snort, recalling how Kasey had treated everyone in high school. James hung around with the same group as her, but it wasn't like they'd been friends. Kasey was your classic mean girl, though James had luckily never been on her radar. She'd only had eyes for one guy—her on-and-off again boyfriend—or anyone she could hook up with to make him jealous. While I'd never been the target of her wrath, I saw what it could do to people. That was something I did not need right now. The more distance, the better.

"Thanks, but I really need—"

"I was so sad when I heard about his car accident on the radio. How's your dad doing? How are you doing? It's been almost a year, right?" She blocked my path to continue the conversation.

I paused and fought back the lump forming in my throat. My knees trembled, but I didn't want her to see how weak I was. The anger from earlier had vanished, leaving only pain and weakness behind. Instinctively, I clutched at my necklace for support and tightened my grip on my basket until my knuckles turned white.

"He's fine. I'm fine. I've just come back for a while to help sort some stuff out." The basket almost slipped out of my sweaty hand, so I shifted it higher on my hip.

"Oh, so you're not staying?" She frowned, gripping my wrist with a fairly genuine smile. "If there is ever anything I can do—"

"Hey Kasey, I found the drinks. Did you want the blueberry or raspberry?" a male voice called from behind her. I peered curiously over her shoulder at another familiar face—the on-and-off again boyfriend. Even though I hadn't seen him since we graduated three years ago, I knew his name was Gray. He had been on the same soccer team as James, and they'd been pretty close.

Messy brown hair fell over his forehead, and he ran a hand through it to get it out of the way. Warm cognac eyes stared back at me, squinting against the fluorescent lights above. He wore a faded blue T-shirt with jeans that hugged his legs to perfection. I'd always thought Gray was good-looking in high school, but now he was borderline gorgeous. He'd gained an inch or two in height and even more in muscle. He waved two drinks at Kasey, his muscles playing under the short sleeves, and my stomach fluttered ever so slightly.

"Either is fine. Look who I ran into!" she said, motioning towards me.

Gray moved his gaze from the blonde beside me and up my body, taking more than a few seconds before landing on my eyes.

"Oh. Uh, hey, Stella." I couldn't read the expression flashing over his face.

I gave him a brief smile, hiking the basket even higher. Gray continued to study me, then inhaled sharply and looked back at Kasey.

"We should get going. I've got a date with a boat, so if you want a ride home, we need to get a move on."

"You're going fishing?" Kasey squealed, running up to him and wrapping her arm around his. What would being pressed against his side feel like? "Can I come? My mom has me working the late shift tonight, so I've got nothing to do until then and I'm bored! It could be like old times." She winked at him. I almost wanted to roll my eyes, but I was slightly swooning over him too, so I couldn't exactly blame her.

"Since when do you like fishing?" he teased, making no attempt to release her grip. Were they still together? They sure were cozy with each other.

"I don't. But I'm bored, so it will do. And Stella just got back! She should totally come. I bet you haven't been up at the lake in years!" Her wide smile was now directed at me, catching me like a deer in headlights.

It took me a second to realize what she had said. My mouth dropped wide open, and I wanted to shake my head no vigorously. When she gripped my wrist, I only stuttered a few strange noises. Gray eyes zipped between us.

"Uh, I mean, I guess?" he drawled, assessing my reaction. I stared at him, hoping he would magically read my mind and speak for me.

"Yay. It will be great!" Kasey exclaimed, dragging me towards the exit.

Damn it, why wasn't my voice working? All I needed to say was no. A simple—

"No," I croaked out, shaking my head as I planted my feet. No, I most definitely didn't want to go fishing with Miss Perfect and her boyfriend, no matter how delicious he looked in those jeans.

"Oh, come on! It will be fun."

"Kasey, she just got back. Let her settle in." Gray's voice rumbled behind me, sending a warm tingle through my core as his breath brushed my ear. When had he gotten so close?

"But—"

"Kase." Gray's hand rested on her bare waist.

She reluctantly let go of me. "Fine. But we can still go fishing, right?" She barely missed a beat as she smiled and continued through the store and away from us.

Gray ran a hand over his face, letting out a long sigh. "Sorry about her. She doesn't understand boundaries."

I shrugged, because what was I meant to say to that? It was a miracle I'd gotten the *no* out.

He glanced at me, but didn't let his eyes linger. The sadness in them seemed genuine enough, and I reminded myself I wasn't the only person who had lost someone. I was about to step away from him and make a run for it when I caught more familiar faces staring at me. A shuddered sigh rolled from my lips, and Gray gave me a strange look.

"You okay?" he asked, his brows drawing together.

I nodded. "I'm fine." *Liar.* I glanced around. "Just people I'd rather not deal with."

"Come on, let's get out of here." Gray turned to me and rested his hand on my lower back. My skin practically caught fire, but I'd let him keep it there as long as no one spoke to me.

If I could be anywhere else, I would. Put me in a deep dark hole and throw away the key for all I cared. It would be better than this. He shouldn't have to rescue me. I wasn't a child, and I should be able to go into a store and buy food without breaking down or freaking out. But things were different here than in LA. I wasn't invisible. Not by a long shot.

I stayed beside him as we paid, happy to hide out if it meant no one asked me questions. He handed me my groceries, and I put them in my backpack as quickly as I could. I didn't care that things were getting squished. I just wanted out of this place.

"You're welcome to come," Gray said, out of the blue.

We were just outside the doors, freedom within my grasp. I peered at him, brown waves falling over his forehead before he swept them back again. I wasn't sure why he wanted me to go fishing with him and his girlfriend. He shook his head with a small grin and the hair fell back down. That mischievous glint reminded me of James.

"If you want to. Fishing is my escape from everything, and it looks like you could use some of that too." He ran a hand over the nape of his neck.

"You're going with your girlfriend. I don't want to intrude. And my bike is here." I gestured towards it and shifted my weight. They weren't the only reasons, but the only two I was going to voice. I swung my backpack over my shoulders, then took a step towards the hunk of rust. I just wanted to be home now so I could throw myself on my bed and scream into my pillow. Why? Anger. Embarrassment. And pain. The answer was always some type of pain.

"Kasey isn't my girlfriend anymore. That ship sailed a long time ago." Gray chuckled awkwardly, gently wrapping his hand over his throat. I followed the movement with my gaze. "But if you don't want to go fishing, that's fine. Let me at least drive you home. It's too hot and you've got your bag weighing you down." I looked back up, and the smile he flashed me this time made my insides tingle. He gestured at the bike. "Want me to grab it?"

"It's okay." I glanced over my shoulder at Kasey by his truck. I wasn't too keen on spending more time with that *perfection*, although they weren't an item anymore. Dating was not on the agenda, let alone with someone from my hometown.

He followed my gaze, releasing a drawn-out breath. "I know she can be a lot, but she's really not all bad. I think you might like her if you got to know her. James got along with her. Somewhat." He smirked, straight white teeth beaming back at me.

"I just want to go home," I said at the mention of my brother, gasping for air as gracefully as I could. That was the cold shower I needed. Gray was a part of James's life that I wasn't familiar with.

James was the reason for all my pain. If he was still here... But no. He left me. Like everyone had. Mom. Dad. James. Dad again. Everyone always left. I was done relying on people to be there for me.

Gray's shoulders sank toward the ground, as did the corners of his mouth. "I promise she won't say anything stupid. Neither will I. All right? Come on. Please? Trust me?" He tried another smile, hesitantly pointing to the bike again.

I nodded and sighed. It was clear he wasn't taking no for an answer. And just because we'd be in the same truck didn't mean I had to make conversation. They'd soon figure out I wasn't interested. I would also be home a lot sooner if I let him drive me, which sounded good.

It wasn't the fact that I wanted Gray to smile again. Just like I most definitely didn't check out his ass in those jeans when he turned, or the way his muscles stretched under his shirt when he picked up my bike. Nope, I didn't notice any of that because that would be stupid on another level.

Chapter Two

- GRAY -

Kasey tapped away on her phone beside me, singing like always to the horrible '90s pop coming through the speakers, while Stella sat quietly in the back with her bag resting on her lap. She had said little since I convinced her to let me drive her home, and I didn't want to press her.

I couldn't imagine what she was going through. James had been a close friend of mine since the start of high school, but I'd barely spoken to Stella before today. With her girl-next-door looks, she'd been impossible to miss in the hallways, but the few times I'd gone to their house, she'd been in her room. Quiet behind a closed door.

She'd always had something special about her, something that drew me in, but her being James's sister made me keep my distance, just like in high school.

And then there was Kasey. Our relationship was always up in the air. When we'd decided to just be friends, my brain couldn't handle a relationship that involved the opposite sex. I wasn't sure I was in the right headspace even now. It felt strange even thinking about it.

Stella sniffed quietly in the back. It pulled my attention away from memories of breakups I'd rather forget. Through the rearview mirror, the stress and tension in her eyes as she glanced around the roads tore at me. A few tears clung to her lashes, and she swiped them away with the back of her hand before they fell. Roads that held happy memories for me must hold so much pain for her. She fidgeted with her necklace, holding her breath as we drove past the high school. It was painful to watch when I knew how pretty her smile could be. James would have hated to see her like this.

"Oh, are you free this Friday?" Kasey suddenly asked me, causing me to jerk. I refocused my attention back on the road.

"Uh, maybe. Why?" I asked hesitantly.

"Mom's… home." She glanced over her shoulder, then plastered on a fake smile. "So I'm going out. And you're coming with me! We could go to Seattle!"

I snorted. "No, thanks."

"Why not? We used to do it all the time!" She slapped my chest with the back of her hand.

"Because I've got work. Then I'm meeting up with the guys at Damien's on the weekend."

"Boring," she huffed, and I couldn't help but laugh.

"Just as going to a club and dancing is boring," I retorted. It was her turn to laugh. It sounded hollow. I peered over at her, my brows drawing together.

"All right. Fine. What about you, Stella? Girls' night out? It'll be epic!" She flung her body around with a hopeful smile. When Stella shook her head, still refusing to speak, Kasey huffed again. "God, you guys suck. I don't want to go alone."

"Then don't," I said, pinching her leg and trying to get a read on her.

She swatted my hand away. "Maybe I won't. Maybe I'll crash your little guy party at the farm."

A snort flew from my lips before I could stop it. "Yeah, I very much doubt that. When did you last go? Do you even remember the way?"

"Oh, I remember all right," she cooed, giving me a teasing wink as she bit her bottom lip. "I remember all about the lake, the barns, the back porch—"

"All right, all right." My cheeks flushed at the memories from a horny teenage time. "That was a long time ago, and we are not together. I'm going there to relax, meaning *you* have to make conversation with someone else too. Like Nate," I told her, hoping it would be enough to change her mind.

Not that I didn't want her there. Well, kind of. Despite both her and Nate being my best friends, they never got along. With the two of them together, I would spend most of my time making sure Kasey didn't rip Nate's balls off or he didn't shoot her. Not the relaxing weekend I was hoping for.

"Ew. Yeah, I'm good. Thanks." She faked a gag, then returned to Instagram on her phone. Her frame shrunk in the seat, and the corners of her mouth turned down. A minute later, we parked outside Stella's house.

"Back in a sec," I told Kasey. She barely acknowledged my words—her mind had already left the conversation. If I didn't know her so well, I might have missed the lip tucked between her teeth and the slight redness forming in her eyes. There was definitely something up. The question was, would she let me in, or push me away like all the other times?

I only allowed myself a glance at the window once belonging to James as I pulled the bike out of the back, wondering if it still looked the same inside.

"Thanks," Stella said, snapping me out of my thoughts. I leaned the bike against the garage and looked at her. She gave a tight smile as tears welled up in her eyes, looking ready to dash inside with her hand already on the door handle.

"No problem." We stared at each other for a moment. I wanted to tell her everything would get better. It probably would. One day, however distant that day may be. But it wasn't my place.

Stella gave me another forced smile, flicking her eyes down to the ground and away from me, and it hurt more than if she had let the tears flow. She retreated inside, softly closing the door behind her. I headed back to the truck, sliding in with a scowl on my face.

Life wasn't fucking fair. James didn't deserve to die so young, and Stella sure as hell didn't deserve to be left without him. I wasn't sure I'd dealt with my own feelings regarding my friend's death. Time stood still, yet moved so quickly. In the months after his passing, there had been tears, anger, more tears, and fights with my friends for no reason. Eventually we got to this. Not okay, but somewhere in that neighborhood.

Before my brain could dive into that dark hole of pain, my phone rang. It was my dad. I contemplated not answering, but ignored that impulse for self-preservation.

"Hi, Grayson, I was hoping you could swing by the house for dinner? Mom misses you." My dad's voice boomed through the truck.

"Yeah, sure, Dad," I drawled. Kasey snapped her eyes to me, her eyebrows drawing together.

"Good. I will let her know." He hung up before I could say anything else, and I reluctantly turned the car around with a long exhale.

"What about fishing?" Kasey asked. She had tucked her phone back into her pocket and a crease lined the middle of her tanned forehead.

"It can wait. But what about you? What's up?"

She turned her head away. Just when it seemed like she was going to ignore my question, her soft voice rolled through the truck. "Just a bad day. A bad week. Am I allowed to say a bad life?" she scoffed, then wrapped her arms around her legs. She rested her chin on top of her knees before tilting her head at me with a faint smile. "I'm okay."

"I'm sorry. You want to talk about it?"

After a sigh, she shook her head. "No, not today. I'm just done with it all." The happy girl sitting beside me a few minutes ago seemed so far gone I almost wanted to pull over and wrap her up in my arms. But this wasn't my fight, just like I didn't have any right to tell Stella it would one day be okay.

Kasey kept her pain hidden from most, only letting me in when she truly couldn't keep it from boiling over. I'd tried to get inside her battered fortress before, but she kept that door so tightly under lock and key that it had almost broken us apart. She was too important for me to lose, so I'd taken a step back.

"Do you want to come with me to my parents? Or I can drop you at the park?"

"I'll come with you. I haven't seen your mom in ages." She gave me another weak smile, then tilted her head away from me to stare out through the window, ending any more conversation.

We drove in deafening silence until we reached my parents' house. My mood was now so low it was dragging on the ground, turning dirty and muddy even though the ground was dry. I would have to try not to take it out on my dad, though that was easier said than done.

We'd never been close. I loved him and all, but he wasn't exactly the warm kind of parent. Since finishing high school, I'd worked at his construction business, and it hadn't exactly been a walk in the park. The first year was rocky as hell—I fucked up more times than I'd like to admit, and my dad came close to firing me several times after costing him both time and money. It wasn't like I'd planned on fucking up. Fuckups just seemed to have a way of finding me. My mom always said my heart was in the right place, but it usually took my brain a bit longer to catch up.

Last summer, after James passed, I tried to force my anger and sorrow into something other than self-destructing by working for Habitat for Humanity in Oregon for three weeks. That summer really changed my outlook on life. I'd taken everything I had for granted, and to help someone at their lowest was a gift.

That's when Nate and I made a deal. We would start our own construction company and help people who really needed it. The people who needed a roof over their family's heads. The people who didn't have the resources to build one themselves. *Not* the people in fancy business suits building their third or fourth home, my dad's usual clientele. I'd spent months working on a business plan, but I was so over my head, it sometimes felt like I was drowning.

Nate tried his best to keep my spirits up, but I would still freak out—just less frequently externally. I didn't do well with pressure or responsibilities, hence the many fuckups from before. It was the same reason Kasey and I had dated for so long. It was easier dealing with each other than risking letting someone else down. I didn't think too hard about why Stella's face popped into my mind, popping the thought like it was a balloon.

I'd tried to talk to my dad about my business idea before, but he never took me seriously. He only cared about the bottom line—the big payday. Taking jobs from people in need would mean fewer mansions and more housing units, and in the end less money. He wasn't interested in that. Dad said I was too young and inexperienced to make it work; that I needed a few more years under my belt before he would even consider my proposal.

That was why I was trying my best *not* to fuck up anymore. It was time to grow up. Making the business plan bulletproof was the only way forward. I hadn't figured out what the steps were or how I would pull it off, but somehow I needed to.

"In my office," my dad called as we entered the house. Kasey headed towards my mom singing in the kitchen while I made my way to the back.

Dad sat behind his office desk, a laptop open and an empty cup of coffee beside him. The familiar smell of old books hit me the second I stepped inside. He'd spent a lot of time in this room when I was growing up. He still did. If he wasn't working on-site, he was in here. He'd built the business from scratch and was proud of that, but it had also meant a lot of dinners where it was only Mom and me.

He moved some papers around before neatly tucking them away into a folder. "So, last week was good. How did it feel?" He peered up at me with a warm smile on his face. My guard instantly went up. There was more to my visit than just dinner. He had that business tone in his voice.

"Uh, yeah, it ran pretty smoothly. We got most of the things done that should have been. I'll drop by the hardware store tomorrow and pick up some more materials." I nervously tapped my foot, attempting to stop by placing a hand on my thigh.

When I'd shown up for work last Monday, I took over as site manager while the actual one was at home with his newborn. Scared shitless that I would fuck something up, I only got through it with Nate's help. He'd been working with my dad for as long as I had and always had my back.

After finding me on the edge of a nervous breakdown, he'd given me some speech about how I needed to man up. Nate was good at that. He didn't give a shit what other people thought—his only concern in life was making sure he always had a good time, whatever or *who*ever he was doing.

"Good, good. I agree. Therefore—" Dad searched for something in his desk drawer. After a moment, he pulled out a document and held it out to me. "I was hoping you would be my replacement in the company. Not now, of course. You would need training first. Lots of training. But I've seen some real improvements in you this last year. Last week only proved as much. I think you're ready to take on more responsibilities."

Responsibilities. I cringed at the word, but tried to make the reaction as internal as I could. I grabbed the paper from him with wide eyes and raised eyebrows. A quick glance over the page helped little with the confusion that must have been clear on my face. My brain was trying to think of all the reasons this was both a terrible and great idea, and I couldn't focus on any words to make out what it actually said. I stuttered as I tried to get my words out.

"So you mean I would..." I pointed from myself to him, unable to finish the sentence. I rubbed my hand against the nape of my neck, my heartbeat skyrocketed, and I stuttered a few more times before ending my attempts at speaking with a chuckle. Shit, I wasn't ready for this. Nowhere near fucking ready.

While it could be a good way to learn more, I only got through last week because of Nate. I wouldn't always be able to rely on him. Fuckups were a major possibility—likely, even—meaning I would let my dad down. Let the company down. Shit.

My dad laughed at my reaction. "That's right. You would take over for me when I retire. Your mom and I have been talking about it, and while I could go until I drop, she's talked me into retiring in ten years. It might seem like a long time still, but there's a lot for you to learn and it would mean the world to me if you could continue to run the company. I built all of it for you and your mom." He leaned on his forearms before continuing. "I know I have been tough on you in the past, but I have only ever done it in your own best interest. And I think you're finally ready to learn now. So what do you say?" He clapped his hands with a smile, oblivious to my panic.

I stared at him, then back at the paper in my hand. My mom came in before I could say anything.

"Oh, darling, have you told him?" She put her hand on my shoulder and gave my cheek a kiss. "Isn't it great? I'm so proud of you. You have come such a long way!" My mom had a different view of me than my dad. In her eyes, I could do no wrong. I was, and probably always would be, her golden boy. It was for her that I forced a smile. For her that I was going to make this work. For her that I shoved my insecurities deep, deep down, where the sun would never shine.

"Yeah, it is," I said, clearing my sticky throat. I needed more time to think through whatever the fuck this situation was before I blurted out something I would regret. My dad wouldn't give me more than one chance to prove myself, so I guessed it was now or never. It was a shame Nate wasn't here to slap some sense and confidence into me again.

My dad stood up and reached his hand out to me. I grabbed it, still in denial of what this would actually mean for me. For us if I screwed up. He pulled me up to stand with him.

"We are *both* so proud of you, my son. I always knew you had it in you." His eyes, wet with unshed tears, cemented the reality.

I pulled my mom in for a hug and kissed her cheek. "Let's go make sure Kasey hasn't burned dinner."

I stopped to take a breath as they left, listening to the pounding of my heart in my chest. I could do this. Right? I mean, it's kind of what I wanted. Kind of perfect. I could learn more about how the business works before I tried to talk to my dad about the business plan again.

Responsibilities. You're gonna butcher this. Shut up, brain.

Chapter Three

- STELLA -

The week dragged on. I barely even noticed the sun going up or down with my nose buried in one book after another. Anything to distract me from the painful memories everywhere in this house—like a weighted blanket I couldn't shake.

The days my dad had told me he was free, he now had to work. He blamed it on his boss, but there was more to it than that. The real reason was probably because he wasn't ready to hear what I needed to tell him. Probably would *never* be ready. Unfortunately for him, I wasn't going anywhere.

I spent most of the time alone in my room or outside on the back porch, where no one could see me. Birds sang in the trees, the leaves rustled in the warm summer breeze, and the quiet hum of nearby neighbors playing in their yards reminded me of a time long ago. It hurt, but it was also necessary.

One afternoon, I found myself at the top of the stairs, standing in front of my brother's bedroom door. Instead of giving into my first instinct and running back to my room to scream angry words into my pillow, I twisted the handle.

The door creaked as it swung open slowly. Hot, stale air flooded out, dust swirling in the light coming through the window. I scanned the room and an unexpected sense of calm washed over me, replacing the angry, electric current zapping all my cells.

Pictures of James and his friends hung on the walls—some with his girlfriend Bee—and there were dirty soccer clothes on his unmade bed and on the floor in the corner. The room looked the same as last year. I guess my dad hadn't been in here either.

When my eyes landed on the brass urn on James's desk, my heart could have ripped out of my chest. Nausea washed over me, and I pressed my hand over my mouth.

My heart raced as I broke out in a cold sweat. Frozen to the ground, I stood there for several minutes, then forced myself to walk over to his desk. I eyed the trash can, knowing I might still need it. Class schedules, workout routines, and paperwork lay scattered all over the right side of the desk, along with handwritten notes for the kids he helped coach in soccer at the elementary school. That's where I focused my attention. Not on the cold brass on the left side of the desk.

His dream had always been to coach kids in the sport he loved. I think he was playing with soccer balls before he could even walk. But not only did he love the sport, he was good at it—maybe not enough to go pro, but he understood the stuff behind the scenes. And he was great with kids. I used to joke with him that he'd end up with an entire herd of his own one day. He would laugh, but I think in the back of his mind, he wanted that. A big family full of love. Something we hadn't had growing up.

His voice became clearer in my head as I read his handwriting. It morphed into a flashback of us doing our homework in his room together; me sitting right here and him propped up with pillows on the bed.

The sound filled the room, and anger flared in my chest. I wasn't sure why, but it was all-consuming for a second. My throat was hot and tight, like someone was holding a searing iron glove over me. I closed my eyes, burning with unshed tears. I could hear his pen tapping on the paper he was holding, and my breath came a little easier through my flared nostrils.

"Hey Stell, who wrote Les Misérables *again?"*

"Well, if I told you, would you remember?"

"If I said yes, would you believe me?"

His laugh echoed through the walls, slowly fading away as the memory passed.

I smiled as I opened my eyes and ran my fingers over his scribbles on the papers in front of me, surprised I wasn't shaking with tears or anger. The warmth from being near his things spread through me, something I hadn't felt for some time.

Temporarily confident, I glanced to my left at the urn, and the sadness swallowed me whole. My chest tore in two, then pressed together so tightly I gasped for breath. I had to get out. I had to be anywhere but here. The moment of relief disappeared as a familiar pain engulfed me.

I ran downstairs to put my shoes on, grabbing my bike from the garage and riding down the street with no direction or destination in mind. Lost to my feelings and painful memories, with tears rolling steadily down my cheeks and dampening my hair. I muttered as my pedals went round and round—angry words about how James had always promised to be there for me. His promises had been lies, and I fell for them all.

I crossed the main road and continued past the park. The chain on the bike clunked loudly, once, twice, and then the pedals spun freely under my feet. Tumbling forwards, I lost my balance and only narrowly avoided face-planting on the concrete.

When I came to a stop, I found myself back near the main road, my legs trembling from exertion. I let my head roll back, puffing in and out through my mouth. It would take me the better part of an hour to walk home, not that I wanted to go back there, anyway. I swung my leg over the seat and dropped the bike onto the grass beside the path. I wasn't sure my legs could keep me upright for much longer, so I sank to the ground with a loud huff.

Removing my phone from my back pocket, I swiped through my photos in search of anything that was my brother. Something to ground me. It didn't take me long to find as I didn't take many photos these days. There were a few of a massive cinnamon bun I'd ordered several weeks ago. Another picture of the sun setting over buildings in LA—beautiful orange and lilac clouds floating against a darkening sky. A video I'd saved from the internet of a duck chasing a dog. That sort of thing. There was no life in the pictures. Until I got to ones from high school.

The girl in the photos looked happy on the outside, but her eyes were empty. I had seen that look in my brother's eyes sometimes, though he always tried to hide it from me.

I wanted to be the girl in those photos again. Even though she thought she was alone, she wasn't. Her brother would have dropped everything in a heartbeat if she needed him. She could lean on him for anything. But with him gone, I had no one to fill that hole. He had been the one solid constant in my life of disappointments. I wanted to laugh hysterically when I thought of my dad filling that hole. He was part of the problem, not the solution.

James was gone. He'd left me just like everyone did. Anger simmered under the surface again, and I tried to blow it out with some sharp exhales through my nose. A video of James popped up as I swiped, the anger quickly morphing into knives stabbing at my heart. Hunched into a ball with my knees under my chin, I pressed play and curled up even tighter.

"Hey, sis, happy birthday! Can you believe it? We made it another year together!" James's smiling face covered the screen, a multicolored, cone-shaped hat on his head. He put a party blower in his mouth and blew it as hard as he could, the noise dreadful. The yellow-and-black high school varsity jacket with signatures from all the players in black marker hanging over his shoulders told me this was the summer after graduation. That jacket still hung in his wardrobe. I had already left for LA when he sent this video. If I could go back and never leave, I would. Choking on an inhale, I stared at the video through blurry eyes.

"I can't wait to see you. I hope you're coming home soon. Dad is his grumpy old self, but I know it would mean a lot to him if you came back. We could go out somewhere and celebrate together! Maybe get a stack of pancakes and bacon at the diner! Anyway, love you, Stell. You're the best twin a guy could ever want!"

The video ended, his face frozen on the screen. I pressed play again and again and again. I held the phone to my ear so I could fill myself with his voice. The pain of my heart breaking mixed with love and anger, and it gripped every cell in my body, pulling me apart. The phone eventually slid out of my hand and landed on the ground beside me. I didn't look at anything as cars drove past, daydreaming into the space in front of me as I berated my brother in my head. Telling him how much I hated him for leaving me the way he did. How he'd lied when he said I'd never be alone.

A blue Chevy pulled up by the road just ahead of me, snapping me out of my trance. I quickly wiped my cheeks in case I was crying, squinting against the blinding sun. Gray jumped out of the truck and hurried over to me.

"Stella, are you okay?" he asked, inspecting my face. The internal screams faded as Gray's voice rolled through my ears, a soothing balm to the pain.

I drew in a deep inhale and motioned to the bike next to me. "The chain broke." That didn't explain why I probably looked like a train wreck. But I was tired. Completely drained. Even talking was hard, though some sadness had lifted off my shoulders and been replaced with love after hearing James's voice. He always had a way of making me feel better, even though I still resented him.

"So you just decided to sit here?" Gray smirked. It made me want to smile back, but my lips wouldn't let me. My jaw ached, so I turned my gaze away. A moment later, he sat down on the grass next to me, his feet planted on the ground and his arms wrapped around bent legs. I picked up my phone from between us.

He jerked when his eyes fell on the screen, but he quickly composed himself when he noticed me studying him. "Remember how nervous he was before each of our soccer games?" He shook his head and let it fall forward between his knees. "I walked in on him puking in the locker room more times that I could count. I had to make sure Coach M didn't know or he wouldn't have let him play. For a confident guy, James sure didn't always act like it."

I tried to picture him in his yellow soccer uniform. I loved it when he came home after practice or a game. He looked so full of life. Tired, but with bright-red cheeks and a sparkle in his eyes that could light up any dark corner. I clenched my fists tightly around my legs, despite trying my best to loosen them.

Gray continued, unaware of my reaction to his story. "But once the game started, it was like all his nerves disappeared. He was in his element. I wouldn't say he was the best player we had," he laughed and nudged me with his shoulder, the scent of fresh pine and coffee rolling off him. "But he was the player with the most heart. He loved the game. He was an amazing teacher to all those kids."

It was like someone gently squeezed my heart. I sniffled. "I loved watching him play because I knew how much he loved it." A tear spilled over my lashes, and I quickly wiped it away.

"Yeah, he really did." I felt Gray's eyes on me even as I hid behind my hair, hoping he didn't notice my deteriorating state, as unlikely as that was. "He was happy, you know? Like really happy. More than I think I had ever seen him. He missed you. He always talked about you, but he was happy. I don't know if he ever told you, but he was talking about asking Bee to marry him."

I remembered Bee. She and my brother had dated throughout high school and were the real deal. You could see it in their eyes. James had this dream where he would buy a plot of land and settle down with her. Where was she now? She'd left town quickly after his accident, just like me, and I hadn't seen or heard from her since. Was she hurting too, or had she moved on? I had a strong anger towards her too, but I wasn't sure why.

I turned to Gray. His brown eyes were filled with both happiness and sadness. It made me feel guilty for hating James the way I did, but reminiscing with Gray helped soothe that angry part of my heart. I wasn't so mind-numbingly broken or alone when he was around. Like I could feel the warmth radiating from his eyes like with James.

We sat in silence for a while longer. Gray picked up small stones from the ground and threw them into the grass. "Do you mind if I ask why you've come back?" He looked between me and the road a few times.

"I'm helping my dad sort out James's memorial. It's been too long. He deserves to be put to rest." I'd rehearsed the words, but it still hurt to say, my voice almost catching in my throat.

"It's been almost a year." It wasn't quite a question or a statement.

My chest tightened, and I slumped my shoulders. With my cheek resting on my knees, I fought back the tears before muttering, "Mm-hmm." My jaw was glued shut and aching again. Not that I hadn't cried since James's passing, but being back here was different, like the floodgates would open and never close. Like if I let myself grieve for James with tears, I'd cry until I was a dry husk.

"I can drive you back home if you want?" Gray rested his hand on my shoulder. The warmth spread through my skin, trying to loosen the death grip around my throat.

I shook my head and turned to look towards the road. "I don't think I can go home right now. There's just too much of him there," I said.

Gray nodded. "Well, you can't sit here all day. And I'm not about to let you walk home with a broken bike. My mom would kill me if she found out." He stood up and brushed the dirt from his faded jeans. "So if you don't want to go home, and you can't stay here"—he gestured to the small patch of grass—"then you can come and hang out at the lake with me. I never made it up there yesterday, but I'm definitely going today. My poor soul needs it." He clutched his heart over his shirt and looked dramatic, making me smile ever so slightly.

I didn't want to smile. I wanted to scream and shout, though nothing but a small sigh escaped when I opened my mouth.

"What do you say? We could swap stories about James if you'd like, or we could just relax in silence."

I took his outstretched hand before I decided against it. It had been nice hearing stories about my brother. Maybe it was what I needed. Maybe it could stop this relentless anger and turn it into love again. I wanted to love James. My rock. My world.

But right now, I couldn't.

"Okay," I said. I drew my lips into a tight line as I nodded.

Gray smiled widely, his eyes sparkling in the sun. Something about them calmed the storm in me. Catching myself staring, I averted my gaze. He grabbed my bike from the ground, and I couldn't stop myself from peering back and glimpsing dancing muscles under his shirt. My heart fluttered. Maybe it wasn't just filled with anger and pain after all.

"This feels familiar. Have I done this before?" Gray asked, a playful tone to his voice. He laughed when I rolled my eyes.

We drove out of town and down towards the lake. James had brought me out here when we needed to get out of the house. For him, that was most of the time. He wasn't good at sitting still. My bike rattled in the truck bed as the pavement turned to gravel. These woods and fields were comfortably familiar, and a small lightness spread through my chest as I leaned my head against the headrest and stared out the window with a small smile forming on my lips.

I had forgotten how beautiful it was here. Forgotten how light my heart could feel.

We took a left down an even smaller dirt road. Before I could ask Gray where we were going, he turned to me with a smile.

"It's usually too busy up by the beach, but there's a part just on the other side. Liam's parents own it. Do you remember Liam Myers? He was on the soccer team too. Tanned guy, black hair. Anyway, it's where me and the guys mostly go to hang out, but they won't be there now."

I nodded. I had a vague recollection of Liam. Worried I would end up with more painful memories of my brother, I didn't think too hard. After a few minutes, we pulled up beside some Douglas firs, and Gray shifted the truck into park. I stepped out onto the soft grass and moved my eyes towards the water's edge.

Grass turned to sand, and waves lapped against the shore with no drone of traffic this far from the roads, only the gentle sound of the water. Birds sang happily as they flew above us, trying to catch flies in mid-air. It was calm. Peaceful. Something I was so unfamiliar with.

Gray grabbed a bag out of the back of his truck and made his way down to a powerboat tied up against a small wooden dock. It looked like it cost more than I'd made in total since leaving high school. And then some.

I followed him, but stayed on the sand as he dropped the bag on the planks, leaning over to untie the ropes. His muscles flexed under his white T-shirt, and if I squinted hard enough, he could almost be James. But he wasn't. James wasn't here anymore.

The urge to scream overcame me again and I opened my mouth, but only a small squeak came out. I slapped my hands across my face and let out a cry. My body didn't know whether to break down in tears or anger, and it was so confusing.

"Hey, what's wrong?" Gray dropped the rope onto the dock and in a few steps, he was in front of me. He grabbed my wrists and lowered my hands from my face, hunching down until we were face-to-face. Unable to get any words out, I focused on his worried brown eyes.

"You look like him. And I... I don't know whether I hate it or love it or..." My voice broke. His hair was a few shades darker than James's, but a similar messy cut. Gray's white T-shirt and faded jeans could have been exactly something James would have worn. I wanted to rip his shirt off and stamp it on the muddy ground under the dock. Set it on fire and watch it burn. Hold it close and never let go.

"Ah damn, I'm sorry." Gray pulled me into his arms, and I allowed myself to grasp his shirt.

Steady as a rock, he stood there while I calmed down, my knees too weak to support me. His scent found its way into my nose and soothed me with each inhale. It was warm, and I could smell his sweat mixed in with whatever aftershave he was wearing. I moved a little closer and gripped his shirt a little tighter. I felt safe here. The kind of safe I had only ever felt with James. That list of people ended there. One. One person. How sad was that?

"If you don't want to be here, I'll take you home," Gray murmured, running a gentle hand down from the top of my head to rest on my back, the touch soothing even though I didn't really want it to be.

I looked past his shoulder and out to the water, weighing my options again. "I think I might just sit here if you don't mind." My voice was quiet and shaky, but at least I didn't feel like screaming.

Gray's warm scent filled my lungs as I wiped tears from my cheeks. I didn't want to pull away from him, but I had to. I couldn't stand here gripping onto him for dear life much longer.

He swallowed, his Adam's apple bobbing against the side of my head. He let his hand drop with a nod and stepped towards the boat again. My legs still felt unsteady, so I sank down and dug my fingers into the warm sand. I stripped off my shoes and socks and sank my toes in too, listening to the waves as they gently brushed against the beach to connect me to the world. The hot summer air danced through my hair and tickled my nose, the external feeling bringing me comfort, though on the inside I still only felt pain.

The sound of Gray chucking his bag back into the truck made me turn around. "You can still go out. I don't mind just sitting here," I called, feeling bad that he wasn't able to go fishing again.

"Ah, it's fine. I've got plenty of time to go fishing." He smiled, but his eyes didn't sparkle. I liked it when they sparkled.

I turned back around with a quiet sigh, not having the energy to argue with him. As he walked up behind me, I closed my eyes and pretended it wasn't Gray but James who sat down with a thud next to me and let out a deep exhale.

"James used to take me to the beach whenever I would come back home," I whispered, my eyes still closed as I clung to the fact I knew wasn't true. My voice was just loud enough to hear over the breeze in the trees. "He wanted me to remember the good side of home, if even for just a little while." He would want me to do so now too. But I wasn't there yet. The sound of James singing rang through my head, the same stupid country music he'd always played. Right now, it gave me a headache.

"James used to come up here a lot," Gray said. "We'd bring some beer and just drink the night away. Those were some good times."

"I could hear him climbing back in through his window sometimes. He always thought he tricked everyone, and I'm sure Dad didn't know, but I did. I would ask him about it, but he would pretend like he was all innocent." Remembering his face and those memories made me smile. A sigh tore out of my chest as some of the tension released.

"Oh, he did? Well, I definitely wouldn't say James was innocent!" Gray laughed and placed his hands as a cradle behind his head.

I turned to him with pinched brows. "What do you mean?" I never thought of my brother as a saint, but the tone in Gray's voice surprised me.

He glanced at me and snickered. "Let's just say..." He faltered, taking a moment to pick his words. "James was usually the instigator of these things. When he wasn't hanging out with you or Bee, he let out his wild side. That was his best side." Gray closed his eyes and grinned. I threw some sand at his leg, knowing he was probably telling the truth. This was my brother, after all—high on life was a state of being for him. "I miss him," Gray said with an exhale. His words shook me to my core.

"Me too." Despite it coming out as a soft whisper, I knew he had heard me when he slipped his hand into mine. Fingers entangled like they had done this a thousand times before. It was comforting to share that burden. It was comforting not to be so alone.

Chapter Four

- GRAY -

My dad's question jarred me from my daydream about bronze curls and sad eyes.

"Uh, sorry. Yes, I ordered the electrical sockets earlier today and confirmed they should be here by the end of the week." Shaking my head didn't make Stella's face go away. It had been firmly lodged in there since our trip to the beach.

"The end of the week, huh?" Dad repeated, rubbing his beard as he looked through the papers in his hand. "That won't be soon enough. We've got the power being installed on Monday, so we could use them sooner. Could you call them back and see if they could rush it?" He nodded, ending the conversation by walking back over to his open laptop.

I picked up the phone and called the supply store. After a lot of back and forth, I got them to agree to the order being delivered on Monday morning, but they were adamant they couldn't get them any sooner. It made me feel useless, as my dad would have been able to smooth talk them into a better deal, but I guess that's why he was the boss and I was still just learning how not to get fired.

Nate walked past the window and shook his head with a laugh as our eyes met. When I'd told him what had happened with my dad, he laughed at my panic for several minutes. Nate didn't understand. He'd never had loving parents who wanted him to succeed, or any parental figures at all. Growing up in foster homes had been hard on him, and though my parents were as close as he got to parental love, he practically recoiled from it. Even with this business plan, Nate only tagged along because of me. He knew I needed someone in my corner.

With the working day over, my dad packed up his bag and left. I slumped down on a chair in the corner, still crunching numbers and trying to re-member where I put that damn invoice I'd seen this morning. My eyes were dry from focusing hard and my hands were cramping from writing too many emails. High on my sixth coffee of the day, it caused my whole body to simultaneously feel wired and numb.

Working in an office was ten times worse than working on-site.

Nate poked his head in. "Was it as fun being the boss as you thought it might be?" he mocked. I kicked at his foot as he walked past, but he jumped out of the way.

"I'm not the boss you think I am. Every sin-gle thing I did was double checked. Hell, probably even triple checked when I wasn't looking. I don't know what I'm doing most of the time." I rubbed my hands over my face several times and exhaled sharply. The caffeine supply would dwindle sooner or later, but having more wasn't smart.

Nate snorted and glanced at some papers on my dad's desk with a grimace. "You ready to head out? Liam's parents are out of town tonight, so there is no way we are letting you get out of this one."

I nodded and Nate's eyes lit up like the Fourth of July. He all but ran out of the office. "Let's do it," I said to myself, trying to mirror his enthusiasm.

Hopefully, a fun night with the guys would distract me from everything. I needed to relax. Maybe things would eventually get easier. If not tomorrow, then the day after. Yeah... maybe.

When I slid inside my truck, the image of Stella sitting beside me made the hairs on my arms stand up. I cracked my knuckles and leaned forward to turn the radio on. I shouldn't be thinking about her the way I was. She wasn't mine to save. If I was one step away from Kasey's problems, I needed to be at least ten to fifteen from Stella's. Preferably on the other side of the damn street.

When we got to the alabaster mansion where Liam had grown up, I spotted my friends through the fence, playing on the outdoor pool table his parents kept under the stone gazebo during the summers. After parking, we headed over to the kitchen where the alcohol was, taking a shot of whiskey and grabbing a beer to chase it. Liam, Damien, and Cody hollered at us to join. We'd all been friends since kindergarten and inseparable in high school. They weren't just my friends, but more like my brothers.

We'd been through it all together. If anyone understood me, it was them.

"Hey guys, go easy on him. He's had a big week at work," Nate teased as we walked out to the back. I shoved him hard, but he just grinned wider, hissing a laugh through his teeth.

"Don't start," I groaned, taking a long sip of my beer. The guys finished their round of pool before I took the cue from Cody to join in. The alcohol helped numb the sad eyes burned into my memory.

Several beers and many missed shots later, mainly from me, Kasey walked in through the gate, a smile spreading across her face as our eyes met. I frowned at Nate, but he held his hands up in front of him.

"Don't blame me," he said. "I didn't invite her."

"I did. Nate said you could use a distraction," Liam responded, taking a step back as Kasey headed straight for me. She jumped up on the edge of the table, taking my beer with a mischievous smile.

"Hi, Kase." I lined up my shot beside her. The ivory ball hit the wrong ball, bounced on the side wall, and rolled down into the pocket. I'd never been good at pool.

"Oh sorry, did I distract you?" Kasey winked at me.

Nate took the cue from me. "Don't flatter yourself, babe. He's been like this all week." He snickered, and I shot him a look, but it only made him laugh harder. Why did the two of them get along when it was to torture me?

"Having a tough week? Something to do with that brunette?" Kasey followed me as I leaned up against a stone pillar.

I glanced around, but only Nate paid attention to what she said with a cocked eyebrow. The rest of them were arguing about soccer. "Yeah, work has been a bit shit," I said, ignoring her mention of Stella. I didn't want the guys knowing about that. The curious look Nate gave me told me I wouldn't get off so easily.

She wrapped her fingers around my arm as she stepped even closer. "Want to tell me about it?"

Even though it had been a joke, Nate wasn't wrong. I'd been off my game all week with the promotion—or whatever it was. And then Stella came along and messed with my head in more ways than one.

Since I'd taken her to the beach yesterday, my mind had been cloudy with memories of her brother. It had been exhausting reliving it all, but it also felt good. My friends missed James as much as I did, but we rarely spoke about it. Liam was still dealing with his own shit, Nate didn't enjoy talking about his feelings, and Damien... Well, Damien could be blunt, to put it nicely. With Cody off at college in Seattle, he wasn't around as much anymore.

But it wasn't just her brother who made my head cloudy. Having Stella wrapped up in my arms stirred something in me I hadn't felt for a long time. Kasey and I had just started dating when I found out about the fights between her and her mom. I tried to help, but ended up making it worse. Instead,

I developed this desperate need to help people. It was another reason to make this business plan work. Stella brought those protective feelings out of me again, and I wasn't sure what to make of it.

I took another sip of my beer and grabbed the pool cue from Nate, but Kasey snatched it with a glint in her eyes. She took her shot and missed, pouting as she handed the cue to Nate. Their shared look was anything but friendly, yet it still made me smile. They could say they hated each other, but deep down, they were friends. She strutted back to me and rested her back against my chest.

I leaned over and whispered in her ear, "Did you miss to make me feel better about my own terrible shot?"

"Gray, I would never," she cooed, waggling her eyebrows at me. Something in the tightness around her eyes didn't sit right with me. I wanted to ask if she'd had another rough day with her mom, but not with everyone else here. Then there was no chance of her opening up.

I finished my beer and put the empty bottle down. I slid my thumbs into her front pockets and leaned my chin on her shoulder. She made a content noise and relaxed against me, watching the guys play out the rest of the game without us.

Nate gave me a look from across the table, but I closed my eyes. He knew all about my relationship with Kasey, having lived through it with me. The good and the bad—mostly the bad. But this wasn't a repeat of what we'd had in high school. Her warm body against mine wasn't turning me on or inspiring fantasies about her. It was calming because she knew me and I knew her, inside and out, outside and in. That was one thing the guys didn't get.

They finished up a few more games before we walked to sit by the firepit. We talked about everything and nothing for several hours and slowly but surely finished the last few bottles of beer.

Kasey was posting a picture of herself on Instagram with her legs resting in my lap and had mentally checked out of the conversation. I traced my fingers up and down her shin as we talked, more out of habit than anything else.

"So Gray, what's this thing that's going on with your dad?" Liam leaned forward on the outdoor couch opposite me, resting his elbows on his knees.

"Apparently, I'm taking over the company. Not sure whose bright idea that was, but I'm guessing it has more to do with my mom than my dad. Knowing me, it will all end up in a blazing fire."

"But I don't get it. Isn't it a good thing? I mean, since you want to do that business thing, it's kind of the perfect scenario. You can learn from him." He took a sip of his beer, rolling his eyes as Kasey giggled at something on her phone.

I knew why Liam was saying what he was saying. He was starting work with his dad at the local high school soon. His dad had been our soccer coach when we went there, and Liam was following in his footsteps, though it hadn't always been the plan for him. Instead of going off to college to be the next big thing in soccer, Liam lost his scholarship and any chance of going pro because of an injury at the end of high school. He was still coming to terms with it, with some days better than others. But soccer was his whole life, from the moment I'd met him until the accident that had nearly cost him everything, and with months of rehab and pain later, not counting the physical, Liam was finally getting to a point in life where he was happy again.

"Yeah, I guess, but... I don't know. I just feel like I'm going to let everyone down." I wished I knew how else to describe it without sounding like a cliché.

"You will be the boss one day, right?" Damien chimed in. A very Damien comment. He didn't enjoy taking orders from others. "That means you get to make the rules. So you can do that shit you've always been talking about. Just got to put in the work." Case in point.

Technically, he was right. But that would be years away. Years of time to fuck up. I tried to find the right words, but the alcohol had definitely impaired my thinking capabilities. I shook my head tiredly, wondering if maybe they were right. Maybe this situation was only as bad as I was making it. It was an amazing opportunity my dad had given me, and all I needed to do was show him he could rely on me. For once in my life, I just needed to not. fuck. up.

The conversation thankfully went in a different direction. I stared into the firepit as the flames licked the surrounding stones, leaning back to look at the sky. The sun had completely gone down, and thick clouds filled the heavens. The night was calm, apart from the odd laugh from the guys.

Kasey wiggled her legs in my lap and moved closer. "I'm cold," she mumbled, so I wrapped my arms around her. She rested her head on my chest and snuggled in with a contented sigh. Having someone to hold felt nice—she probably needed that too.

Damien and Cody called it a night a while later, and Liam, the self-appointed designated driver, offered to give them a ride, and Nate excused himself to go to the bathroom when the others left.

As soon as they were gone, Kasey snuggled even closer to me and moved my head to face hers. "Tell me what's wrong."

I gently kissed the back of her fingers. "I'm fine, really."

She sat up and frowned. "It's that girl Stella, isn't it?"

Her words took me by surprise and I choked on my inhale. "What? No, why would you think that?" I turned to face her as she pulled her legs away from me.

"I saw the protective look in your eyes. It's usually just directed towards me," she mumbled and shot me a quick glance, filled with the same insecurities I had seen in high school.

Everyone thought Kasey had everything figured out, but that was far from the truth. And if she felt her security was threatened, even if we were only friends now, she might lash out. Stella did not need that right now. And there was definitely nothing between us. Yeah, she might look like a cuter version of Megan Fox—her red eyes and nose somehow just making me even more attracted to her—but she was

James's twin sister. It didn't matter how good it felt to hold her. Bro code.

"I just wanted to get her out. You've heard the talk this whole last year. She doesn't need to hear that. She and Bee did the right thing by staying away." I caressed Kasey's knee and tried to get her to look at me, but she kept her eyes glued to the fire. "Anyway, you know I've always had a thing for brunettes," I taunted, knowing I was pushing her buttons, but I couldn't help myself.

She punched my shoulder, and I wrapped my arms around her, tucking her close.

"What about you?" I whispered into her ear as I moved her hair out of my face. "I can tell something's up."

She sighed heavily and curled up closer. "Nothing new. Just the same old, same old. Had a fight with my mom again about Dion, but she never listens. Nothing ever changes. It's only getting worse."

I stroked the top of her shoulder, and she took a shuddering breath. Ever since we were little, she'd had a complicated relationship with her mom, and it took a turn for the worse when her baby brother was born a few years ago. I wanted to tell her everything would be fine, but she wouldn't believe me.

Kissing her head with a sigh, we both soon drifted off to sleep.

When I woke up, the sun was about to rise, a gentle orange hue hanging in the air. Kasey was still wrapped up in my arms, and Nate was fast asleep on the lounge chair with a cushion over his face. Liam was nowhere to be seen, but he'd probably gone inside when he came back from dropping the others off and found us all asleep.

I carefully lifted myself from behind Kasey and stood to stretch. With a few hours to kill before work, I headed in search of food. As I entered the kitchen, I found Liam picking up the beer bottles from last night and putting them in a big bag. His black hair was wet, giving away the fact that he'd had a shower after he woke up. Lucky guy. I would have to go to work like this.

"Hey, I didn't know anyone was awake." I yawned and slid onto the bar stool by the kitchen island.

"I thought it was best I cleaned it up before my parents get back. You know how my mom can get with a mess," he said with a nervous chuckle. "So, are you back together with Kasey?" Liam nodded towards the sleeping girl outside.

"Nah, that ship sailed a long time ago. She's a friend and nothing more."

"Are you sure she knows that?" Liam raised his eyebrow, studying me.

I nodded quickly. "Yeah, don't worry. We're not doing that again." I scratched my chin with a tired smile.

"Good. She's not the one for you. She's too irritating." He chuckled as he walked outside with the garbage.

Liam poured us some cereal, and we passed the time by talking soccer for an hour before I went outside to nudge Nate. He groaned and slapped wildly at me, but I continued.

"Go away," he grunted.

I poked him again and again. "Get up."

He finally sat up and glared at me. "You suck. You know that, right?" He yawned and flicked his eyes toward Kasey, still asleep on the couch. "Oh shit, she's still here? I thought she would have left last night." His eyes weren't exactly wide open in surprise as sleep was still trying to drag his ass back down onto the lounge chair.

I nodded with a sigh. "Would you mind getting a ride from Liam? I should probably get her home. She had a rough day yesterday."

Nate looked from me to Kasey while shaking his head. "You sure you know what you're doing? She's too fucking annoying. And don't go thinking with your dick like you did in high school."

"People keep telling me that," I said with a small laugh. "Don't worry, I'm not getting back together with her."

Nate didn't look convinced, making a point to glance down at my crotch and then back up, shaking his head at Kasey before walking into the house.

She looked peaceful in her sleep, like she didn't have a worry in the world. I liked that Kasey. The one who could let loose and have fun, not the one who carried the weight of the world on her shoulders.

I walked over to her and kneeled on the ground, tucking some hair behind her ear to slowly wake her. When there was no life, I squeezed her shoulder.

"Hey, wake up," I whispered.

She stirred with some cute groans, scrunching her nose at the rising sun. "Is it already morning?" Her eyes were stress free for a moment.

"I'm afraid so. Want me to drive you home?" She flicked her eyes to mine, suddenly filled with anguish. "Let me drive you to my place. You can stay there as long as you want, but I need to get to work or Dad will kill me."

"Thanks," she whispered, the tension still weighing her down. The smile she gave me didn't look real at all.

We caught Nate before he left and all drove back to our place. As soon as we'd gotten our first paycheck from work, Nate and I moved in together. I honestly couldn't imagine living with anyone else. Nate was the closest to my brother out of all the guys. He could be a real dick, but he'd burrowed his way too deep into my heart at this point.

Kasey grabbed an old sweatshirt from my closet and curled up in front of the TV with a big mug of tea, disappearing into her own world while Nate and I got ready for work. He had given me several looks throughout the morning, but I wasn't in the mood for his grumbles.

When we got in the truck, he turned to me. "You sure you know what you're doing? I know you said you're fine, but dude, she's in your clothes. And she's not moving in," he added quickly. "You might enjoy dealing with her bullshit, but I don't." He pointed his thumb toward the door with a grimace on his face, his damp blond hair standing in all directions.

I grinned at him and started up the engine. "Don't worry, she's not."

"All right. And don't think I forgot about her comment about a brunette. You seeing someone you haven't told me about?"

I forced my face not to change when I thought of Stella. I couldn't tell Nate about her. Not yet. It was still too confusing. "No, it was just some girl from high school I hadn't seen in a while. You know how jealous Kasey used to get." I peered at Nate, hoping he'd believe my white lie.

He shrugged and turned forward in his seat. "Whatever. If you do, don't fuck her on the couch. Or the kitchen." His face twisted up. "My room is also off-limits."

I choked on a breath, laughing at him. "Why the fuck would I sleep with someone in your bed?"

He smirked. "Role-play and all that shit. You know the girls go wild for me." He waggled his eyebrows. I smacked him on the chest hard enough that he coughed.

"Dickhead." Until this moment, I hadn't thought of Stella and sex in the same sentence. Playing with the image as we drove to work gave me a semi, one I had to hide from Nate when we got out of the car.

Chapter Five

I t was early in the morning, but my racing brain wouldn't let me fall back to sleep. I got up with a huff and headed downstairs, stopping at James's door. The familiar anger returned, but there was also something else, something warmer. It had started when Gray told me stories about my brother.

I hadn't let myself really remember James as a person. It was easier to be angry or hurt. To hate him when my heart couldn't grasp loving anyone ever again. Being back in town made it harder to do that, so I could understand why my dad was struggling to let go of his pain. It engulfed me wherever I went.

I was in the kitchen when there was a low rumble in the driveway. I walked over to the window overlooking the front of the house. Gray's Chevy was parked on the road. He got out and lifted my bike from the bed, walking it over to the garage and leaning it against the brick wall. I barely even remembered coming home from the lake that day, let alone the fact he still had my bike.

He stood on the drive with his hands deep in his pockets, then sat down and hung his head between his knees. Before I knew what I was doing, I tiptoed out into the hallway and slipped my shoes on.

Gray jumped up when he heard me. "Damn, I'm sorry. I didn't mean to wake you." With an apologetic smile, he placed his baseball cap back on his head, causing the ends of his hair to press over his forehead and brows. He tucked his hands into the front pockets of his shorts again and hiked his shoulders up to his ears. This guy wasn't just hot—he was the kind of hot that could also look really adorable without trying. He dipped his tongue out to wet his lips, then raked his teeth over his bottom one with a smile.

I rubbed over the ache in my heart. It was nice seeing him again. Even with my dad in the house, I felt cut off from the rest of the world. Lonely, the word that always haunted me, along with *pain*.

I moved closer. "That's okay. Thanks for bringing my bike back," I said with a weak smile.

"I fixed the chain and greased some parts. It should be like new." Gray took some slow steps towards me. My body copied his movements until we were only a few feet apart.

"Thanks. You didn't have to do that." I wanted to move closer, but I didn't really have a reason to.

"Don't worry about it. If I can ever help, just let me know." He tilted his head to the side as he spoke and walked backwards towards his truck, his eyes still fixed on me.

"Gray..." I called out as he placed his hand on the handle. The sadness in his eyes tangled with the words in my throat, but I forced them out. "Thanks for being there for my brother." I swallowed the lump left behind, unable to even force a small smile. All I could do was try to keep the tears from spilling over. I wasn't sure what it was about being near Gray that made the anger go away, but the tears left behind weren't better. Just different.

He looked at me for several seconds, then nodded with his lips thinned. He opened the door, but before he sat down, he glanced back at me. "I'm headed to Damien O'Donovan's farm to hang with the guys. You're welcome to join us. I know it's probably not your favorite activity, but I don't like the thought of you sitting in that house alone. It might get rowdy"—he smiled sheepishly as he bit his lip and flicked his eyes towards the ground, a simple gesture that did something to my insides—"but maybe you could see the type of life James had with us here."

Nothing came out when I opened my mouth, unsure if it was something I wanted. It might completely break me. Talking about memories was one thing, but being in places with a lot of him was beyond daunting. Gray and I stared at each other for a few more seconds.

He shook his head when I didn't reply—couldn't reply. "Nah, don't worry. It was a stupid thing to ask. I'll see you around." He widened the truck door and slid into the driver's seat.

I took a few tentative steps towards it. I was curious about the life James had lived here without me, and the thought of feeling close to him again overpowered the fear. With James's friends by my side, maybe it wouldn't be so bad. His room couldn't stay this way forever. His soul would eventually leave it, and then what would I have left? More anger and pain. I had to move past that at some point.

I'd reached the passenger window by the time the truck rumbled to life. Knocking on it, I dropped my hands shakily by my sides, my stomach swirling out of control. Gray rolled the window down and turned the radio off, running his hands over his shorts as he waited for me to say something.

"Could you give me a few minutes to get changed?" I asked. I really hoped I wouldn't regret this. The smile Gray gave me filled me with some confidence, along with a warmth that rolled through my belly.

"Take your time."

I regretted my decision to come with Gray almost instantly. I'd been picking at my cuticles since we started driving, a bad habit I'd never been able to shake. My fingers were sore now—little bits of blood seeping out of my skin. After a long and uncomfortable silence, he had leaned over and turned the radio on. It wasn't the type of music James used to listen to, much more punk rock than bluegrass or country, but it was better than silence.

The road turned into a dirt driveway, with nothing but fields on either side. At the end sat an old farmhouse with a cute cornflower-blue door, old wooden benches, and a rocking chair on the beautiful front porch. There were several barns and workshops with big openings that showcased the clutter of things packed inside of them and a chicken coop off to the side of a field with horses. A group of guys stood in the shade of a tall tree. The sight of them caused my stomach to somersault.

"If at any point you want to leave, just tell me," Gray said, breaking the silence between us. His eyebrows drew together, and he had a look of concern in his eyes that did little to relax me. He parked the truck next to the others before continuing. "They can be loud, but they're good guys. At least, James seemed to think so." He tried a smile, but it looked pitiful and soon morphed back into a frown.

I bit my lip and nodded. His eyes drifted down to my mouth as his frown deepened even more. I guess he could tell I was worried. We stepped out of the car together and the guys instantly started shouting for Gray.

"Hey, here he is! Man, I thought you'd be here hours ago." A sandy-haired guy walked up to Gray and slapped him on the shoulder. "Taking your sweet time bringing the goods! We've been getting by on beer alone." He was tall and muscular, looking a perfect image of a lumberjack. His hair was soaking wet, and the water dripped over his ripped flannel shirt as he shook his head from side to side. He looked familiar. I must have seen him around high school, even though I'd mostly kept to myself.

"Yeah, yeah, whatever, Damien. Still got a long day ahead of us." Gray playfully pushed his friend and nodded to the other guys in greeting.

Damien noticed me standing by the car and pulled Gray to the side. They whispered about something, but Damien soon backed off when Gray fixed him with a firm look. Gray waved for me to come closer—I wasn't sure I wanted to. The truck had been comforting until now, but it was time to leave that safety behind. My knees tingled, threatening to give way as I took a tentative step forward. God, this had been such a bad idea.

"It seems we've got some company today, guys! This here is James's sister, Stella. I hope we're all going to give her the welcome we would have given James, so throw me a beer, would you?" He motioned towards the other three guys, and one of them grabbed a beer out of a cooler and threw it to Damien. He handed it to me, still dripping with water from the melting ice it had been sitting in.

"Thanks," I said as I took the beer and popped the top. I didn't sip it, but just the act of opening it felt like the right thing to do. With my dad being an alcoholic for most of my life, my relationship with drinking was strained, to say the least.

Gray stepped closer and rested his hand on my lower back. My cheeks flushed at the softness and I moved even closer to the safety. If I didn't have the truck, I guess Gray would have to take that spot. I was determined to get through the day. Or at least a few more hours. If I could feel closer to James for a little while, that was all I could ask for.

"This here is Nate Keyes," Damien pointed to the dark-blond guy standing a few feet away, wearing a navy T-shirt that left little to the imagination. He winked at me, and Gray tensed. I definitely recognized Nate. He was the playboy in high school and had tried to talk to me a few times. Actually, when I think back, it had definitely been more flirting than talking, with winks and innuendos. He'd quickly lost interest and moved on to some cheerleader instead. It hadn't been that I didn't find him attractive, because he definitely was—probably even more now than in high school as he filled out his shirt with bulging muscles. But he was confident and lively, and I was neither of those things. People who were brash made me feel uncomfortable.

"And then we've got Liam Myers and Cody Brooks." Damien motioned to the other two.

Liam was a raven-haired, lean but muscular guy in a gray top who had a scar on his right knee. I vaguely remembered him hurting himself during a soccer game at the end of senior year.

Cody was shorter, with medium-brown hair that curled up at his ears. He wore a baseball shirt a few sizes too big, hanging loosely over his shoulders, and after giving me a smile and wave, he turned to look in another direction, not staring like the rest of them. Hallelujah.

I'd seen them all in high school, but I didn't know them. I never hung out with my brother and his friends. He wanted to move on, and my pessimism brought him down. Of course, he had never said that. He didn't have to. But I hadn't wanted to be a bother, so I stayed away.

Liam and Nate nodded at me, and then finally went back to talking to each other. They were dripping in sweat from the summer heat, and the back of my neck was heating too. The gentle breeze that blew over the yard only brought more hot air, and the warm hand on my back wasn't helping things, but I never wanted it to move. With it, I might be able to do this. Without it, I'd be alone again.

"Now that we're all here, let's head out. The ATVs are behind the barn, so let's load up the truck!" Damien whistled and waved his finger in the air. Nate, Liam, and Cody grabbed the coolers of beer by their feet, along with some long duffel bags, and chucked them in the back of Gray's truck.

"We'll drive out there and they can take the ATVs." Gray squeezed my waist to grab my attention. His touch made me jump as it sent another flurry of heat through me. He held my gaze for a moment, then dropped his hand from my waist as if he'd been shocked. Coming here had definitely been a bad idea. A bad idea in more ways than one.

I couldn't get attached to Gray or anything else in this town. A week or two more, then I'd be back in LA. It was easier to move on there. This place would always hold too much of James.

"Hey, wait up. I ain't riding with Cody!" Nate came running up behind us and playfully smacked Gray on the back of the head. Gray laughed and punched at him, but Nate jumped less than gracefully out of the way. He winked at me as he held open the door to the front seat so I could slip in.

The three of us got into the truck. Gray stared Nate down through the rearview mirror, sharing a silent conversation until Nate held his hands up innocently.

"I haven't said anything, man." He was sitting back in the middle seat with his legs spread wide and a devilish glint in his eyes.

"Said what?" I asked and looked between them, trying my best not to wring my hands.

Gray threw another scowl at his friend, but Nate just leaned forward between us. His face was so close to me now that I could smell his aftershave. It was spicy but clean, tingling my nose and setting my senses on fire. I shifted to the side to create some space and gave up trying to keep my hands still—I shoved them between my thighs instead.

"Well, we don't normally bring dates or girls on these sorts of things, except for Josie, Damien's cousin, and maybe sometimes Kasey. You know Kasey. You were in cheerleading together, right?"

I shook my head. "I was never a cheerleader."

"Anyway," he said with a shrug, barely taking in my comment. "Her and Gray used to be a thing back then, so she was always around. Even Bee didn't really come up here much when..." His voice quickly trailed off when he realized where he was taking this conversation.

I would not scream.

I would not cry.

I couldn't breathe.

My eyes burned, and I had to blink furiously to get the tears to retreat. I couldn't take more than tiny breaths in through my nose and by this point, my lungs were burning.

"This isn't like that," Gray growled. I peered at him as he focused on reversing around the barn, but I couldn't quite read his expression. "I just wanted her to get a taste of what James got up to when she wasn't here, you know?" He took a sip from a bottle of water and shifted back into first. He glimpsed at me, but his eyes didn't linger. Was he angry at me or at his friend? Maybe he already regretted bringing me here. That would make two of us.

"Yeah, yeah, I'm just teasing you, buddy." Nate slapped Gray again, who let out a grumble. They shared another silent stare, then Nate scoffed and shook his head, leaning back in his seat and looking out the window.

Bad idea was playing on repeat in my head. Bad because I didn't know these guys that well, bad because tears were still burning behind my eyes, and bad because I wanted to be near Gray, as he was the only thing that seemed to calm me.

At least I didn't have painful memories everywhere I looked because I'd never been here before. The place was beautiful and serene, and the fresh air did relax me some. Where there had been nothing but fields before, now there was nothing but forest as far as I could see, which honestly wasn't that far as the undergrowth was thick and the hills rolling.

We drove for a few minutes on an old dirt track, the truck jumping up and down over roots and dried-out puddles. I had to give myself a pep talk when another moment of hesitation washed over me. I thought about asking Gray to drive me back home, but I could almost hear James in my ears egging me on and I said nothing.

He would have wanted me here. I know he would have. It brought a tiny smile to my lips. But he wasn't here to experience this with me. We could have had this if I hadn't left. Suddenly, the anger that was normally directed towards him turned to me. Yes, he might have been the one who left me in the end, but I left him first. The smile faded into a frown as tears pricked my eyes.

Chapter Six

We pulled up to an opening where Cody, Damien, and Liam had parked the ATVs. They were having an argument about who got to go first, pushing each other playfully as they threw insults around.

Nate jumped out of the truck with his beer lifted high in the sky and shouted, "Hey, I haven't got a go yet. Get out of my way!" He pushed the other guys to the side and jumped on an ATV before they could stop him. They laughed and flipped him off as he drove off at full speed down the track, dirt flinging up behind the wheels and leaving a cloud of dust.

"You okay?" Gray asked, nudging my leg with his hand. We were still sitting in the truck.

I nodded, not trusting my voice. He smiled when he slid out of the truck, jogging over to the others and knocking into them, then motioned for me to join them when he noticed I hadn't moved.

"So, Stella, have you ever driven one of these before?" Gray smirked as he wiped some sweat off his forehead, swiping his unruly hair back.

"You're not expecting me to drive it, are you?" I walked towards them and crossed one arm in front of my body, trying to create a shield between us.

"It's easy. Come here, I'll show you." Gray walked over to the ATV and hopped onto the seat. "This is the gas, and this is the brake. You turn the engine on"—he turned the key in the ignition and it sputtered to life—"and then you pull the clutch in, click with your foot, and..." He turned to me, grinning at the blank expression on my face. "Yeah, okay, maybe we'll take it slower. Why don't you get on the back and I'll drive?"

I hesitated, shifting my weight from one foot to the next. "James did this with you guys?" I squeezed the beer can in my hand and clenched my jaw as I said his name. The pain was almost debilitating, but I did my best to hold it at bay. I wanted—needed—to be stronger than this.

Gray turned the engine off, shifting to look down the track. The guys had taken the truck and driven off after Nate, leaving us standing in the clearing alone. I was walking or getting on the ATV—that fact hadn't eluded me.

"I, eh... He changed a lot throughout high school. He grew up, and he moved on from everything."

It was like a stab to the heart, but it was true. James had moved on from our terrible childhood, something I never truly did. I inhaled sharply and my vision blurred. Gray jumped off the ATV and took my hand in his, pulling me to sit with him on it. His touch helped, but it wasn't enough to stop the pain.

"I don't mean you didn't," he grumbled, letting go of my hand to sip his water. Missing the touch, I stared at his hand longingly but didn't reach out. That would be weird, right? "I just mean..." He fumbled with his words, letting out a huff. "He wanted to live life to its fullest. He liked to have fun. You know he used to sneak out at night, right?" Gray gestured to the ATV with a careful smile. "We would be out here most weekends. But whenever you would come to visit, we didn't hear a word from him. It was like he had two lives." He wiped some sweat off his brow, studying me.

I scraped my foot in the dirt. He was right. James was different with me than anyone else. He wasn't just a brother or a friend; he was my protector. I'd never asked him to be—he'd taken on that role all by himself. But when he wasn't looking after me, he went out and continued to live his life. Part of the reason I left for LA was so he wouldn't have to be responsible for me anymore.

I hadn't lived while I was there; I'd ran from the past. James hadn't. He owned who he was, and he wanted me to do the same. He had asked me to join him and his friends more times than I could count. It wasn't his fault I refused every single time. Maybe if I had stayed here, things could have been different. Even now, I was holding on to the anger and pain. For what? To punish him, or to punish myself?

Gray nudged my ankle with his boot and tried to catch my eye. I looked at him, wishing that if I just stared long enough, he would turn into James.

It wasn't fair, but I wanted it for just a moment. To have him here again. To not feel *this* anymore. Gray reached out to wipe a tear from my cheek, and a smile formed on my lips. He'd been so good to me. I felt protected when his warm cognac eyes stared back at me—less alone.

"Okay," I said, tears still clogging my throat. A spark lit in his eyes. I took a slow breath and looked at the beer can in my hand. He took it from me and placed it on the ground.

"I'll get you water in a bit, all right? I should have asked what you wanted to drink earlier. That's my bad." He squeezed my wrist, and the pain softened into a swirling in my belly.

I wiped my sweaty palms on my jean shorts. Just for today, I would try to live without regrets. Well, for a few hours. I'd made it this far. If my brother had trusted Gray, then I could too. Gray swung his leg over the ATV and patted the back, and with a deep breath and another cautious smile, I swung my leg over too.

"Don't worry, I'll take it slow." His grin was mischievous as he turned the engine on and it made my stomach flutter even more. I slid my feet in behind his, my toes only reaching the back of his heels. "Grab on to these or me," Gray said, tapping the metal railings on either side of my legs.

I nodded, and a nervous noise rolled from my mouth as he drove down the track. I was thankful he was going slower than the other guys, as even at this speed, it was bumpy as hell. The trees weren't exactly blending into mush in the corner of my vision, but the wind pulled at my hair and I had a tight grip on the railing.

"See, piece of cake!" Gray cheered over the engine noise and his wide smile brightened my own. We eventually stopped at the top of a hill. The engine sputtered as he shifted into neutral, and he turned to me with a glint in his eyes. "You ready for this? It's going to go faster now. Tell me if you don't want to."

I bit my lip with a smile and nodded. His eyes zoomed in on my lips and his grin widened, making his eyes sparkle. They were beautiful. It sent a shiver through my body, but I told myself it was nothing more than adrenaline. Confusing feelings I hadn't felt in a long time for something other than pain and sadness wasn't smart.

I was close to James out here, and that's what I needed to focus on. I closed my eyes for a moment and imagined him sitting in front of me. The part of me that was angry we never got to experience this together got shoved away for now.

The ATV jumped forward with a roar. I reached my hands around James's stomach. I mean, Gray's stomach. His damp T-shirt stuck to my arms, his hard abs constricting under my touch. They stretched and moved as we went faster, sending a frenzy to my core. I was desperate to slide my fingers under the fabric. Gray cheered as he sped up and we flew down the woods much faster than before.

I grabbed on tighter as the feeling of weightlessness filled me and we were no longer touching the ground. My chest was pressed tightly to his back, and my lungs filled with his masculine scent. It was like an eternity before we landed. When I finally opened my eyes, the guys were up ahead, hollering and raising their beer bottles as we pulled up next to them, skidding in the dirt.

"Hell yeah!" they shouted, and Cody ran up to high-five Gray. He gave me a toothy smile before retreating to his friends.

I reluctantly released my grip around Gray's stomach, and he swung his leg around so they were on one side of the vehicle. His eyes twinkled with adrenaline, and his hair was now completely dry of sweat from the ride, but very tousled. Reaching my hand out to run my fingers through it would be a bad idea, right? Yes, very. Another bad idea. My brain was all over the place today. Maybe I was trying to distract myself, but touching Gray like that would be inappropriate. It didn't mean a woman couldn't daydream, though.

"So, how was your first ride?" He smirked. I snapped out of my thoughts with a blush, studying his hand as he flicked his hair from his face. He caught a bottle of water Damien threw at him, taking several long mouthfuls and exhaling sharply at the end. My legs were unsteady as I swung them around to meet his. Our knees touched, and I moved to the side.

"It was all right, I guess," I said, with a small smile that quickly broke into a grin.

Damien whistled as he threw me a water when Gray nodded my way. "Dang girl, I almost forgot you were James's sister! But I can see the resemblance now. That same fire in your eyes." The guys laughed while unloading bags from the truck.

Gray watched me, but I kept smiling. What might have once brought me to tears somehow only made me feel even closer to James. Maybe it was because of where I was, or because of his friends. I lifted the bottle to my lips and the cold water swirled in my mouth as I closed my eyes, feeling James right here with me. My heart constricted, but not from pain. Only from love. I rubbed my hand over the left side of my chest, allowing myself to enjoy that feeling.

Gray shifted next to me and then jumped to his feet with a groan. When he reached down into the truck bed, I admittedly checked out his ass and toned legs. If I wasn't already sweating, the sight of more muscle moving under sweaty skin definitely would have pushed me over the edge. He pulled out a long camouflage bag, walking over to dump it by an old barn near a field. His shorts stretched against his backside, sending a pulse to my core. I tipped my head back to tear my gaze away, pressing the cold bottle against my neck to feel some relief.

"Dang, you make a grown man weak doing shit like that, girl!" Nate hollered as he unloaded the last bag from the truck.

I sat up straight, dropping the bottle to my lap. My cheeks flushed and my heart raced as I looked in the opposite direction, not wanting to make eye contact. I wasn't sure why his comment made me react like that. He'd basically only mimicked my thoughts about Gray.

When Nate walked away from the truck, I dashed over to it and slid into the passenger seat, needing a moment to compose myself. I was being ridiculous. I knew that. He was only doing the same flirting he had done in high school. But with no hot cheerleader to steal his attention from me, it was overwhelming. *Steal* was probably the wrong word, as that implied I wanted his attention. I would have happily shoved him at them.

As I closed the door, the glove box fell open, and a piece of paper dropped onto the floor. I reached down to pick it up. It was a photo of all the guys holding up mason jars filled with water. Well, it probably wasn't water, but the clear liquid could have been anything—most likely moonshine. Damien, Nate, Cody, Gray. And then my brother. He stood on the right, smiling wide, with an intoxicated look on his face and his brown hair pointing in all directions. The look reminded me of my dad, but Dad rarely smiled when he was drunk. James's looked warm and playful, just like I remembered it.

"Hey, you all right?" Gray leaned in through the window. The smile he'd worn faded when he saw the photo in my hand. His face tightened and he held his breath as he looked from it and back to me a few times.

"When was this taken?" I asked and handed it to him with a shaky hand, feeling the tears already trying to claw their way out of my eyes. Despite feeling good for a while, seeing his face had been a shock.

Gray opened his door and slid in beside me. He hesitantly took the photo from me and rested it on his leg, shifting restlessly in his seat. "Summer after graduation. It was the end of a seventy-two-hour bender up by the lake." He glanced at me and handed the picture back. His cheeks flushed red, and it traveled down his neck. The worry in his eyes overpowered his embarrassment.

Scanning the photo, I saw the boat behind them, along with the beach covered in beer cans, dimly lit from a bonfire in the background. A warm tear ran down my cheek. I quickly wiped it away, but more followed.

"Come here." He shifted closer to me and pulled me into his arms. I sniffled and wiggled my hand free so I could continue to stare at my brother while Gray's warm arms created a safe cocoon from the world, but there was no protecting me from the internal pain. A whimper slipped out of my mouth, the tears flowing heavier and faster.

"I hate him. And I hate myself. All of it. It's my fault." Stuttered words followed by more whimpers rolled out of me. Gray tightened his arms with each one.

"None of this is your fault," he pleaded, his deep voice rumbling against the side of my head and his hands tangling in the hair hanging over my back.

"Yes, it is." I pushed him away and looked into his eyes. "If I hadn't... If I had just..." My throat closed so tightly it was a miracle I could breathe. Or maybe I wasn't. Everything hurt so much, it was hard to tell. I dropped my eyes back to the photo.

Gray sighed and reached for the ignition. "I'm taking you home. I don't know what I was thinking when I brought you here."

I didn't stop him. I didn't know if I wanted to stay or go. All I could do was stare at my brother's face.

Gray shouted at his friends that he'd be back, and then we drove down the same path we had taken with the ATV. I let the tears flow freely now, unable to even lift my hand to fasten my seatbelt, so when we got to the road, he reached over and buckled it for me. I clung to the photo, my breath catching in my throat as I curled up as small as I could on the seat and held the picture against my chest while clutching my necklace.

It wasn't fair. None of it.

Some time later Gray nudged me, and I opened my eyes, still filled with tears that had yet to fall. We sat outside my house, and it looked just as empty as I felt.

"Do you want me to walk you in?"

A wave of sadness washed over me when I turned to look at Gray, making me feel even weaker. He looked so sad. So hurt. I hated that he had to see me like this.

Gripping the door, I got out of the truck. Gray dashed around to my side and let me support myself against him. Even now, his touch tried to ease the pain, but it was no use. I held on to the picture and my necklace as I lay down on my bed, a blanket hugging me but it didn't feel comforting. How I ended up here, I wasn't sure. I didn't remember walking through the door, or trudging up the stairs and past my brother's room.

"I'm sorry," Gray whispered before he left. Clomping footsteps sounded through the house, followed by the slamming of the front door. "Fuck!" rang through the air from outside, followed swiftly by a bang. The Chevy's engine roared as it sped down the street, leaving behind a silence so deafening I thought I had lost my hearing.

It was like no time had passed at all. Like it was just yesterday that I got the news about James's car crash. Everyone had said it was nothing but a tragic accident, that no one was to blame. But how was that possible? We lost a life that day. The purest of souls gone in the blink of an eye. If I had been there, maybe he wouldn't have been driving down that road. Maybe I could have stopped it all from happening.

Chapter Seven

The guys were asleep under some pine trees when I got back. I sank down beside them, bouncing my foot on the ground as I berated myself for bringing Stella here.

It had been stupid. So *fucking* idiotic. My need to be with her had overpowered my brain.

My muscles were as tense as the string on a bow. I didn't know why she affected me so strongly. I sat there, internally screaming, as I finished a bottle of beer in just a few minutes. It didn't make me feel any more levelheaded.

"Hey, you're back," Damien groaned as he woke, rousing everyone else. Cody was the last to stir when Liam kicked his boot.

"Where are we off to next?" I asked, gripping the beer tightly. Damien looked at it, and so did I. My knuckles were white but also bruised. He frowned.

"Are we not talking about what happened?" Liam chimed in from my side. I glanced at him, my hand twitching involuntarily.

"Yeah, dude, it was weird how you two just took off suddenly. Did you guys...?" Nate humped the air, laughing. I stared him down with a clenched jaw and a glassy stare. He quickly stopped, frowning and looking more concerned than the others, but there was also curiosity in his gaze. The same curiosity he'd had when Kasey mentioned a brunette and when Stella stepped out of my truck at the farm. He was trying to put two and two together. I didn't even know what it equated to at this point, but it definitely couldn't make four.

"She wanted to go home. Nothing else to it." I looked at them all until they nodded.

"What about the damage to your truck door? That off-limits too?" Nate pointed to my truck and then at my knuckles. I ignored his question in favor of sipping my beer.

I hadn't exactly planned on punching my truck. In hindsight, it wasn't the smartest thing to do. But I'd been so agitated after leaving Stella on her own that it just happened. All I had wanted to do was make things better for her. It was my fault she'd broken down. If I hadn't dragged her out here, none of it would have happened. I was better off leaving her alone, no matter how much I wanted the opposite. But just like with Kasey, I had to learn when to let go. It wasn't my fight.

My chest constricted. Fuck, I wanted it to be my fight.

"Well, let's head to the river for some fishing then, boys!" Damien broke the tense silence, rounding us all up. We grabbed our bags, then set off down a small path.

After a few minutes of walking through the woods, we got to the river. Nate normally sat with me while I fished, but he lay down beside Cody instead. Despite that, I could feel him watching me, blue eyes boring a hole in the back of my neck. The rapid water tried to drown out my worries, and it worked to some extent. I didn't grab the fishing rod so firmly my hand ached, and the entire day went by blissfully slow.

Josie, Damien's cousin, showed up a few hours later with some food—a true blessing. No one caught anything more than some plants and driftwood. We all blamed it on the weather. It was either too hot or too windy. We couldn't decide.

We talked about soccer. About Liam's dad finding the trash bag full of beer cans, and what Cody was doing at college. Normal things. Cody smiled at Josie a lot. Probably—definitely—more than he should have. He'd had a thing for her since before we were teenagers, but had never been brave enough to do anything about it.

It was for the best. Her father, *Pastor* Andrews, would never let her go out with one of us. He thinks we're all degenerates. And I didn't really blame him, to be honest. We always drag Josie into some problem or another with our stupidity.

And then there was Damien. Her cousin disguised as an overprotective brother. It was mainly because of him she was off-limits. Bro code was most definitely a thing with her. I was pretty sure Damien would only be happy if she became a nun and never talked to guys again. The image of Josie as a nun made me chuckle, as she was always dressed in the most brightly colored and adorable outfits she could get her hands on.

After we'd finished eating, Josie said she would take the stuff back to the house for us and Cody graciously offered to help her. Damien didn't react, but he'd never noticed they had a thing for each other. I shook my head as Cody went with her, her giggles rolling over the water as they disappeared out of view. They weren't exactly discreet.

The rest of us packed up our fishing gear and headed back to my truck and the ATVs. We drove farther down the track, shouting and screaming as we egged each other on. I finally felt like I could smile instead of tense up when I thought about Stella and how her hair had looked as she stepped off the ATV. The way she clung to me for dear life had sent a bolt of lightning through me. I'd enjoyed that. A lot. So much so I'd been sporting a semi that I'd tried desperately to hide. Her rubbing her chest hadn't helped things.

Although I probably shouldn't, I toyed with that image for a moment. My shorts tightened again.

With the sun setting over the trees, we needed to get a bonfire lit. Damien showed us to an empty backfield where he and Nate built the bonfire, and the rest of us unloaded the alcohol. Damien pulled a lighter out of his back pocket, starting the fire all around the base of the pile they'd created, then rested his hands on his head with a low whistle. The sun dipped down below the horizon, and the warmth that spread from the fire caressed my face.

I sighed deeply, then looked at all my friends. We were all thinking the same thing. The pain etched on their faces was the same I was feeling in my chest—the clawing, burning ache of missing someone. We hadn't been able to bring ourselves to light a bonfire here since losing James. Thinking about it in terms of years and not months or weeks was wild. But I guess life moved on, whether you wanted it to or not.

It was one reason I had asked Stella to come. I wanted it to be something she got to experience, but I was still kicking myself for believing it wouldn't hurt like hell for her.

I locked eyes with Nate, and even his were red and glossy. He gave me a small smile that didn't reach past his lips and raised his moonshine jar to me in a silent toast. I nodded, grabbing one for myself and raising it towards the bonfire.

"To James," I said, fighting to keep my voice steady.

"To James," they said back in unison.

Through the flames, I almost thought I saw him. Brown hair pointing in all directions—the wide grin, his default look, beaming back at me. As the fire danced, his face disappeared with the flames. I smiled as I looked up at the sky, now filled with stars, and whispered, "This is for you, Junior."

I woke up with a splitting headache and the sun glaring down on me. The entire weekend was a blur, and flashing images were all my thumping head summoned. Brown curls, too much moonshine, and not enough sense to know when to stop doing stupid things.

I smiled, slowly opening my eyes to find Damien passed out next to me. I nudged him and he sat up, mirroring me by tightly clutching his head.

"Ow," he moaned with one eye squeezed shut, the other one barely open. He chuckled at the same pained expression on my face.

"Where is everyone?" I asked.

Damien had managed to barely pry open both eyes, and he looked like he was regretting his choice. "They must have left." He brushed some grass from his shirt as he stood up on wobbly legs with a nauseated groan, leaning over on his knees. I stood with him and felt around for my phone, pulling it out to find it dead. Great.

"Nate wouldn't have left without me."

"I don't see him."

"Helpful," I groaned. "What time is it?" I was already pretty confident I wouldn't like the answer.

Damien dug through his shorts and pulled out his phone. When he winced and then smirked, I was close to throwing my fist into his face.

"Tell me."

"Almost midday. Shit, your dad is going to *kill* you." He looked all too pleased about my looming demise.

My heart sank in my chest, and I could have thrown up. I was suddenly stone-cold sober. Tight panic spread through my chest when I realized what my dad was going to think. It hadn't even been a month, and I'd already screwed up.

"Fuck, fuck, fuck, FUCK!" I shouted as I ran up the hill to my truck, my headache trying to split my skull in two. I slammed the gears in reverse, leaving Damien laughing at me in the yard. Nate's car wasn't here, which meant he'd already left. Why the fuck hadn't he woken me up for work? *I* was going to kill *him*.

I plugged my phone in to charge on the console, flicking my eyes between it and the road as I waited for it to start up. No matter how many times I slapped my face, I couldn't wake up, still hungover and probably a little too drunk to drive. There was a diner farther up the road, so for everyone's safety, I pulled in to grab some coffee.

A happy-go-lucky lady took my order, then slid a cup of black coffee over to me. I barely let it cool before gulping it down. Just how completely and utterly screwed I was became apparent when I glanced at the clock. The coffee in my stomach tried to come back up.

I would just have to come clean to my dad when I got back, and maybe he would understand. Unlikely, but it wasn't like I had any other choice.

A woman in the corner caught my eye. Her wavy mocha hair framed her sunglasses, her face almost hidden from view. I didn't recognize her at first. Stella gave her order to the same lady who took mine, and as she followed the waitress with her gaze, she looked in my direction. She snapped out of her daydream when I gave her a quick wave, blushing adorably as she smiled back before turning her attention to her dad.

A warm feeling spread across my chest. I enjoyed seeing her smile, and that made me uncomfortable. I tried telling myself I was just happy to see her okay after this weekend's fiasco, as there was no fucking way I was going to develop feelings for my dead best friend's twin sister. No way in hell. If Josie was off-limits for Cody, Stella was on another fucking level. All the guys would beat me up if I did anything stupid.

A minute later, she got up from her seat and made her way over to me. I'd almost hoped she wouldn't, but couldn't help the nervous flutter running along my spine when she sat down beside me.

"Hi," she said. She fiddled with a napkin on the counter, avoiding my gaze. I couldn't see her eyes through her sunglasses. Why she was wearing them indoors?

"Hey," I replied. What could I say after what I'd put her through? Sorry didn't seem quite enough. Hair fell over her face when she tilted her head down. My hand twitched at the thought of tucking it behind her ear.

"You look rough," she teased once she looked back up, gesturing to my stubble. She pushed her sunglasses higher on her nose, and through the reflection I glimpsed dark circles under her eyes.

My chest tightened and the need to hold her got even stronger. Shit, this was bad. I shouldn't be reacting this way to her. I forced a smile. "Yeah, I've, uh... just left Damien's." She smiled back at me, but it looked as forced as mine felt. "I'm sorry, by the way. I shouldn't have dragged you out there. It wasn't my place."

She sighed. "It was my choice. I just didn't know it was going to hurt that much. Some of it was nice."

I studied her face, knowing she wasn't telling me the whole truth. She looked so small in her seat. All I could think was that I wanted to hold her and make everything better. Not that I could fix anything, but that was beside the point. I almost felt James's eyes watching me from above, burning like a cattle prod on the top of my head.

"Either way, it was stupid of me to offer," I said as I finished the last bit of coffee, sliding the empty cup away. I still wasn't sure I should be driving, but I didn't want to sit here with her any longer than I needed to. "You'll be okay. It might not be soon. It might be a long time from now. But you will get there." What the fuck was that bullshit? It had come out before I could stop myself.

"I just said that to my dad," she said with a sour chuckle. "I just don't know if I really believe it. That one day it will hurt less. I can't even figure out if I want to cry or scream." Her words sounded raw and honest.

My chest almost caved in. I looked away, tensing my fists into balls by my sides. After a few deep breaths, I moved my eyes over the diner and landed on her dad. He was watching us with a curious look, a newspaper folded in front of him. It was definitely best I left.

"I'll see you around."

"Wait," she blurted. "Would you tell me some more stories about James? It might be too much for me to experience it, but I want to know. I need to know. Maybe it's the only way I can ever move on." With a napkin ripped to shreds, she moved on to her cuticles, still not meeting my gaze as she spoke. It made me want to say no even more, but I couldn't.

"Give me your phone."

She pulled it out of her back pocket and handed it to me, her light touch setting my arm on fire in lots of tiny explosions. She pulled back and wrung her hands in her lap, a soft shade of pink tinting her nose and cheeks. They looked even silkier than her hands. I cleared my throat to remind myself where we were—and who she was.

"This is my number. Call me anytime." I reached for her hand, craving that sensation again. I gave it a small squeeze, relishing her soft skin before I had to let go. The top of my head and my neck burning broke the spell I was under. "Say hi to your dad for me." She gave me a small nod and I couldn't help from reaching out and squeezing her shoulder before I left.

Fuck, I was on thin ice. I pressed on my bruised knuckles in another attempt to clear my mind, but it did little to help. I'd never felt this way before. The closest thing I could think of was with Kasey. That need to be near someone, so close that all you could breathe was them. But this was even stronger than that and not mixed with teenage hormones.

And it wasn't just the feelings scaring me. It was how easily she seemed to make me forget reason.

I couldn't let myself do that. She was hurting. She was James's sister. There was no way I would cross that line. My dick would just have to get with the program.

Chapter Eight

- STELLA -

"Who was that?" My dad probed in forced nonchalance as I slid into the seat opposite him.

"That's Gray, James's friend. They used to play soccer together." I gulped the orange juice, tapping my nails on the glass.

"I thought he looked familiar. What did he want?"

I'd learned to keep things from him a long time ago, but it was easier when he was drunk. I wasn't sure why I didn't want to tell Dad the truth. "He was just asking some questions about the memorial."

My dad's face softened, and he took a sip of his coffee. "Is he coming on Sunday?"

I tried not to let it take my breath away—thinking that this was the week I'd be saying goodbye to my brother forever. Until now, I'd told myself he was just in his room, which on some disturbed level was true. He'd always been home. But it was time to let him go. It wasn't doing anyone any good.

"I don't know, but I'll ask him if I see him around." I was hoping he would show up. Not just for James, but for me. I wasn't sure I could get through it alone after breaking down so many times since coming back.

We sat in silence until our pancakes arrived, then both picked at the food. Neither of us had an appetite anymore. An unknown amount of time passed with the food getting cold on the table, and then my dad looked at his watch and sighed.

"I should probably get going. My shift is starting soon and I'm working late again tonight. Do you want me to drive you home?" The way he didn't meet my eye made me think he wasn't working late, but I didn't have the energy to fight with him. He grabbed his wallet and left some money on the table before glancing at me.

"I think I'm going to walk home. Some fresh air might do me good." I smiled tightly.

My dad checked his watch again. "Are you sure? It would take you an hour to get home."

I smiled and assured him I would be fine before giving him a hug. He walked outside and slid into his car, giving me a wave through the window. I gave him one back, though my hand dropped as soon as his back was turned. The waitress walked over to my booth to clear the plates with a chipper smile.

"Thanks," I said.

She stacked the plates with one hand and grabbed the glasses with the other. "Anytime, darling!" Her sprightly voice echoed in my ears, and I longed for a time when I could feel happy again.

I pulled my legs up under my chin and watched the other customers in the diner. My right cheek rested on my knees as I scanned the room, families coming and going as I daydreamed. My gaze eventually landed on a blue Chevy just in view at the far end of the parking lot. I was pretty sure it was Gray's—the side just as dirty as I remembered. I grabbed my stuff and exited out of the front doors.

I found him asleep, his hands resting on his knees and his head tilted back. His lips were slightly parted, and I wondered for a moment what they would taste like. I shook my head to rid myself of that thought. Not getting attached or involved. I tapped on the window, and he blinked his eyes open, looking at me with a confused, tired smile, then rolled the window and rubbed his face while yawning.

"Shit, I guess I must have fallen asleep." His rumbled voice sent a shiver down my spine, lodging itself in places it shouldn't.

I rested my fingertips on the rolled-down window and leaned my weight back on my heels, unsure of what to say. He twisted to the console to check the time and a tightness spread across his features. He suddenly looked wide awake, and he rubbed both hands over his face.

Turning the engine on before looking over at me, he asked, "Where's your dad?"

"Gone to work." Maybe. Or he just decided he needed a drink. I dropped my fingers from the window and took a step back.

"So you were going to walk home again, were you?" Gray shook his head at me, leaning over to open the passenger door. "Hop in. But I can't take you home right away. I need to pick up some deliveries first." My feet moved before my brain had decided if it was a good idea or not. "What would you ever do without me, huh?" He squeezed my leg for a moment too long when I sat down, then reached to turn the radio on. My skin burned where his touch had been, lingering until I wiped it away with my hands.

He mumbled along to the music on the radio, glancing at me every now and again with a smile. When he smiled, I wanted to smile back. That was an alien feeling.

"Did you have a good weekend?" I picked at my nail polish, keeping my eyes fixated out the window.

"Yeah. Whenever Damien's dad isn't around, we usually spend most of our time there. It got a bit wild." He chortled.

"And what about the dent on the door?" I quizzed, lifting my eyebrow. I'd noticed it when I walked up. "Did you slide into a tree?"

His smile faltered briefly, but it was enough for me to notice. "Nah, that was all me," he answered, tightening his grip on the steering wheel and pretending to look at something in the rearview. He changed the radio station a few times, and a song stuck out to me, grabbing at my heart.

"Stop, go back," I squeaked.

Gray went back through the stations until I gasped. I curled my legs up under my chin and continued to stare at the dashboard. It was one of James's favorite songs, "*Somewhere on a Beach*" by Dierks Bentley. I couldn't even count the times this song had been playing from his room. I closed my eyes. I swore I could hear his voice, right there in the truck. But I wasn't sad. Or angry. There was a lightness in my chest.

"James liked this song, didn't he?" Gray gently drummed away on the wheel as we turned into a large warehouse parking lot.

I leaned my cheek on my knees so I could look at him. The sun beamed through the window, blurring everything but his silhouette. I pretended for a moment that James was sitting right next to me—that he wasn't gone. And it kind of worked. If I squinted, he looked just like my brother. Another wave of calm washed over me, spreading over my scalp in a tingle.

"You okay, Stella?"

I blinked a few times as my eyes adjusted to the light. My heart fluttered when Gray's face came into focus, his worried eyes studying me. The song ended and the radio host took over so I reached for the volume and turned it down low, leaning back in my seat.

"I'm good. I haven't listened to James's music in a long time. Even before his... I would only hear it when I came home, which wasn't very often. My home wasn't really full of happy memories." I picked at some dirt on my shoe. Why had I felt the need to tell him that?

Gray sat there for a moment, then reached for the door. "I have to grab some stuff, but I will be right back." He sounded hesitant, echoed in his tense movements.

I forced a smile as he jumped out, knowing I had overloaded him with information. He tapped the hood of the truck twice as he walked past, heading into the warehouse. The faint sound of the radio suddenly annoyed me, so I reached over and turned it off. Looking around to see where we were, it seemed we had parked outside a trade store. People came and went, some carrying bags, while others dragged large carts to their respective vehicles.

Several minutes passed and there was no sign of Gray, but a man was heading toward me from the store. It was Nate, and I tried to make myself smaller in my seat. Maybe he hadn't seen me yet. Unless he'd looked in the mirror, he might have thought the truck was empty. Before I could get my hopes up, he called out for me.

"Hey, Stella, what's up?" he drawled, jogging the last few steps over to me, then knocked on the window. I reluctantly reached for the button and the window rolled down. Nate leaned into the opening and clasped one hand with the other. He was so close I could smell him—all of him. Yup, he still smelled divine. "Fancy meeting you here. I was sad when you left us at the farm. I was hoping you'd stay all weekend." He winked at me playfully. A drop of sweat rolled down his neck, his arm muscles flexing under his ripped flannel shirt.

"I had somewhere to be," I said, continuing to pick at the dirt on my shoe.

"Why are you hanging out in Gray's car? He's working today, right? Or did he actually up and quit?" He flicked his head toward the empty driver's seat. With a smile, he shifted his weight closer to me.

He knew how he affected me and seemed to enjoy the power.

"He's just giving me a lift home. He didn't say anything about quitting." I bit my lip as I glanced toward the entrance of the store. There was still no sign of Gray.

"All right." Nate exhaled, running his hands through his sweaty hair. He was busy looking the other way, so I allowed myself to gawk for just a moment. His blond hair danced over his eyebrows in the wind, and I traced the contours of his perfectly shaped nose and cheekbones with my eyes. He wasn't just attractive—he was stunning. Statues would have been made of him if this wasn't the twenty-first century.

Finally, Gray appeared in the distance. I let out a thankful breath, and Nate noticed and chuckled.

"You're dead to me," Gray hissed as he walked behind Nate, dumping the box in the back of the truck. His words surprised me but it didn't seem like it did Nate.

"Oh, relax. So I let you sleep a few more hours. You needed it."

"I also need my job," Gray snapped. It only caused Nate to laugh. "What are you doing here, anyway?"

"Your old man sent me. He found more things wrong with the wires in the house and you're not picking up your phone. So I had to drag my ass out here to grab the parts." He playfully punched Gray's arm before nodding toward me. "Got some lovely company, huh?"

Gray's face firmed up, and he clenched his hands into fists. "I'm just giving her a lift home," he replied and fixed Nate with a stare as he walked around to the driver's seat. "You didn't rat me out, then?"

Nate chuckled and tipped his head back slightly. As he wiped some sweat from his neck with his top, he revealed several glorious inches of ripped abs. I didn't know where to look, but when I drifted my eyes to Gray and he saw my flushed cheeks, I knew that was *not* the right place. I dropped my gaze to my lap instead. I wonder what might hide under Gray's shirt. His was looser than Nate's, yet it was easy to see defined abs under that fabric too. That thought only made my heart race and a tightness spread to my core, pulsating and warm.

"Yeah, that's what Stella said. And no, I covered for you and said the electrical company sent the products to the wrong store, so you had to drive a few hours to get them. I wouldn't leave you hanging like that, dude. I ain't stupid." Nate frowned at Gray, who looked sorry for his earlier outburst. "How long until you can drop the parts off? Your old man was looking antsy when I left, and I don't know how much longer he will believe my lie if you don't pick up your phone."

"I won't be long. I've only got one more stop to make, but I should be there within an hour," Gray said with a nod. "And thanks. I owe you one." He slid in next to me, his shirt showing sweat marks from the summer heat, just like Nate's. I went back to the thoughts of what was underneath but now envisioned it slick with sweat, and I firmly crossed my legs. My hormones weren't able to handle the testosterone in and around this truck, as evidenced by my thudding lady bits.

"All right then. Make sure you get back to your dad. I don't like being the go-between for you two." He tipped an imaginary hat to me with a wink, his other thumb in the belt loop of his faded jeans. "Miss."

"See ya," I said, smiling sheepishly.

"Let's get you home," Gray mumbled under his breath. The wheels spun in the grass as we drove off, country music playing softly through the radio again. Gray gripped the wheel tightly, his eyes glued to the road. Hoping to ease the tension, I turned toward him.

"So you work for your dad?" I trailed my eyes down from his face and over his broad shoulders and muscular arms, sucking my bottom lip into my mouth.

He nodded and let out a sigh, smiling at me. "Yeah, my dad decided that when I didn't go to college, I would have to work at his business. He's training me to take over one day."

"Oh, that's cool. What does he do?" I kept letting my eyes wander. I'd noticed Gray was attractive before, but right now, he looked delicious enough to eat. It had been a while since I'd been with a guy. After James's passing, it hadn't been on my mind. No wonder I was sitting here thirsting over Gray like this. I needed to get those thoughts under control.

"Construction, focusing mainly on residential properties." It sounded robotic.

"Nate said something about you quitting?"

He scoffed. "Yeah, I've thought about it. Though, it's more likely I'll be fired."

"Why?" I frowned.

"Because I screw up a lot." Gray bit back a smile. "Not by choice, more like it's in my DNA. Dad promoted me the other day."

"That's great!"

He raised his eyebrows like he didn't agree. "Maybe. I'm trying to see it that way, and not like it gives me more chance to fail. Nate is the only thing keeping me together at the moment." This was Gray falling apart? Wow, he must think I look like a train wreck. He stared at the road for a moment without speaking, something clearly on his mind. "Try to ignore Nate," he finally said. "He's a bit of a ladies' man. A guy like him and a girl like you would never work." My lips snapped shut and I quickly dropped my gaze to my hands. "Shit, I didn't mean it to come out like that." He scratched his jaw, struggling for words.

"It's okay. I know we're not in the same league—"

He snorted and glanced over at me. "Please tell me you're joking?" He looked at me with an incredulous smile, raking his eyes over my body before capturing my gaze. It set my skin on fire, the pulsing between my legs starting back up. "You really believe that?" I couldn't speak for fear I'd squeak or say something inappropriate, so I nodded. He flicked his eyes back to the road and chuckled. "Nate would love to think he could have a girl like you, but you should have nothing to do with the likes of Nate."

I frowned, trying to make sense of what he had just said. "A girl like me?"

"Yeah, you know..." He shifted in his seat. A mischievous smile tugged at his lips and he raked his teeth over the bottom one. "Innocent, sweet, beautiful. The girl-next-door type. Those types are like magnets to guys like Nate. But trust me, nothing good could come from that. Once he's had his fun, he isn't the staying kind."

"Oh..." I mumbled, turning back around in my seat to face forward. I was suddenly boiling hot. Had he just called me beautiful? I'd never thought of myself as ugly, but I liked the idea that Gray found me attractive.

We turned onto my dad's street a moment later. I should say something, but I didn't know what.

"Thanks for the ride," was all I could manage. I reached for the door and slid down to the ground, tucking my hands in the back pockets of my jeans to stop from wringing them.

"No problem." Gray gave me a heated but playful look I was sure I wasn't making up. My heart fluttered as we stared at each other. He broke the tension by shifting the truck into drive. "Don't forget to call or text me. Whatever. If you're ready to hear some stories about James, that is." He cleared his throat and grinned. "It's nice to reminisce about him."

"I will," I said, tapping the back pocket where my phone was resting. I probably wouldn't. After all this, I was better off staying far away from Gray and all of his deliciousness.

"See you around, Stella."

Even the way my name came out of his mouth made my body tingle now. He turned his truck around and drove down the road. I didn't want to linger on his words for too long. They'd start to mean more than I was sure he'd meant them to. My horny brain couldn't tell the difference between a flirty comment and whatever was lodging itself in my heart. And between my thighs.

Mrs. Johnson's face pressed up against the glass across the road gave me the cold shower I needed, and I turned on my heel. I was confused. Gray was trying to be a nice friend to his best friend's sister. That's all. And either way, I was in no state to be in a relationship, much less with someone from here. I still couldn't wait to get out of this place.

I was halfway up the stairs when I froze. I hadn't thought about one painful memory on the drive with Gray. I'd been too focused on him. Mixed emotions washed over me—guilt at the top of that list. My brother's memorial was in a few days, and here I was wondering if Gray had the same sexual thoughts about me as I did him.

I was the worst sister in the world.

I stopped by James's room and poked my head in. The warm air quickly filled my lungs and tears pricked my eyes. I needed to feel him close to me again. I didn't want to let myself forget him. Ever.

"Do you remember that time Mr. Jackson called Dad on us after he found us skipping class? We were only about twelve, hiding near the blackberry bushes past the soccer field."

A tear rolled down my cheek as I closed my eyes. His voice was as clear as day.

"I remember," I replied, rolling my eyes. *"You were worried about a history test and you made me go with you to hide. I'm not sure how your genius plan was meant to end, but I'm sure it wasn't being dragged into the principal's office to do the test right there and then."*

"No, it wasn't." James chuckled from the bed. *"But I passed it, didn't I?"*

"Only just," I teased.

I kept my eyes closed tightly, not wanting this moment to end too soon like so many others had. The pain ripped at my heart, but I needed it to. I needed it to wash away any feelings I shouldn't be having.

"I think it was a pretty good day. I got to spend some time outside with you and passed a test. Not sure what else I could have asked for."

"I'm guessing you forgot about the week of grounding we got when we got home?"

"Oh, I didn't forget. But then I never really followed any of Dad's rules."

His voice distorted and faded away into an echo. I opened my eyes to stare at the unmade bed, willing the memory to come back. It didn't. I walked over and slid in under the covers. The scent that was more dusty than James-smelling filled my nose and the tears fell just like clockwork.

Chapter Nine

- GRAY -

T he entire drive to work, I was thinking about Stella. The way she blinked her big, innocent eyes back at me when I'd blurted out she was beautiful. Fuck, it had made my dick twitch. The brief telling-off I'd given it as I left the restaurant clearly hadn't helped. Now I didn't just want to wrap her in my arms and tell her everything would be okay. I wanted more. I wanted her lips on mine and her body pressed so firmly against me I could feel every dip and valley that hid under her clothes. I wanted to see if her body flushed as pink in other places as her cheeks. My semi wasn't just a semi anymore; I was uncomfortably hard.

When I got to the office, my dad was on a business call. He waved me away, giving me another few minutes to find the confidence to tell him the truth, confidence I hadn't quite found yet. My mind was still wrapped in brown curls, and it made it hard to think.

I dropped the box off outside and went to find Nate. He was lying on the kitchen floor, covered in dust and dirt and installing some pipes under the sink while loud music played through his phone on the counter. He stopped to play air guitar when the solo came on, singing the notes out loud. Even that didn't make me smile.

"Hey," I grunted. Maybe Nate could give me the telling-off about Stella that I desperately needed.

"Hand me the slip joint, would you?" Nate asked, holding out his hand as he stabilized the pipes with the other. I handed it to him, then sank to the floor. "Thanks." He shifted sideways so he could reach farther in under the sink. "So last night, huh?" He grinned as he appeared from under the cabinet and punched my leg. I chuckled with a sigh.

"Yeah, I honestly don't remember any of it." I rubbed my hand over my face.

"Probably for the best. It wasn't pretty." Nate laughed. He collected all the tools together and dumped them in a bag. "Talked to your dad yet?"

"He's in a meeting."

"And what are you going to say?" Nate lifted his eyebrows. We got up off the floor and I followed as he went outside to turn the water on.

"I don't know... If I tell him the truth, he'll fire me." I sighed and nestled my hands into the pockets of my shorts. "He won't take another fuckup."

"No shit." Nate snorted. After turning the water on, he looked through the kitchen window to see if anything was leaking.

"I know what you're going to say," I interrupted before he could say anything else.

"Oh, you do?" His grin grew wider as he filled up a bucket of water.

"You're going to tell me to lie and move on. And maybe I should. It would absolutely break his heart if he knew the truth."

"Dramatic, but go on," Nate mumbled, rolling his eyes as he turned off the tap, the bucket now full.

"So maybe you're right. I just need to keep my head down, suck up the fact that I've got responsibilities now, and get on with it. And try my best not to fuck up." I ran my hands over my face, blowing air through my fingers.

"You make a good point," Nate drawled as he tried to contain a smirk. "But I was going to ask about Stella." I tried to cut him off, but he kept talking. "She's James's sister. What the fuck, man?"

"I know, I know." I squeezed my head between my palms. "She's alone and I don't like it. I just feel bad for her. That's all." Great, now I was lying to Nate too.

"Whatever, dude. Not your responsibility."

"I don't want to talk about it." I didn't want to lie again.

He snorted and shook his head at me. "Oh, we're going to talk about it, all right. But not here. Not now."

I peered at him, confused about why he was giving in. Too late, I saw the sparkle in his eye and the full bucket of water in his hands. He flung the whole thing at me, ice-cold water soaking me from head to toe. I exhaled sharply as it dripped down, my muscles contracting and shaking. I punched towards him after the initial shock of the cold had gone, then grabbed the hose and turned it on to full. Nate laughed hysterically as he ran from me.

"Grayson?" my dad called from behind me. I stopped immediately and turned the tap off.

"Dad," I stuttered, dropping the hose to the ground and wiping my wet hands on wetter clothes. This was not a good look.

He looked me up and down, but instead of getting angry, he laughed and called over my shoulder, "Good one, Nate!"

Nate cautiously came back from around the house with his grin plastered all over his face. "Thank you, sir." He bowed and headed back into the house. I glared at him over my shoulder.

"So, son, did you get the parts? I heard you had some issues at the store this morning?" My dad waved at me to follow him back to the office. Playtime was over.

"Uh, yeah," I answered, squeezing water from my T-shirt. "They mixed up the stores, so they sent it to their southern branch. It took me several hours to get there. I had to take the back roads after an accident on the highway. My phone is dead, so that's why I didn't call you." I shook more water from my hair as I followed him. It plastered to my face, so I swept it back with my hand.

"But you've got the parts? The electrician is on his way, so we need them." I pointed to the box outside the office and he sighed. "Oh, great. The owners are coming over later too, and I want to make sure we can show them some actual progress." He didn't bat an eyelid at the story Nate had manufactured. I didn't know if I was relieved or more stressed. I hated lying to my dad, though it was easier than telling him the truth.

I changed into some spare but dirty clothing I had in the back of the truck, then spent the next hour going through paperwork. A spotless white car pulled up outside, and my dad sprang up as a couple stepped out. The woman carried a shiny sable bag, and the soles of her shoes flashed a vibrant red before landing on the ground. She didn't look pleased to be standing on the gravel.

My dad left to give them a tour of the building site. I sat down on the chair behind his desk to help sort out the invoices and bills stacked high. It was something he hated to do, and I still felt bad about lying to him. I took a sip of my extra-strong coffee, feeling a fake sort of energy buzz through my body, though the hangover was definitely still present. A few minutes later, the couple left and my dad returned to the office, mumbling to himself as he entered.

"How did it go?" I got up from his chair.

"They seemed happy with the progress. They did, however, change their minds on the bathroom tiles, so we are going to have to return them and find new ones." A grunt rolled from his chest.

"What was wrong with them?" I refilled my coffee and handed my dad another mug.

"There is nothing wrong with the tiles. We showed them all the samples, and they picked one. Ordered and delivered last week. But I guess now that they've seen them, they don't like them anymore."

"Fucking rich people in suits don't give a fuck—" I muttered before I could stop myself. My dad glared, and I sank lower in my chair, snapping my mouth shut. My dad had spent damn near a fortune to have them sourced, and now they didn't want them anymore. It was a good thing I hadn't been there when they told him because I probably would have said something stupid.

He grunted again, half in agreement, and looked around on his desk. "Have you seen the invoice for the tiles? I swear I had it just a moment ago." From the filing cabinet behind him, I grabbed the paper he was looking for. He gave me a thankful smile and picked up the phone from his desk. He glanced up and held the receiver out to me. "Here, you do it. It's time for you to have some more responsibility."

That word sent a chill down my spine like it always did. "Are you sure?" I hesitantly grabbed the phone and paper from him. I wasn't sure I could smooth talk the supplier into taking the stock back. With my dad watching me from across his desk, I sure didn't want to fuck up.

"Yes. I see so much of myself in you, and you're ready. Just try to keep the swearing to a minimum." He smirked from behind his mug, but it wasn't all a joke.

I dialed the number, resting one hand on the back of my neck and bouncing my leg up and down.

The next few days went by quickly. I kept my head down to make sure I finished all my tasks I had for the day, not wanting to let my dad down and also to avoid more thoughts of Stella. I wasn't successful in the latter department, though Dad seemed genuinely proud of me for once. It was strange to know I'd made him feel that way. He probably wouldn't be so happy if he knew the truth about why I was late Monday morning.

Before I knew it, the clock struck five and my dad collected his things. As I headed out the door, Kasey was standing by my truck. Her eyes were red and her arms were wrapped around her body as it shook. She threw herself at me as soon as I got to her and cried into my shirt.

"Hey, hey," I shushed and stroked her hair. With one hand, I opened the door to my truck, then lifted her up on the seat. Her whole body vibrated against mine. I tried to catch her eye, but she wouldn't let go of her grip around me.

"I-I hate her. I hate her so much," she whimpered. I wiggled out of her arms to take her hands in mine.

"Did you guys have another fight?" I asked, knowing she was talking about her mom.

"She is just such a bitch," Kasey spat out, the words both sharp as daggers and tremblingly weak. "She never came home last night, so I had to stay in and take care of Dion for her. And because I had to stay in and look after him, I didn't make it to work. Now I'm in trouble with my boss. *Her* boss. When she finally showed her face this morning, she didn't even bother saying hi to Dion. She just went straight to her room. He was so happy to see her, but when she ignored him, he wouldn't stop crying. I've been trying to keep him occupied all day, but all he wants is his mom." She nodded behind me. I glanced over my shoulder to see the little boy playing in the dirt by the side of the makeshift parking lot.

I turned back around with a sigh and pushed her legs into the truck. "Let's go. You guys can come and hang out with me tonight." She attempted a smile, but it wasn't believable.

I walked over to Dion and kneeled down on the ground in front of him. The little boy, not much older than three, squealed when he saw me. His shiny black curls bounced against his dark skin. He was wearing jean overalls with a green dinosaur T-shirt underneath, dirt already covering most of him. Kasey and Dion didn't share the same dad. Her dad had stuck around for a few years when she was younger, but no one knew who Dion's dad was. The guy probably didn't even know he existed.

"Gray!" He wrapped his little arms tightly around my neck. I hugged him back as I picked him up.

"What do you say the three of us have some ice cream at my place, huh?" His eyes went wide, and he nodded enthusiastically. "And you can have as much as you want. I won't tell anyone," I whispered into his ear. He giggled and squirmed in my arms, absolutely delighted with the idea. I carried him back to the truck, placing him in Kasey's lap while I dug around for the car seat in the back of the truck. Since Kasey was a staple in my life, that meant Dion was too. He didn't ride in my truck often, but when he did, I did everything I could to make sure he was safe.

He leaned in to whisper to her, and she gave me a look. "Oh, he did, did he?" She sniffled, wiping the last tear from her cheek with a tiny smile. I waggled my eyebrows at her, not even pretending to look innocent.

I texted Nate to say I was leaving, but I didn't tell him why. He'd either find out when he got home later or I'd tell him in the morning. He'd probably be pissed that I ditched him for Kasey, but I didn't really have a choice right now.

Kasey ran inside the store and bought ice cream, while I kept Dion busy. He went from laughing to crying in a few seconds, and my heart broke for him. He kept asking about his mom, and I didn't know what to say. Kasey finally came back and showed him the ice cream, which made him smile and my heart hurt a little less. I'd known Dion since he was born—he was basically my nephew.

She looked exhausted when she sat down, but did her best to smile. She wanted to protect her baby brother at any cost, but she had to look after herself as well. I wasn't about to say that out loud, though. We were in a good spot right now.

We spent the evening playing in the backyard and eating ice cream until Dion fell asleep. She tucked him in on my couch, then came out to sit with me.

"He's out like a light," she rejoiced. "Thanks for helping. I didn't know where else to turn."

"It's all good. You guys are always welcome." My phone vibrated in my back pocket and I picked it up, revealing a text from a new number.

New number

> Hi Gray, it's Stella. You said I could text if I wanted to hear any stories about my brother. So I guess that's what I'm doing.

That warm feeling spread through my chest again. It would have been a lie to say I hadn't hoped she would contact me. I looked up at Kasey, but her eyes were closed, soft snores vibrating through her mouth. She'd had a long day, so I carefully stood and walked to the front of the house, pressing the call button on my phone and waiting as it rang.

"Hello?" Stella answered after a few seconds. She'd been crying—her nose sounded blocked and there was a soft shakiness to her breath. Fuck if that didn't make my chest ache.

"Hey. You all right?" I dug the heel of my boot into the soft ground. A twig snapped under my foot and bugs darted towards the safety of some rocks.

"I-I've been better," she said with a quiet sniffle. "I was going through our old photo albums"—her voice caught in her throat—"and I looked through th-them all, but I felt like I needed more. Are you busy?"

I turned and looked behind me at Kasey, then walked farther down the drive. "No, I'm not." A small smile that shouldn't be there spread across my lips. "What do you want to know?"

She was quiet for a moment. "I'm not sure," she concluded. Her soft voice did something weird to my chest. More of a lightness than the heat I'd felt before, but I pushed it away before I could think about it too much.

"Well," I began, "do you remember back in freshman year when it was soccer tryouts? Coach M, Liam's dad, is good friends with my dad, so I thought for sure I would have a spot on the team. I used the least amount of effort when warming up, and I accidentally kicked the ball the wrong way. It ended up rolling down into the muddy creek behind the field. It pissed Coach M off so much that I had to run suicide drills for an hour. Fifteen minutes in, this other guy joined me. I don't know what he'd done to deserve Coach's fury, but we bonded over our physical pain. That was how I met James. I'd seen him around, but we didn't have any of the same classes. Anyway, as I'm sure you know, we both ended up getting a spot because we didn't stop running for the entire hour, earning Coach's respect again." There was silence on the other end, and I worried for a moment that she'd run away from her phone. "You still there?" I asked hesitantly.

"Mm-hmm..." Her voice was shaky, but she didn't sound like she was crying. That was a good sign.

I was silent for a moment, not sure if I should continue or not. "After that, we were inseparable. He fit in with my friends right away." I smiled, thinking back to how young and stupid we used to be. "He could always smile, no matter what." A laugh escaped. "I don't know if you remember the time he had to wear an ankle brace for a few weeks. Middle of summer?" I asked and waited for her reply.

"Yeah, I remember. He'd fallen while out running and twisted it." Her voice was clearer, and it almost sounded like she was smiling. My heart thudded weirdly again, and I pressed my hand over it, hoping it would make it go away. It didn't.

"So he never told you about our little trip to Damien's then, I guess."

"No, he just said he'd tripped on a root in the woods." She drew out her words as she realized her brother must have lied.

"We'd been out there, kind of like when you came, just to mess around on the ATVs and have a good time. James decided he was going to do the jump standing up. We were a few beers in at that point, so we didn't really have the sense to make him stop. But he did it. He stood up on the ATV as he flew over the jump. Landed it perfectly with the biggest fucking smile I'd ever seen. But when he got off"—I paused with a smirk as I pictured James jumping off the vehicle triumphantly—"he slipped on a root and rolled down a small bank. So I guess technically he didn't lie to you?"

"Yeah, I guess," she giggled. Damn, that was a wonderful sound after hearing her cry. "I miss him so much. I feel like I'm drowning." In the space of that sentence, she was crying again. I bunched up my fists, wanting to punch something. Anything. Hearing her giggle had been like music to my ears.

"I know you do. He was a great friend, so I could only imagine what an incredible brother he was." The back of my throat burned and there was a tremble in my voice that I couldn't stop.

A noise from behind me pulled me back to reality. I spotted Kasey through the window as she leaned over the couch to pick up Dion. If she wasn't here, I probably would have driven over to Stella's house, and I wasn't sure that was such a good thing. My sexual attraction to her was turning into something more. Thin fucking ice. I grimaced up at the night sky, knowing James was watching.

"I should go," I said. I wanted to stay on the phone for longer, but it was better if I ended this call before some otherworldly force ripped me in half.

"That's okay," she whispered, clearing her throat. "Thanks, you know. For being there. My dad... Never mind."

"Anytime." That was more true than I wanted to admit.

I slipped the phone back into my pocket and headed in. Dion was asleep in Kasey's arms while she collected all her things from the coffee table.

"I should probably get him home." She yawned and rubbed her eyes. I reached over to get her stuff together. She gave me a thankful smile, followed by another yawn.

She was beyond tired, and though I wanted to offer for them both to stay here, she wouldn't agree to that. Dion needed clean clothes and a bath. The small two-bedroom house I shared with Nate only had a shower, not to mention the fact he wouldn't be too happy if she was still here when he eventually showed his face.

We headed out to my truck. Dion didn't stir from his sleep as she tucked him into the car seat. She stroked his dark, curly hair and gave him a gentle kiss on the forehead—a fierce, protective love flickering in her eyes.

We didn't talk on the drive, and when I parked in front of her mom's trailer, Kasey's face turned hard. She took a moment before heading towards the door with Dion in her arms, poking her head out after a few seconds to wave goodbye. I wanted to go in and help her work through the shit with her mom, but she wouldn't want me to. It was a part of her life she wasn't willing to share. I hated she felt she had to carry that burden alone.

Despite it being late, I had no desire to go back to my house to sleep. Before I realized where I was driving, I'd turned onto the familiar road where James used to live. I didn't know if I was here for him or Stella. It confused the shit out of me.

I parked a few driveways down from his house, far enough away not to feel like a stalker, but close enough that I could see it clearly under the dim streetlights. There was a light on in his room facing the front, but the rest of the house was blanketed in a darkness that sent a chill down my spine. She was in there. Alone.

The window slid open, and Stella's hair blew gently in the wind as she curled up on the windowsill.

I picked up my phone but stopped before calling her. What would I say? *Hey, I'm parked up outside. Want to join me?* I shook my head and threw it on the passenger seat with a groan. Fuck, I shouldn't even be here. As I put the truck in reverse to leave, my phone beeped and I stopped to check it.

It was a text from Stella with a picture of James. He was covered head to toe in mud. I chuckled with a lump in my throat and studied the picture for a while, resting my hand holding the phone on the top of the steering wheel. He looked so young, not much older than ten—not at all the wild teenager I remembered.

Stella

Thanks again for the story… It was nice to dream I was somewhere else for a moment.

I shouldn't do it and tried to stop myself. I really, really did. But I just couldn't. I pressed call and waited a few seconds for her to answer.

Chapter Ten

I opened the window in my brother's room and sat on the windowsill. The fresh evening breeze danced in, replacing the stuffy air that had collected from the summer sun. I hugged his pillow to envelop myself in his scent. It was fading, but if I took a deep breath, I could still smell it. Scrolling to the image on my phone that I had found in a photo album, my heart leaped in my chest.

It was James from many years ago. We'd been out playing in the rain, jumping in muddy puddles like kids do. Then we trailed mud throughout the house, soaking the living-room carpet and couch. Mom was furious with us, but in his drunken state, Dad had thought it was hilarious.

I sent the image to Gray. Hearing more about James made me feel like he was still here. I had good moments sprinkled in with the many bad. At least it was more than I'd had before coming back. I owed a lot of that to Gray. Without him, I'd probably still be bitter and angry.

My phone vibrated against the wooden windowsill, and Gray's name flickered on my screen. I answered it hesitantly.

"Gray?" I bit my lip. Maybe I'd upset him by sending the image.

"Hey, I, uh, I'm just checking in on you, making sure you're, uh, okay."

I straightened and hugged the pillow tighter. "I'm fine. Thanks again, by the way."

"That's all right," he said. I could hear his smile and it softened my chest. "How are you and your dad holding up?"

I sighed as I looked out of James's room. My dad was somewhere downstairs, passed out drunk. I had hoped to talk to him when he got back, but he got to the bottle first. "If I'm honest, my dad's falling apart. I'm not sure if James told you or not, but he... drinks... a lot. Mostly when he's sad, and I don't really remember a time when he wasn't."

"Yeah. He told me a couple of years ago when it was really bad. He's not violent, right?" Gray sounded worried.

"No, no," I quickly replied. "He's not like that at all. He just cries and shuts himself off. I don't see him very often."

"Shit, that must be so lonely."

"Sometimes," I lied. There wasn't really a moment in this house when I didn't feel alone. Had I really felt less alone in LA, though?

"Well, I, uh..." He hesitated. "If you ever want to get out of the house, just let me know. We could drive to the lake or something. Maybe finally go fishing." He sounded like he was smiling again. I envisioned it tugging on the corners of his mouth, and a surge of heat ran through me.

God, that sounded good. It was so claustropho-bic here that I wanted to scream just to break the silence. Being with Gray had been the only time I hadn't felt completely alone.

"Sure. How about now?" I slapped my hand over my mouth. There was a moment of silence, and I wished I could take the words back. "I mean, never mind—"

"Okay," he interrupted, catching me off guard. "I'll pick you up in a few?"

"Okay," I stammered sheepishly, sliding off the windowsill. We hung up, and I stared at the phone, trying not to panic.

Shit... now what? I looked down at my clothes, an old T-shirt of James's and a pair of plaid pajama bottoms. Not exactly how I wanted him to see me. Grabbing a pair of jeans from my room, I slid them on and ran a brush through my hair, then stopped to look at myself in the mirror. Why did I care what I looked like? Gray probably didn't.

When I came downstairs, the TV in the living room was playing and my dad was fast asleep on the couch, a half-empty bottle of beer in his hand. I took it before it fell and made a mess, then pulled the blanket over him as he mumbled incoherently.

Gray stood by his Chevy, parked in front of the house when I opened the front door. He took off his ball cap, running his fingers through his hair before slipping it back into place with a smile. "Hey. I was in the area already." His face was tilted down and his shoulders were pulled up tight. Was he nervous? He waved his hand at his truck. "Want to go for a drive, then?"

Before I could change my mind, I dashed the few steps to Gray's truck and jumped into the passenger seat, smiling just as nervously at him.

"Where do you want to go?" he asked as we slowly rolled out of the neighborhood.

"Anywhere." I didn't care where we went. Anywhere but here sounded good to me. So we drove. We didn't say much, but the silence wasn't awkward. I didn't feel the need to speak, and the few glimpses I threw in Gray's direction told me he was comfortable too.

A gust of wind tousled my hair. I reached my hand out the window and spread my fingers wide. Free. I felt free. Not from pain—I wasn't sure I ever would be—but less weighed down by everything.

When we came to a stop at an intersection, I pulled my hand in with a contented sigh. Gray looked over with a calm smile and pointed to the sign ahead.

"Which way?"

The sign pointed in opposite directions. Left to loop back towards the other side of Waterbury, or right to take you towards the mountains. I stared at the sign before looking at him again. His cognac eyes sparkled in the dark, the hairs on my arm standing to attention, like an electric buzz had rolled through me.

"Keep driving."

His smile grew wider as he turned right and we headed even farther away from town. I peered over at him. He had thrown his cap in the backseat, where surprisingly, a child's car seat sat. I would have asked why, but I didn't want to break the tranquil hum of the engine and the tires along the road. His brown hair blew freely in the wind, and he had his elbow resting out the window.

He caught me looking and smirked before turning his eyes back to the road, swapping his hand on the wheel to rest one on the top of his thigh. I yearned to reach out and hold it. To know if the spark that ran through me from his touch was stronger than the one his eyes set off in me.

"There's this place close to here where we could stop. It's a car park where you can see for miles. If we keep driving, I'm going to need some coffee." He yawned and rubbed his hand over his jaw. I followed his every movement with fascination.

"We could stop for a while," I replied, looking over at the time on the dashboard. We had already driven for over an hour and it was nearing one in the morning.

We drove for a few more miles before Gray pulled into a parking lot, seemingly in the middle of nowhere. The headlights briefly illuminated a sign that said *Welcome to Eagle Viewpoint - Mount St. Helens National Volcanic Monument*. The moon hung high in the night sky, with no clouds or streetlights to hide the stars. They twinkled merrily, all of them so bright against the vastness of space.

I followed Gray as he led me across the open space to a lookout point, my jaw dropping as I swept over the landscape in front of me.

"Oh, wow," I whispered. Gray let out a rumbled chuckle behind me that made my cheeks heat. I walked over to a rock and sat down. There was nothing but mountains and valleys as far as the eye could see—the volcano standing proudly in the distance completely mesmerizing me with its snow-covered ridges standing out against the polka-dot sky.

Gray came to sit next to me. "It's pretty, isn't it?" he whispered, nudging me with his shoulder.

"I've never seen anything like this. I'm not really an outdoorsy person." He laughed at me, and my cheeks flushed even more. A fresh mountain breeze rolled over us, making all the hairs on my arm stand up.

"Did you see that?" Gray pointed up at the sky with one hand and rested the other on my leg. "Ah, you missed it."

"Missed what?" I tried to ignore the heat from his hand on my thigh. He shifted his thumb as he leaned backwards, and I had to force my leg not to twitch.

"An owl or something flew right over your head." He moved his hand as he turned to see if he could spot it again.

"Ew. I hate big birds." I tucked some hair behind my ear and looked around cautiously. A jagged part of the rock dug into my lower back. I winced and shifted forward.

"Come with me." Gray jumped to his feet and jogged back over to the truck. The sudden feeling of being alone crept in, and I swore I could hear twigs snapping in the dark behind me.

"Gray?" I squeaked as I got up and followed. He turned the truck around before jumping back out, grabbing a hoodie from the backseat and lowering the tailgate.

"Jump up. It will be much more comfortable." He patted the truck bed.

Thankful to have somewhere more comfortable to sit, I climbed up less than gracefully while he made it look like it was the easiest thing in the world. Wafts of his warm and woodsy scent filled my lungs as he stretched his arms above his head and yawned. It made my head a little cloudy and my thoughts went places they probably shouldn't.

"Me and the guys go camping near here some-times, but it's been a while." He leaned on his hands behind him with a sigh, tipping his head back.

"Sounds nice." Did James ever go with them? He probably did. While I was never really into the whole nature thing, James went on a lot of trips with his friends. I much preferred to stay inside to read or watch films. Our parents had rented a trailer a few times when Mom was still in the picture, but I had been so young I barely even remember what it was like. Camping or having a mom. As I opened my mouth to ask about James, Gray spoke.

"There it is again." He pointed at something in the sky. I searched, hoping the owl would be far away.

"I don't see it." He grabbed my hand and tried to point in the direction, but all I could focus on was his touch. Warm and steady.

"Ah, that's all right. We probably scared him off." He shifted farther back on the truck bed, then lay completely flat on his back with the hoodie as a pillow. I lay next to him and he pulled it over so we could share. I was so close to him I could hear his breath as it rolled through his nostrils. Heat radiated from his skin, but I refused the pleasure of snuggling up against it.

"Do you know any of the constellations? I didn't pay much attention in school." He chuckled close to my ear as he scanned over the night sky.

I smiled. James had been the same. If it had nothing to do with soccer, he wasn't interested. For me, the more studying, the better. It meant I didn't have to focus on what was going on at home. I oriented myself for a few seconds before I found a familiar cluster.

"That's Orion." I pointed, and Gray followed my finger with his eyes.

"Oh yeah, that's the dude with the bow, right? I remember him." He smiled proudly, glancing at me. Warm breath rolled over my face, but the warmth traveled much farther south. "So if that's Orion..." He looked back up. "Then that's Cassiopeia?" I looked at where he was pointing and smiled when I saw the W-shape.

"Yep, not bad. You haven't forgotten it all!" I pulled my legs up and rested my hands on my stomach. Our shoes and elbows touched. I thought about moving mine, but didn't want to make a big deal about it.

"I love looking at the stars. Makes me feel really calm, you know?" Gray shifted to get more comfortable and his arm pressed against me. Shivers ran through me—or was that him? "It's really cool that you're named after stars." A sarcastic snort escaped me, and he turned to look at me with amusement. "What's so funny about that?" He poked my ribs, then rested his hand behind his head.

"My dad would always make fun of me and tell me they named me after his favorite beer. Not as cool when you say it like that."

He shrugged and snickered. "Yeah, I guess that makes more sense." I gently kicked him, trying to contain a grin.

We went back to trying to find some more constellations, but I struggled to remember a lot of them too. It was late, and I was tired, not to mention the fact my brain was high on Gray's nearness. I had still been unsuccessful in my attempt to get my hormones under control. In my defense, Gray was a special kind of eye candy, not to mention he had a very sweet side that I wanted to get to know better. But I was still leaving soon, so nothing could happen between us.

Before long, there was a gentle snore next to me. Brown hair rested on his forehead and his soft lips were open. I closed my eyes with a smile and sighed. I'd forgotten about the real world for a moment. About the pain. It had been peaceful to feel like me again—I couldn't remember when I'd last felt that way. I made the mistake of thinking about my brother, and it was like someone was trying to rip my heart out of my chest as a flood of aching washed over me. A few tears spilled over as I stared up at the stars. They were all blurry now.

Another tear rolled down my cheek as a falling star shot across the sky. I didn't know why, and it would probably have sounded really cheesy if I said it out loud, but I tried to imagine it was James up there saying hi. That maybe he hadn't left me down here all alone.

"Hi," I whispered. Another star shot above my head. My chest tightened, and the tears rolled faster. I thought about a life without him, and panic spread through my mind. It had always been us. The two of us. Now there was only me, something I would have to get used to. I turned away from Gray and quietly sobbed into the sleeve of his folded-up hoodie.

"Stella." He stirred behind me as my cries turned to sobs, and pulled me back to face him. His eyes were tired and sad, but there was no pity. Only genuine sadness. It didn't ease the tears, but I wasn't sure anything could. Two muscular arms wrapped me up as I rolled my face into his shoulder, pressing my lips against his shirt. He said nothing, running a soothing hand up and down my back. The touch was both comforting and not at the same time. Letting myself feel calm in his arms was like a betrayal to James, but I soon relaxed into him and wiped away the tears with the collar of my shirt.

"I'm sorry for crying all over your hoodie."

A quiet chuckle rolled through his chest. I was gripping onto his shirt. Quickly letting go, I peered up at his face. He was looking up at the stars again, but soon shifted so he was facing me. One arm stayed under my head as a pillow, while he rested the other on my waist.

"I never want you to feel sorry about being sad. You need to grieve." His eyes locked with mine. He wiped a tear from my cheek, letting his eyes drift to my lips. "But I wish I could make you smile. It's beautiful."

Inch by inch, the distance between us disappeared. I'm not sure if I was moving closer or he was. When his breath pulsated over my lips, they quivered. His lips touched mine gently at first, and it was like I was on a cloud of feathers. He held me closer to him with his hand on my cheek, and I bunched my own hands back up in his shirt.

He tasted even better than he smelled, a hint of something sweet lingering on his lips, like strawberry and vanilla. A moan spilled from me as he ran his tongue along the seam of my lips, and I let him in without hesitation, the sweet taste intensifying as he caressed my tongue with his. The arm under my head tensed, caging me between hard muscle and soft lips. He leaned over me slightly, resting his weight on his forearm while I still held onto his shirt, almost desperately so. I didn't want this moment to end, but it was giving Gray the wrong idea. Giving my brain and heart the wrong idea.

I dipped my head to the side, quickly sitting up and away from him as I tried to control my racing heart. This couldn't be a one-night stand. It also couldn't be anything more. I was leaving in a week. He was my brother's best friend.

Oh my god, why had I let him do that? Stupid hormones.

Gray was blinking hard when I peered back at him. He sat up, running a hand over his stubbled jaw, then reached out as if to run it along my back, but he let it fall, fisting his fingers by his leg.

"I'm sorry. I just... got lost in the moment. Sorry," he muttered, flicking his eyes between me and anywhere else.

I pulled my knees up under my chin and wrapped my arms around them. My heart still wasn't in control from that simple kiss, and while most of my body wanted more, my brain was smarter than that. I glanced back at his lips. Hopefully, it was.

He leaned back on the truck bed and let out a sigh as he ran his hands through his hair. "Let me know when you want to head back."

"I can't go back to that house yet." I shook my head. While staying here with him longer wasn't smart for my heart or my body, it was a lot better than sitting in the house alone. "Would you tell me some more stories about James?" That would distract me from the luscious lips I craved another taste of.

After a moment of silence, Gray spoke, his voice softer now. "One summer, the guys and I went camping for a few days. We'd packed up everything we needed and set out first thing in the morning. We hiked for a few hours into the woods before finding the perfect spot next to this lake to set up camp. James and I grabbed our fishing rods and tried to catch something to eat, but the fish were not biting that day. I gave up after about an hour and headed back to the camp to cook some of the food we had brought with us.

"As I went to get some water for the pot, James shouted from his spot up on a rock. I looked over just in time to see him lose his balance. He fell straight into the water, splashing around like mad." Gray flung his hands around, pretending to be James. I smiled. "He climbed up on the rocks with a smallmouth bass gripped in his hands. The smile on his face"—Gray turned to me with a grin and showed with his hands how big the fish had been—"was something I will never forget. He was soaking wet and all tangled up in his fishing line."

I giggled, imagining James. A slicing pain ran through my body, but it didn't hurt the same. Because of Gray? Maybe. I shifted my hand away from where it had been resting on the truck bed beside his. He moved with me—on purpose or not, I wasn't sure.

"The other guys mocked him, as friends do. But he was so happy with his catch that it didn't bother him. I think that was the only fish we caught that entire trip."

"When was this?" A chilly breeze blew across the car park and I shivered.

"Come here." Gray motioned for me to lie down with him, giving me a cautious smile when I eyed him. "Just for warmth. I promise." His smile looked genuine, as did his eyes. Maybe the kiss hadn't meant anything to him. My heart sank.

I gave him a small smile back, and I rested my head back on his arm. The warmth from his body spread to mine, and he grabbed the hoodie from underneath his head and laid it down over us. The safe smell of him enveloped me. It was good. Too good.

"Thanks," I whispered.

"It was after graduation. We cut the trip short, as James insisted he had to go home. You were coming to visit, I think. But we didn't really mind. We knew how much he had looked forward to you coming back."

"Really? I don't remember that." I glanced up at Gray, pulling the hoodie closer to my face as the wind blew over us again. The bridge of his nose jutted out from his face, cutting the night sky in half. I traced the outline of his face, eyes magnetized to his lips again.

"Yeah, but it was all right. Like I said, we all knew how excited he was to see you again, and it's not like we didn't have all the time in the world that summer."

I felt bad for taking James away from that. We continued to share stories about him for a while longer until I fell asleep. Gray's gentle breathing, accompanied by his scent and the rumble of his voice through his chest, lulled me to sleep—a much more peaceful one than I'd had in a long time.

Chapter Eleven

- STELLA -

I woke up a few hours later as the sun crept over the horizon. It blinded me, despite trying to shield my eyes with my hand. I was still laying on Gray's shoulder, and by the sounds of it, he was asleep. His rhythmic heartbeat against my ear was soothing.

A warmth lodged itself in my heart as I peered up at him, remembering the kiss from last night. It might not have meant anything to him, but at least it showed me I could feel something other than pain. That I wasn't completely broken.

Eventually, I got up and watched the sunrise from the edge of the tailgate. Gray stirred behind me, but didn't quite wake. I looked at his face and a small smile spread across mine. He'd been so good to me, and we didn't even know each other that well. I couldn't mess that up by confusing my feelings for something they weren't. He could be a friend, but nothing else.

Sliding off the truck, I turned my head back to the sunrise. Birds sang in the trees nearby and an eagle cried somewhere far away, echoing across the valley. This really was paradise.

"Good morning." I turned my head back around. Gray leaned up on his elbows, squinting against the sun with hooded eyes and mussed hair. He smiled, and I awkwardly returned it.

He jumped down to the ground and stretched his arms out in front of him with a groan. His T-shirt rode up, and I couldn't stop my eyes from going there. Shit. His abs and a delicious V played peek-aboo under his shirt. With no control over my reaction, I licked my lips. My whole body burned, and my heart beat between my legs. What was wrong with me? Friends. Friends, friends, friends. How else could I spell it out?

He walked over to stand beside me, darting his eyes along the ground.

"Everything okay?" I asked.

He looked over at me, the power in his eyes almost flooring me completely. "The kiss... I, uh..."

"It's okay, really."

"No, I..." He sighed. "I shouldn't have done that. You're hurting, and I feel like that was kind of taking advantage of you."

"You didn't. I... liked it. The kiss I mean. It was a good kiss." God, I sounded like I was still in elementary school.

Gray didn't seem to notice my word vomit—a smile on his lips as he cleared his throat and a red tint colored his neck. "Cool. Me too."

His brown hair blew in the gentle breeze, brushing the top of his eyebrows. He took a small step closer, and before I could get my hopes up that he was going to kiss me again, I turned away, staring out over the volcano. I didn't want him kissing me again. Okay, that was a complete lie, but I couldn't see how another kiss would do anything but make me fall deeper for a guy I couldn't be with. LA was my future. Taking care of my dad was my future. Not happy endings with a hot guy.

"We should head back. It's quite a drive." Gray nudged my elbow, then turned to the truck, closing the tailgate and hopping in the driver's seat.

I took one last look at the volcano, my heart sinking in my chest. This life wouldn't be my future. I wasn't sure what my future exactly looked like, but it for sure wasn't this.

We drove in silence, slowly descending the mountains. Gray yawned and rubbed his face to wake up. I peered at him, taking him in as the sun hit him just right. Why did I feel so calm whenever I looked at him? Why did I want to tell him to pull over right now and straddle his legs to finish what we barely started last night?

I twisted my head the other way, scratching my cheek with the back of my hand as I tried to get a grip on my emotions that were running rampant.

"You okay? You've been quiet. Was it the… you know. Again, I'm sorry." Gray tried to catch my eyes, but I kept looking the other way.

"Yeah, I'm just tired." I paused. "We're okay, right? I mean, after…" Apparently, I couldn't say the word now either. Stuck in this confined space, all my senses were hyperaware of all of him.

He smiled, a beautiful, calm smile. My heart thudded violently, and I was surprised he didn't hear it. "Yeah, we're good."

"How much longer until we get back?" I needed to get out of this truck and away from Gray before I did something foolish. Right now, I wanted to know if we could ever be more than just good.

"An hour maybe. Probably just before six." He tapped away to the radio on the steering wheel. I let my eyes linger for longer than I should have. "When does your dad leave for work?"

"Uh, it depends," I replied. "I don't know if he's working late or not."

Gray tried to talk to me every now and again, but I didn't know how to answer. I could barely look at him without my mind running off to places it shouldn't. When we pulled onto my dad's street, his car wasn't there, so he must have already left.

Gray parked by the side of the road and waited for me to step out of the truck. As I slid out, I eyed the plant pot by the door—the one that usually had the spare key hidden under it. It wasn't in its normal spot. I walked over and tilted it to the side, feeling under the cold terracotta for the key. It wasn't there. I walked up to the door and tried the handle, praying it would be open. When it wouldn't budge, I dropped my head back with a groan.

"Everything all right?" Gray leaned his wrist on the wheel, a smile spreading across his lips at my predicament. It wasn't as upbeat as before, barely reaching his eyes.

"Locked out."

"Come on." He jumped out of the truck without hesitation and walked over to the tree near the garage.

I watched him, confused for a moment. What was he doing? Did he seriously think I was going to climb up there? The first branch was high up. "There is no way I can reach that," I said.

Gray looked at the tree, then back at me. "Hmm, yeah, that's not going to happen, is it?" He chewed on his lip, my thoughts needing no further push to run wild again. "Here, I'll pull you up to the roof."

He jumped to grab the lowest branch and quickly pulled himself up. It didn't seem like the first time he had done this. It was too effortless. No one should be able to climb trees that quickly and look sexy while doing it. His muscles fought against the fabric of his shirt.

Friends...

He made his way onto the roof from the branch, then reached a hand down for me. I raised my eyebrow and stared at him, unsure if the plan was as good as Gray thought.

"Come on, I've got you." He smiled reassuringly.

I didn't have much choice. Dad wouldn't be home for hours and I wasn't too keen on spending the entire day with Mrs. Johnson. I looked around to make sure no one was watching, especially my elderly neighbor, then jumped to grab his hand.

He held on tightly and pulled me up as I used my feet against the garage wall. I grabbed the ledge with one hand, pulling myself up the last bit. It took me longer to get up than him, but eventually I made it, and he rested his hand around my hip as he made sure I was steady on my feet but the touch only made me more unsteady. More needy.

"See, told you." He wiped his hands on his jeans as he walked over to James's window, wiggling it at the corner. It slid open easily. Too easily.

"You've definitely done that before." I shook my head with a smile and walked over to the window.

"Ah, maybe once or twice." He winked at me, sending my heart racing once again, then he took a step back so I could get in through the window. I swung my legs over the windowsill, his hand resting on my lower back now. Because of that, I almost fell into the room, stumbling to get my balance. When I turned around, Gray was smirking at me.

"Thanks, by the way..." I trailed off.

"Happy to do it anytime. You're all good now, though? I mean, you don't mind me taking off? I've got work and I need about five cups of coffee before I'm functional." He yawned.

"No, you go. I'm fine. Sorry you didn't get much sleep."

"Don't sweat it. I had a good time"—he shot me a heated look—"and I've made it through a full day of work on less." The look quickly turned into a friendly smile. Maybe I had imagined it. He climbed back down the tree and I found myself mesmerized by muscular legs in tight jeans. I was screwed, utterly and completely.

"Are you coming to James's memorial on Sunday?" I called when he got to the truck. Tears instantly burned in my eyes and I clutched onto the windowsill for support. The thought appeared and left my mouth before I even knew it was there.

His shoulders jerked, and he paused. "Yeah, we'll all be there."

"Thank you. He would want you there." I stood by the window as he drove off, then kicked my shoes off and slid into James's bed. "I want you there."

With each day closer to the memorial, I broke a bit more. I'd thought I needed this when I came back, but now I wasn't sure if I'd be strong enough to get through it. The anger that had once fueled me was gone, and only pain remained. Maybe this was the new normal. The new me.

Being alone hadn't helped my downward spiral. Dad coped by spending as little time at home as he could. I'd lost track of whether he was at work or "working." I guess it didn't really matter right now. We were just counting down the hours.

I wanted to reach out to Gray, but my growing feelings toward him stopped me. And the kiss. It had been amazing, but it shouldn't have happened. Once Dad and I got to LA, I wanted to forget about this blip of time and move on with every part of my life. That was my future. Though, being wrapped in Gray's arms was something I daydreamed about more than I cared to admit. I held onto the thought of seeing him on Sunday, but hated knowing that he'd have to see me so weak. It wasn't a question of if I would fall apart, but how badly.

When I woke up on Sunday morning, I was numb all over. My feet were heavy as I slid out of my brother's bed, thudding down each step of the stairs like my legs were made of lead. Dad stood by the sink with the tap running, scrubbing the same plate over and over and his empty, red eyes fixated on nothing outside. I walked over to stand next to him and he snapped out of his trance, putting the plate down.

"Hey, darling." His smile was crooked, alcohol on his breath. My heart sank.

"Have you already had something to drink?" I nudged him to the side and took over.

He slumped down on the kitchen chair. "No, no. I mean, just a little, but I'm good." His voice shook as he spoke, and he tapped nervously on the table, rubbing his other hand over the back of his neck.

I sighed, finishing the last few dishes and placed them on the drying rack. It was eight in the morning. Three hours to go. Tears burned in my eyes, but I couldn't break down in front of my dad. I'd made it this far. I could go one more day. At least a few more hours.

I peered over at him. He looked so small in the chair. His back was hunched and his eyes were just as bloodshot as mine felt, raw and hauntingly empty. I excused myself and made my way upstairs to have a shower, turning the water to extra hot as I let it rain down over my face and hoping it would somehow wash away the pain inside. It didn't. I stood there. I thought of James and a piece of the wall I was trying desperately to keep up fell. My chest was hollow, yet somehow so heavy, and every single cell in my body hurt.

I allowed myself a few more tears as I stepped out of the shower, then tried to pull it together. I caught a glimpse of my bloodshot eyes in the mirror, puffy and sore from rubbing them in my sleep. But I was too tired to care. About anything. I just wanted today to be over. I wanted to be back in LA, where I could bury my head in the sand again.

The sound of bottles clanged through the hallway downstairs. A lump formed in my throat, and I ran out of the bathroom.

"Dad, please don't," I pleaded, halfway down the stairs. I found him next to the cabinet where he kept his whiskey, grabbed the bottle from him, and slammed the door shut.

"I-I'm f-f-fine, I pr-promise," he stuttered. Tears flowed down his cheeks as I pulled him to me and squeezed hard. He felt even smaller in my arms than he looked. The anger returned, and I just wanted to scream and shout at James again for leaving me here to deal with everything on my own. My dad softened in my arms and stepped back from the cabinet. I forced my angry words back down and took a breath to compose myself.

"Dad, you need to do this for James." I gulped. My words hurt us both, but I didn't know what else to say. He needed to say goodbye today or he would never forgive himself. I might never forgive him.

"Why don't we go for a drive? Let's just get out of the house."

He sighed with a quiet, "Okay."

I gently pushed him towards his room to get changed before running upstairs for my stuff. I didn't bother reaching for the hairdryer after slipping on a black dress, rushing back downstairs as I zipped it. My dad stood in front of the hallway mirror, struggling to put his tie on.

"Here, let me," I said, taking it from him.

He stroked my cheek, and a small smile spread over his lips. "My little girl, you look all grown up. I love you."

I swallowed hard, mirroring his smile. "I told you, Dad, I will always be your little girl. I love you too." That would never change. Even though he wasn't the best dad in the world, he was *my* dad. And he was all I had.

I went through the mental checklist of everything we needed, silently thanking myself for packing the car the night before. My dad slid into the passenger seat without complaint. He wasn't in any state to drive. With my shaking hands, neither was I. But at least I wasn't drunk.

I fastened my seatbelt and looked at my dad. He stared out through the window next to him, with the same hollow look from before. It chipped at the wall around me, cracks appearing deeper and wider. Falling apart was imminent, but I didn't know how irreparably yet. Only time would tell.

We drove around town in silence. I was too emotionally charged yet somehow too drained to hold a conversation, the silence drumming in my ears.

Soon, it was ten-thirty, and we needed to make our way to the church. My hands did their best to stop me at each turn and my heart beat faster the closer we got. When the car came to a stop, I had trouble breathing. I glanced at my dad again, but he looked no different. I wasn't even sure he knew where we were.

Keep it together, Stella. You can do this.

A pastor waited outside the church for us, a comforting smile on his face. It made me want to turn and drive off, but I stepped out after taking several breaths to calm myself, though I could barely fill my lungs. They still burned and constricted painfully with each exhale.

He walked over to us and took my hand in his, resting another on top. "Hello, I'm Pastor Andrews. I will lead the memorial today. Let me show you inside where you can sit down for a moment." Green eyes tried to tell me everything was going to be okay, but no part of my brain believed him.

I couldn't move my feet, frozen to the ground. My heart raced, and I shook my head firmly. Going into the church would be too claustrophobic. I needed to be out in the fresh air, or I might suffocate.

"You can sit down at the memorial tree, if that would be preferable," he said, his smile fading into a thin line of understanding.

I nodded, and Pastor Andrews walked down a gravel path. I laced my fingers with my dad's, needing some support. The first glance towards the cemetery broke another piece of the wall. A tear fell with it, though I quickly swiped it away. My dad's hand shook violently, and I wasn't sure mine was any steadier. Tears blurred my vision, which at this point was probably a good thing, as the painful world around me faded away. We could get through this. Somehow. Today was not about us. It was about James.

It was a two-minute walk before the pastor stopped near the edge of some woodland. White wooden chairs were lined up in front of a young tree. Pastor Andrews seated us at the front. "I will be back momentarily. If you need anything, anything at all," he said, looking between us, both unhearing, "please come and get me." He gently bowed his head and walked back towards the church.

I fixed my eyes on the ground but slowly lifted them to take in my surroundings. We were at the edge of the cemetery. Tree-covered hills loomed in the distance, Mount St. Helens standing proudly beyond them. My mind wandered to Gray for just a moment before I continued to sweep my eyes along the landscape. A small pond glittered in the sunlight farther down the hill, and ducks bobbed along the surface. This place was as pretty as a picture. James would have loved it here. A flurry of tears fell from my eyes.

"Shhh..." My dad squeezed my hand and gently kissed my shoulder. He tried to soothe me, but it only made the crying worse.

"It's not fair," I sobbed, leaning against him. He retreated to his seat, clutching his head as he sobbed.

I truly was alone. James was gone. My dad couldn't pull himself together enough to realize I needed him. I *needed* him! Mom hadn't responded to the invitation to come say goodbye to her son. Not that I wanted her here. I only wanted people who loved him to be allowed to say their goodbyes.

Footsteps came up the gravel path, and I turned. Gray, Damien, Liam, Nate, and Cody came walking down the path, their expressions tense and mournful. I was out of my seat and running straight into Gray's arms before my mind caught up. I barreled into him, and he held me so tightly I could barely breathe.

"Hey," he whispered in my ear, nestling his cheek against my hair. "You're all right." He stroked my back as I clung to him, tears soaking into his black shirt.

"I'm not. I can't do this," I sobbed, shaking my head furiously.

Somehow, he tightened his grip even more. "You can."

"I can't."

He tried to pull me away, but I pressed my face into the crook of his neck. Here, the world around me wasn't real. He mumbled something to the guys, and they walked to sit down. "Hey, look at me." I shook my head. He wiggled his hands between us and took my face in his hands, tilting it up. "You can do this. We're right here with you. All of us. You're not alone in this. I've got you. Trust me." He kissed my forehead, then fixed his eyes on me again. They were bloodshot, his nose tinted a soft shade of red.

Little by little, I calmed down as I stared into his eyes. I wasn't completely alone. "Thank you for being here. James would have—" The words stuck in my throat.

He gave me a small smile, wiping a tear from my cheek with the pad of his thumb. "He was like a brother to me." He clenched his jaw. "Come on, let's sit down."

I let him lead me back to the chairs. He sat down right beside me and I rested my head against his shoulder. The guys whispered to each other, and it was a nice quiet noise. It slowed my racing heart, as did the small circles Gray drew on the back of my hand.

"He would have loved this spot," he said, his lips brushing against my forehead.

I took in a shaky breath. "Yeah, he would have."

The footsteps of a few more guests came down the path, mostly faces I barely recognized. Mrs. Johnson was among them, as were a few teachers from school. Behind them was Pastor Andrews, carrying James's urn.

I burst into sobs again. They were more violent this time, my body shaking uncontrollably even though Gray supported me against him. He seemed to want to shield me from the pain, but there was nothing holding it back anymore.

The walls fell. More like disintegrated. Smashed into so many tiny pieces, I wasn't sure they could ever be put back together. Every part of my body exploded and imploded at the same time. Sharp knives dug into my lungs, deflating any air in them. Razorblades cut at my heart, and I thought for a moment I might bleed out. That this would be my last resting spot too. Air rushed into my lungs as I saw stars, only to be expelled just as quickly.

I looked over at my dad, a redhead sitting beside him. She looked about my age, but I didn't know who she was. She rested her hand on my dad's back and stroked it calmly. His head still rested in his hands as he rocked back and forth, tears flowing as freely as mine were.

"That's Josie, Damien's cousin. Pastor Andrews is her dad," Gray whispered. His voice sounded distant, almost inaudible over the ringing in my ears. I nodded and looked away, snuggling even closer to Gray. I was glad someone sat with my dad, because I couldn't let go of Gray. He pressed his lips to my ear, his hands tangling in my hair that swung in the breeze. In his arms, I was a little less beyond repair. It still hurt, but there was something about his warmth that reminded me there would be a life after this. Maybe he could help me pick up the pieces.

No. That wasn't a good idea. LA was the plan. There, I didn't need these pieces anymore.

The urn now rested on the ground beside the tree. Pastor Andrews started the ceremony, but my ears rung and my heart beat so loudly I couldn't hear a word. I slipped my hand out of Gray's, digging my fingernails into my palms. I needed to feel something else. A different pain. Anything. I bit down on my tongue, then my lips, but no pain was enough.

Gray was also crying. A spasm rolled through his body with each sob he tried to contain. The seconds dragged on, somehow turning into minutes. The pastor spread the ashes around the tree and scattered some dirt on top. A new terror spread over my chest, and Gray had to stop me from jumping up. He wrapped his arms tighter around me and pulled me onto his lap. I think he said something, but I couldn't hear him.

They needed to stop. I wasn't ready. If I let them finish the memorial, James would truly be gone. No words rolled from my mouth as my throat wouldn't open—the only thing that came out was a small whimper. Gone. Just... Gone.

Pastor Andrews soon finished his speech and walked over to sit with us. The guests left, and the clearing fell into silence again.

I flicked my head around to Gray. "I can't go." My words failed me as a breath caught in my throat. "I can't leave him here..."

"That's okay. You can sit here for as long as you want," Pastor Andrews said as he sat down beside his daughter, a calming presence in the turmoil inside of me. My mind raced from one thing to the next as I struggled to focus.

"And I'm not leaving until you are," Gray said, squeezing me and pressing a light kiss to my ear.

"None of us are," one of the guys chimed in from behind. I hadn't even known they were still there. I wasn't sure who spoke. Peering over my shoulder, I felt a little less lonely with their tear-streaked faces looking back at me. They didn't look as scary as when I had first seen them at the farm.

"Thank you." The words struggled past the lump in my throat.

A tiny hummingbird landed on the tree branch, polishing its beak on the bark. Its shiny green and pink feathers danced in the sunlight. My breath caught in my chest when its eyes fixed on me, the bird completely stilling. We stared at each other, my soul being pulled toward the bird.

"My boy," my dad cried, almost ripping me open again.

Gray's warm embrace somehow held me together. I rubbed my thumb over Dad's beard, seeing the love pouring out of his eyes as he looked up at me. An unfamiliar, calm feeling spread across my chest when I turned to look back at the tree. The bird tilted its head, then fluttered away, swooping down over the field and the lake until it disappeared in the distance.

This was what James would have wanted.

This was what he deserved.

He wasn't gone, he was home.

I slowly eased myself from Gray's arms, and he helped steady me. With weak legs, I slumped to the grass, delicately running my fingers over the brass plaque engraved with his name and a simple quote James had said to me many times. I couldn't think of a better way to give him the goodbye he deserved.

James Riley Harris

Never regret something that once made you smile.

Chapter Twelve

- GRAY -

Seeing Stella completely and utterly broken damn near killed me. No matter how close I'd held her, she still cried, still fell apart right in front of me, like sand sliding through my fingers, like water dripping from the sky. Her hair blew in the wind as she sat by the tree, letting her fingers run through the grass. I didn't like her sitting there by herself, but I think she needed that moment with James.

"Hey, G?" Damien whispered. I turned to him. "Do you want us to stay?"

Josie had left Stella's dad's side and was clinging to her cousin now. Both their eyes were bloodshot. It might have been the first time I'd ever seen Damien cry. I'd known him since kindergarten, but he was usually the kind to keep things bottled up.

I wiped a tear from my cheek. "No, you guys head out. I'm gonna stay and keep an eye on her. Drop my truck off at her house?"

He nodded, tapping Nate on the leg. Nate nodded too, then they all stood up. One by one, they walked down the path towards the parking lot.

I got out of my seat and walked over to Stella. She turned her head to me when she heard me coming, nothing but sadness in her eyes.

"I don't want to go," she whispered.

"Then we stay." She leaned against me as I sank down. I brushed some hair out of her face, wanting so badly to take it all away. I'm not sure how long we'd sat there when her dad got up. He held his hand out to her, and she took it. They whispered something to each other, taking a moment to just look into each other's eyes. She then turned to me.

"Will you take us home? I can't drive, I can't..." Her words tore from her chest and she snapped her eyes far into the horizon.

I nodded and reached for her hand. I felt better having some part of her tucked against me, and if all I could have was her hand, I'd take it. We left, but didn't make it far before Stella turned to stare behind us. She took a shuddering inhale, then steeled herself and kept walking.

I lifted her hand to my lips and she gave me a tiny smile, barely even worth the name. Her dad got in the back of his car, and Stella slid into the passenger seat. The keys were still in the ignition. She must have forgotten to bring them with her when they arrived. The drive back was silent, apart from quiet sobs from both of them. I kept her hand in mine, our fingers intertwined over the middle console. I didn't ever want to let go.

When we got back, her dad all but jumped out of the car and dashed inside. The sound of clinking bottles rang through the air, then the TV turned on.

I sighed, walking around to Stella's side to open her door. She got out on unsteady legs, an emptiness covering her eyes. She wasn't looking at anything, barely even acknowledging me as her eyes drifted past my face.

We walked inside, and Stella led me out onto the back porch. She almost fell down into a sun chair, and I dragged one over to sit down beside her. By the time I sat down, she'd curled up into a ball, her forehead resting against her knees. She fidgeted with the necklace dangling from her neck, her other hand wrapped tightly around her legs. I rested my hand on her wrist, leaning back in my seat.

"What have you got there?" I asked.

She lifted her head slowly, like it weighed a hundred pounds. The metal shined in the light as she held it out, but she didn't answer me. Her tears came harder, shaking her body. I pulled on her wrist and she came to me easily, sinking down on my lap and wrapping her arms around my neck. More tears soaked into my shirt, seemingly never-ending.

My heart broke for her, for the pain she would always carry.

For the friend I'd lost, the one who was taken way too soon.

For the life he should have had, filled with love and joy.

A few raindrops fell from the sky, pattering against the roof. Hours passed, and Stella eventually fell asleep on me. It was restless, her body twitching and jerking, but at least she was resting. Some sleep was better than nothing.

She suddenly jolted awake, a cry coming out of her as she looked around.

"Stella, you're okay. You're home," I said, turning her face to look at me. "I'm right here."

She looked through me for a moment, then she registered me. "I dreamed..." She shook her head and closed her eyes tightly.

"Come on, let's get you inside," I said. It was late now, the moon and stars covered by a blanket of clouds.

"I don't want to sleep. His face..." The words broke away again.

"Then no sleep. But let's go lie down. Somewhere more comfortable." My back was killing me, but if she wanted to stay out here all night, I'd let her.

She nodded and slowly stood up. I held my hand near her waist in case her legs gave out, and we walked inside. She didn't look into the room where her dad snored—she just headed up the stairs. When she went into James's room and slid into his bed, I hesitated for a moment. I couldn't leave her alone, but lying beside her in my best friend's bed just seemed plain wrong.

I tucked her in, her eyes closing almost instantly, then sat right beside her on the floor. She wrapped her delicate hand around my wrist, and I didn't have the heart to pull away. Despite saying she didn't want to sleep, she drifted off within a few minutes. It didn't take long before I joined her.

I glanced at the clock on the bedside table when I woke. Nate would just be heading off to work. As if on cue, my phone rang in my pocket.

"Hey, where are you? I'm just about to head out the door," he said when I answered.

I left the room before I replied. "You go. I'll call my dad and let him know I can't come in today." I glanced over at Stella, her back towards me, and lowered my voice. "I can't leave her alone."

"All right, if you're sure. I'm not sure your dad is going to take it well. Don't you have that thing today?"

Shit, I had completely forgotten about the meetings. Dad wanted me to meet some contractors we used regularly to get to know them better. "I'll make something up. If he asks, please don't say anything," I urged.

"I've got your back. But it ain't my fault if you get fired, all right?"

Nate hung up, and I walked farther down the hall, not wanting to risk waking Stella. I pressed call with a lump in my throat. This wouldn't end well, but how could I leave her? Her dad was no use, still passed out in the living room. If anything, he was making things harder for her by being so distant.

"Hi. I was just about to call you," my dad answered before saying goodbye to Mom.

"Hi, Dad. I know—"

"Grayson," he interjected. "It is very important for both of us that you show up today. I don't want to hear any excuses. I have already told the contractors that I will introduce you as the future owner of the company, so if you don't show, imagine what that will look like. Yesterday was difficult for you, but sometimes we need to do things that are hard. This will be a valuable lesson for you."

I opened my mouth, but slowly closed it again, glancing behind me towards James's room and clenched my fist. "When is the first meeting?" I asked, my jaw clenching so tightly it was hard to speak.

"At twelve. You can come in then. That should give you a few more hours to sober up. But make sure you're there." He hung up swiftly.

Of course Dad didn't understand. This wasn't about me, and it sure as hell wasn't about me being either too drunk or hungover to get to work. I wanted to throw my phone on the floor and shatter it into a thousand tiny pieces. But it wouldn't make me feel any better. I slid it into my back pocket and rubbed my face before walking back to Stella.

I found her in the same position as I'd left her. The same one she had been in all night. Her eyelashes fluttered gently against her skin, and she looked peaceful. Breathtaking even with puffy eyes and a pink nose.

My feet against the hardwood must have woken her up. Her bloodshot eyes fell on me as she looked around distantly, like she wasn't actually here, but her shell was. She bit her lip nervously, and I stared a little too long. The need to wrap her in my arms and try to make everything better again reappeared, but I forced myself to focus.

"How are you feeling?" I tucked some hair behind her ear as it fell over her face.

She grabbed my hand and held it against her lips, closing her eyes again. "Please don't go. I don't want to be alone."

It broke me. I didn't know I could hurt more for this brunette than I already was, but somehow she found a way. "I'm not going." She opened her eyes to look at me as I sank down on the floor.

"Did you sit on the floor all night?" Her eyes went wide.

I gave her a smile. "Yeah, but it's all right. I've slept in worse places."

She sat up and looked at the bed, then slid her legs out. Her dress rose around her waist, but I forced my eyes not to linger. I already felt like a dick for having these feelings towards her. I wouldn't make it worse by staring at her underwear.

"You can sleep in my bed," she whispered. She stood up, and the dress fell down over silky legs.

"Honestly, I'm fine. Are you hungry? Let me make you something to eat."

She shook her head. "I feel nauseous." She left the room, turning left to head to her own bedroom.

Despite saying I was fine, I was craving the soft comfort of a bed. Maybe I could lie down for a few hours. It had nothing to do with the fact that I wanted to hold her, touch her, feel her as she drifted back to sleep herself. I pulled my phone out and set an alarm, knowing I'd have to either get up and go to work later or call Dad again, then slid in beside her.

She turned and rested her head on my chest before I had even got comfortable, tucking her petite
body against me. I froze for a moment, then gave in
to the sensation and wrapped her up in my arms.
She fit perfectly. When I glanced down, she was
looking up at me. Big, glossy eyes scanned my face,
landing on my lips and stayed there. I swallow hard.
She sat up, her hand still resting on my chest.

"Stella, what—"

Her warm lips found mine in a flurry of heat,
soft and plump as she dragged them along mine.
I bunched my hands in the covers, not allowing
myself to feel her. We couldn't do this, especially not
after what she went through yesterday.

"Please," she whispered, breath a silken touch on
my skin. "I need a distraction."

Her tongue grazed my lips, chipping away at my
resolve. "Stella, we can't do this." I shook my head
and reached my hands out to grab her face. She allowed me push her away, but began sobbing almost
instantly.

I sat up and pulled her into my arms, and she
ended up straddling my legs. She wrapped her arms
around me and buried her face in my neck while I
ran my hands over her back as she let out more tears.

"It's going to hurt," I said, "but you can get through
this."

She tightened her grip on me and shook her head.
"I don't think I can. I'm alone. This hole in me... It's
sucking me in, and I can't stop it. I can't *breathe*." She
leaned back and looked at me. Her lips were swollen

from biting them, and they trembled as she stared at me. "I just want the pain to end."

I wiped a tear from her cheek. "It will. I promise. One day—"

"I don't want one day. I want it to stop now." Her voice was impossibly weak as she shut her eyes tightly.

I leaned my forehead against hers. "If I could take even a small part of it for you, I would. But you're strong. You can do this."

"Not alone. Mom left me. Dad left me. Now James. I have no one."

"You have me," I said. I wasn't sure how much of me she wanted after her reaction to our kiss under the stars, but I'd give her whatever she would take.

Her eyes fluttered open, releasing the built up tears. "Then kiss me. Take it away, if just for right now."

Her breath fanned over my lips as she spoke. Heated words turned into heated eyes. Her chest moved closer, and I was suddenly all too aware that she was only wearing a dress. Her tears had been enough to distract me, but with her in my lap, telling me she wanted me, my mind raced.

I should have said no, but my mouth didn't connect to my brain. Stella ran her gentle hands around my neck and tilted my face to hers. She pressed her lips to mine again, and I opened for her, gliding my tongue along hers in a soft caress. My hands stayed firmly on her waist, needing her to set the pace. If she wanted to stop, we'd stop. That was the smart thing to do, but smart had gone out the window when I climbed into bed beside her.

Her tongue entwined with mine, the sweetest taste I'd ever experienced, setting my taste buds on fire as she took what she needed. She sank down in my lap, the crotch of her panties settling against my tightening jeans and forcing a moan to rumble through my chest. Instead of shifting away from me, she began to rock her hips, despite my efforts to stop her with my firm grip on her waist.

"Stella," I said, trying to move my growing erection away from her. Fuck, it felt so good.

When she came up for air, her movements only got faster. Her previously glossy eyes were molten hot as she stared into mine and bit her bottom lip, sucking it into her mouth. She took my hand and guided it under her dress, pressing it firmly against her bra, pressing my fingers into the lace fabric, warm and velvety skin teasing my fingers along the edge. They were round and full, pushing firmer against me as she arched her back. She didn't let go of my hand, so it stayed there, caressing gently at first, then rougher.

I was lost to her. So far gone any thoughts of stopping had long gone.

A moan fell from her mouth as she rolled her head back, pressing more firmly against my jeans. I thought for sure I was losing blood flow to a very important part of my body, but watching her free of pain was enough for me not to stop her.

"Gray," she moaned, rocking faster, taking the pleasure for herself.

She was stunning, her hair a mess around her shoulders and her silky legs on either side of my lap. I gave up the pretense than I wasn't enjoying this and claimed her neck, sliding my hand around her back and keeping her tucked against me. She whimpered as I sank my teeth into the delicate skin where her throat and collarbone joined, peppering it with kisses and licks after. She tasted divine, like the sweetest fruit, yet one that should be so forbidden. I moved my hips to rock in time with hers, our bodies finding a shared rhythm of pure pleasure. It didn't take long for her to reach breathlessness, and she dug her nails into my back.

"Gray, I'm..." she panted, but the words didn't come out, eyes barely opening as she gasped.

The beautiful brunette came undone in my lap, her hands gripping my neck me so tightly they would leave marks, tugging and pulling, pushing and holding. I lifted her head to kiss her, devouring her moans with my mouths. I wanted to feel her ride through the aftershocks as she grappled onto me. Her breath mingled with mine, so hot it was like she was breathing fire yes it didn't burn. She trembled for almost a minute before stilling in my arms, a softness blanketing her face. Only then did I release her mouth, savoring each taste of her before it melted on my tongue.

I hadn't found my release, which in these tight jeans was a good thing. But watching her was all I needed. I tucked some hair over her shoulder, not sure what to do now. She darted her eyes to my chest, then to her lap before crawling off me. There was a wet patch on my jeans that almost made my dick explode, but I quickly averted my eyes.

Fuck, I had never experienced anything like that before. And that scared me. As did the closed off look in Stella's eyes as she sank down on the bed beside me, her arms wrapped around her legs. Silence filled the room, the quiet sound of the TV rolling through the floor from below.

My mind was racing, as was my heart. I wanted to reach out for her, but she looked so closed off I didn't think I could.

"Are you okay?" I asked, shifting a little closer. The throbbing in my jeans softened with each passing minute, yet the memory of her on me never would.

She closed her eyes tightly, a tear spilling over. "I don't think I know what okay means anymore." She glanced at me through her hair. "I'm sorry, I don't—"

The doorbell rang downstairs, cutting her off. Stella left without saying anything else. By the time I stood, she was already by the front door, mumbling voices joining the gentle chatter of the TV.

Well, fuck... What had just happened? I probably should have stopped her. No, I *for sure* should have stopped her. If the kiss had been taking advantage of her sadness, this was so much worse. If James knew, he would have killed me. The other guys too.

I needed to talk to Stella. We needed to figure out what this was, if it was anything at all. I headed down in search of her, finding her standing in the hallway with an older lady.

"I've brought you cinnamon buns and some freshly made strawberry fizz. Come on, let's go sit down." The lady walked through the house like she'd been here before, her eyes landing on me as I got to the bottom of the stairs. "And who's this strapping young man?" She quirked her eyebrow as she took me in.

"Mrs. Johnson, this is Gray. A... friend of James's." I couldn't read Stella's expression, half of her face hidden behind her hair.

"Well, I'm glad you weren't alone. Come, let's eat outside. You must be starving." The lady chatted on as she headed towards the back patio. Stella followed quietly behind, and I reached for her hand as she walked past.

"Please talk to me," I pleaded.

"I'll call you. Okay? I just need time. I can't do this." She rolled up on her toes and gave me a quick kiss on the cheek, then darted outside.

Every fiber of my being wanted to follow her, force her to talk to me. But she'd just put her brother to rest yesterday, so if she needed time, I'd give her time. Hopefully she didn't need too much.

Chapter Thirteen

My dad was waiting for me outside the office, clutching two cups of coffee. He smiled when he saw me, visibly pleased I had showed up. Nate stopped unloading boxes at the far end of the long driveway and stood to watch me as I climbed out of my truck.

I yanked the coffee from my dad without saying a word. During the drive over, my confused feelings had turned into anger at myself for letting Stella get under my skin. For letting her do that when she wasn't in the right frame of mind. She should have remained James's sister, but there was no way she would ever be just that again. I couldn't erase her taste, erase the phantom pain from my hardness trying to rip my zipper apart.

Dad frowned, fixing me with a narrowed look when he noticed I was still dressed in the same neat clothes as yesterday, though they were much more wrinkly now. "We have some things to do before our first meeting in thirty minutes. And you should get changed." I kept flicking my eyed towards the house where Nate was working. My dad must have noticed, as he said, "Go talk to him. I'll be inside when you are ready." He slapped me on the back and walked into his office, leaving me standing alone with my coffee. I wandered over to Nate, who dropped the boxes he'd been moving when he noticed me.

"So, you're here." He wiped the sweat from his forehead with the back of his arm.

I threw the coffee mug into the trees next to me, suppressing a yell, then rubbed both my hands over my face, leaning my back against the pallets next to me. "I'm such a fucking idiot," I growled, not sure I should tell him the whole truth.

"What did you do this time?" he grunted, rolling his eyes.

"Nothing, just... I don't know. She kissed me." There was no way I was telling Nate the full story.

"She kissed you or you kissed her? There's a major difference there," Nate said, barely looking up from what he was doing.

"She kissed me. I think. Fuck, I'm so confused."

Nate put the tools down and turned to me, crossing his arms over his chest. "Dude, I knew this was going to happen as soon as Kasey mentioned her."

"Knew what?"

"That you'd go thinking with your dick again. But with you, your dick somehow morphs into your heart. So you want to tell me again how it was just her kissing you?" He raised an eyebrow, daring me to tell him anything but the truth.

"Grayson!" my dad called from the office, sparing me from words I didn't want to say out loud yet. Lies I didn't want to tell him. I spun on my heels as Nate let out a snort.

"We're not done with this conversation," he called before I walked inside the office.

I didn't think we were, but right now, I needed to put all of this Stella shit to the side and focus on work. If she needed time, I needed to occupy my brain with something that wasn't her because she was still all my brain could focus on.

Dad looked up as I walked in, pointing at his desk. "See this here? Tell me what you think." He took a step back.

I was expecting to see more invoices or an error. But on his desk was a logo, the company's current logo, with one very important difference. The company's name had always been Rafter Construction, but now there was a *& Son* added. I almost choked.

"So, what do you think? I had someone sketch it up last night."

I glanced over at him and saw his proud smile, picking up the paper to inspect it. *Rafter & Sons Construction*. The truth was, I wasn't sure what to think. About anything. About work. About the new name for the business. About Stella and what I wanted us to be. So much for focusing on work.

I shrugged. It clearly wasn't the answer my dad had hoped for as red rose on his neck.

"You had a hard day yesterday. I understand that. But sometimes you need to separate work and personal. Understood?"

Anger rose in my chest. "Like you did? Is that why you were never around?"

My dad looked like he was ready to blow, and he slammed his fist down on the desk. "I'm willing to give you the benefit of the doubt, only because of James."

"You don't know what the fuck you are talking about," I growled, tensing my hands by my sides.

The calm voice that followed sent a chill down my spine. "You will come to the meetings. You will smile. You will do whatever fucking thing I ask you to do. If not, you are done. Is that understood? I cannot keep hoping you will grow up one day. That times has passed. It is now or never. Do you understand?"

My chest heaved up and down as we stared at each other. Little by little, the anger faded. It wasn't my dad I was angry at. I wasn't really angry at all, just confused. Nodding, I tilted my head down. Apologizing was one step too far, especially when I hadn't done anything wrong. But I wouldn't fight him. Not when the real fight was still blazing inside.

The first few meetings went by in a rush. I tried to take in as much as I could, but it was overwhelming. My dad kept a close eye on me, and it forced me to focus on business. It was only several hours later that I remembered Stella. It knocked the wind right out of me, and I had to excuse myself from the office. I hovered my finger over the call button on my phone, but then I pushed the phone back down in my pocket. She said she needed time, so I had to give her that.

Dad looked up at me when I walked through the doors. It was clear he had something on his mind as he watched me with narrowed eyes.

"What's up?" I asked, trying to sound as normal as I could. The tension between us could still be cut with a knife.

"I've been thinking," he said, tapping his desk. "You did well in the meetings, but I can tell your heart isn't in it. I gathered as much from your earlier outburst. I shouldn't have yelled at you. Maybe I'm still asking too much of you. You miss working on-site, don't you?"

I stopped in the middle of the room and glanced out the window. It would be a lie to say there weren't days when I wished I could just drop all of this and work with Nate, but that certainly wasn't why I'd fought with him. And him giving me an out was like he was giving up on me. I was a disappointment, yet again. My heart sank.

"I, eh... I mean, yeah, a little. But I'm getting better at it. Used to it," I added and ran my hand through my hair. It wasn't a lie—I didn't want to add more to the pile. My dad nodded. I worried for a moment that I'd said the wrong thing again.

"For that reason, I was thinking you could work in the office with me three days a week, and two days a week you could work on-site?"

I didn't know how to reply. Was this an olive branch, or a way for him to save face for the business?

"It's okay. I get it. When I was younger, this wasn't exactly what I wanted to do either, and I guess I kind of forgot that over the years. I used to have ambitions bigger than the skyscrapers in New York City, but we're all different." He nodded towards the door. "Go on, I'll see you back here tomorrow." He narrowed his eyes and pressed his lips together.

He wasn't doing this for me. I knew that look in his eye—one I'd seen many times before. Disappointment. I'd hoped each time it would be the last, but apparently old habits die hard.

"All right." I stared back. I still wasn't ready to apologize, so I headed out the door. My steps were even heaver now. Maybe working with my hands would help me forget about this morning. Stella's face flashed across my mind, and that thought quickly went out the window. While she figured out what she wanted, I could hopefully get this part of my life sorted.

But what did *I* want?

I walked up behind Nate, who was installing kitchen cabinet doors.

"So, I heard your shouting contest with dear old pop. What's up with that?" He wiped his hands on his worn jeans, peering over his shoulder at me.

"Just me being me," I grunted. "My dad's letting me work on-site two days a week. I let him down, and he was quick to show me that." I took a deep inhale before continuing. "Fuck, everything is so messed up right now."

"Everything?" He threw the screwdriver at me as he went to pick up another cabinet door.

"Yep. Want to go for a drink tonight?" I asked, deflecting his question that I knew held more weight that it first appeared.

Nate grinned and nodded enthusiastically. "Hell yeah! Damn, it's been a while since we've gone out together. But don't think for a second we're done talking about Stella."

"I don't. Just don't mention it to the others yet. I need to figure this out."

"Whatever," Nate replied. "She's just a girl. Don't let her fuck with your head when you're close to sorting shit out with your dad." It was too late for that. "You okay, though? Yesterday was fucking tough, but... I don't know. You seem to carry the weight of the world on your shoulders lately. Reminds me of when shit when down with Kasey in high school. Stella can't take that."

Her face once again flashed before me, but I pushed it back down, further into the darkest corner of my mind this time. "I'm fine. I'm not trying to hurt her. I just... I don't know. Can we talk about this another time?" I rubbed my hands over my face. "I need to get my head straight first."

"I'm telling you. Girl problems aren't worth it."

"Like you know anything about that, anyway. The only girl problem you have is what girl you'll be sleeping with this weekend."

Nate winked at me. "We all have our roles to play." I pushed him, and he laughed.

A small lightness spread through my chest at his grin. Maybe I was putting too much weight on all of this. Stella was just a girl, after all. Fucking gorgeous and incredible, but if she wasn't interested in me like I was in her, I'd have to respect that. Better not go losing my heart to someone who didn't want it.

Chapter Fourteen

- STELLA -

The next few hours went by in a blur. Mrs. Johnson tried to get me to eat and drink, but I couldn't stomach it. I spent most of the day outside in the yard with her—the stench of alcohol was too strong in the house. She didn't mention it, but then she was probably used to seeing my dad like this.

As the sun set and the stars came out, she made me promise to come over if I got too lonely. I nodded, but had no plans to do so. Right now, I needed to be alone with my thoughts. I needed to figure out what the hell this thing was between me and Gray, and if it changed anything about my plans to go back to LA.

Kissing him had been a distraction at first, but then my body took control. It was like I needed him to breathe. Like he was holding me together when all I was doing was falling apart.

But I couldn't just think about myself. Dad still needed me, whether he wanted to admit that or not. I'd let him have some time to himself yesterday, but it was time we talked about the next step. About possibly going to LA. My stomach twisted in knots when I thought about not seeing Gray again, but I had to focus on Dad first. If that was what he needed, it was what I would do.

"Hey, Dad?" I mumbled hesitantly and gently knocked on the door frame to the living room.

He turned his head to me and tried to shake himself awake. "Oh hey, darling!" He went to stand up but tripped. A bottle of whiskey fell from his hands, shattering on the corner of the coffee table. Glass shards flew around him, and the rug soaked with alcohol.

"Dad," I groaned, walking over to help him before he sliced his feet open. "Sit down!" I yelled when he almost stepped on the glass, and he fell back onto the couch.

"I'll clean it up," he slurred. I was tempted to leave him to deal with his own shit, but I couldn't.

"Just sit there until I've got all the glass, okay? Dad, there's something we need to talk about."

Glazed and glossy eyes met mine, struggling to keep me in focus as he swayed sideways. "About what?"

"We need a fresh start. Both of us. Maybe somewhere new."

He looked at me, confusion in his drunk eyes. Maybe now wasn't the best time to talk about this, but at least I had planted the seed. "A fresh start? Where? I can't just-just up and go. I've got the house and work."

"Those things aren't important. We need to move on, Dad. Do you really think we can do that in this town?" I swiped a tear from my cheek. He pondered my words while I carefully picked up all the pieces of glass, nicking my fingertips on a few sharp edges. I sucked on the blood as I waited for my dad to respond.

"Can we talk about it tomorrow? I've got work," he said, standing up.

"Dad, it's almost ten at night. You don't have work."

His gaze floated from me to the darkness outside. "Oh." He lay back down on the couch. "In the morning then." His lids closed, and he was snoring within seconds.

I stood up and took the glass outside, stopping to inhale the fresh air. I didn't want to go in the house. It felt so… dead. Cold and empty. Like there was no soul left. My bike leaned against the side wall of the garage, teasing me with freedom. I swung my leg up and over the seat, pedaling down the street with more energy than I had to spare.

My legs went round and round as I headed up the hill to the water tower. It would be empty up there, something I both hated and needed. Despite the crescent moon, it was hard to see where I was going, and the bike rattled as the road turned to gravel. Reaching for the brake, my hand slipped as the front tire hit a big hole. The bike disappeared from under me, and I landed on the side of the dirt path with a thud, rolling down the ditch. Air rushed out of my lungs, twigs digging into my sides until I finally stilled.

I lay there for a moment, unable to move. Every cell in my body hurts. Why was *everything* so painful? I slowly turned to my side and pushed myself up from the ground. My hands and knees were scraped and my top had a tear across the front. With a gentle poke, I pressed my fingers against my ribs to check if any were broken, but they only felt bruised. I pulled some leaves and twigs out of my hair as I scrambled up the ditch to my bike. The front wheel was bent out of shape, and the chain hung off the back. I definitely couldn't ride it back home.

A warm breeze played with my hair as I stood there with no more tears left to fall, probably too dehydrated at this point. I stumbled my way to the water tower, leaving my bike on the ground behind me.

Slumping to the rocks with a wince, I held my hand against my ribs. My scraped knees burned as I picked at them, but I welcomed it. It was new. It was tangible, and once I'd healed in a few days' time, it wouldn't hurt anymore. Maybe that's how my grief would fade. One day it would heal, and all that would remain would be a scar. Though it would take a long time.

I stared out across the town as moonlight danced over the buildings. I saw the high school where James and I had spent several years together. The field where I would cheer him on at his games. The park where we'd had picnics when we were younger. My mind played through all the memories we'd had in this town. Maybe I had been wrong before. Maybe James never left this place, and his life was still here. If I left, I wouldn't have to face the memories again, but that would also mean leaving James behind.

Could I do that? Did I want to do that? No. That was the one thing I was sure I didn't want.

But that didn't mean I knew what the next step was.

A pair of headlights from a car came up the dirt road, generic pop music blasting through the speakers. The door slammed shut, and a couple walked down toward another lookout point on the opposite side of the water tower. It didn't take long before they were making out, moans floating through the night.

My mind drifted back to Gray on my bed. I still wasn't sure what to do about that situation. If I was completely honest with myself, I liked Gray. A lot more than I should. But he was here. In a town I hated. My heart sank when I realized going back to LA would mean anything between us would be over. Yet I also didn't see how carrying on was going to work.

A voice I recognized rang through the night. I turned my head to look in the couple's direction, and sure enough, it was Nate. His blond hair was unmistakable, as was his laugh at something the girl said. Not wanting him to see me, I got up to leave, keeping my hair covering my face as I hobbled down the path. I didn't get far when he called out.

"Stella?" I tried to pick up the pace, but my body hurt too much. I turned around when his jogging footsteps came toward me, knowing I wouldn't be able to out-hobble him. "Hey, why are you here?" He stopped in front of me and his eyes went wide as he took me in. "Shit, what happened? You've got blood and cuts all over you." He reached out but quickly pulled back as if worried he'd hurt me.

"I fell off my bike. I'm fine." He dashed around me and blocked my path when I tried to leave.

"That doesn't look fine. Let me drive you home."

I stared at him. Not only were his eyes glossed over, his breath stank of alcohol. It reminded me of Dad and bile rose in my throat at what would meet me when I got back. "You're drunk."

His cheeks flushed red, and he tugged on the ends of his hair. "Yeah, I guess I am. But I didn't drive. It's not my car. It's... the girl... uh... Shit, what was her name again?" he muttered to himself. I tried to walk past him, but he didn't let me. "Come on, you can't walk all that way home in the dark."

"Watch me," I said, continuing on.

"Let me call Gray. He can—"

"No!" I exclaimed, way too loudly and slightly shrill. "No, I'm fine." I wasn't ready to face him yet.

Nate studied me, a crease between his brows. "All right. Then I'll walk you home. It's too late for you to walk on your own. I don't want to know how the fuck you got here, so don't tell me. I'd rather be blissfully ignorant," he grunted.

He was right. I didn't even have my phone if something happened. "Fine. But no talking. I'm too tired."

"Sounds like my kind of conversation," he said, grinning as he fell into step beside me. I glanced at him, quirking my eyebrow.

"What about your girlfriend?"

"Who?" He looked at me like I had two heads. I motioned to the car and the girl still lying down in the grass beside it. "Oh, shit! Uh, wait here. Don't go." He jogged back to the girl. It was too far away for me to hear what was said, but the slap across his face rang loudly through the silent night. It brought a smile to my face, but I scrubbed it off when the car flew past, her middle finger pointed at me through the open window.

"That went well," I teased, peering over at Nate when he caught up with me. I was surprised he'd stayed with me rather than go with his not-girl-friend.

He smirked and rubbed his reddening cheek. We walked in silence for a while, Nate opening and closing his mouth as if to say something several times. In the end, I'd had enough of the inhales and drawn-out exhales.

"Spit it out."

"What's up with you and Gray?"

I swallowed. Did he know about me dry-humping his best buddy? Embarrassment flooded my cheeks, and I was suddenly boiling hot. "Nothing."

"Uh-huh. That's why you panicked when I said I'd call him to come get you?" He grabbed my arm and we came to a stop. I shifted my weight from one foot to the other, trying to avoid meeting his prying gaze. "He didn't even have to tell me about your kiss. I could tell as soon as he showed up at work today that something was up. He wouldn't have flipped on his dad like that for no reason." Nate lifted his hand and pulled a stick from my hair, twirling it between his fingers.

I stayed silent, and when Nate realized I wasn't going to say anything, he sighed and kept walking. We stopped at the bottom of the driveway, staring up at James's window.

"That's his room, right?" he asked.

"Yeah." I wasn't exactly about to invite him inside, so I settled on saying, "Thanks for walking me back."

"You gonna be okay on your own? I can come in and help you clean up." He looked genuinely concerned, blond hair falling over his eyebrows drawn together as he dropped his gaze to my scraped-up knees. He looked so different from the confident playboy I'd always seen him as.

I nodded. He turned to leave, but I called out to him before he got more than a few steps away. "Nate?" He spun back to me. "Don't mention this to Gray."

He tilted his head as he studied me, but didn't promise me anything as he said, "See you around."

My dad opened the door before Nate could leave. He was still drunk, his eyes distant. "Stella? What are you doing out here?"

"Just talking to a friend, Dad." I peered towards Nate.

"I woke up and you weren't home. I was worried you'd gone back to LA and left me here alone," he said, somewhere between a joke and true concern. "Honey, I need you to know—"

"Go to sleep, Dad. We can talk in the morning when you're not drunk."

"I'm Nate Keyes. You must be Mr. Harris," Nate said, suddenly right beside me. I jumped at his nearness and the brush of his firm chest to my arm.

My dad leaned against the door, blinking firmly at Nate. "Oh, call me David."

"Nate was just leaving," I said, giving him a firm push towards the steps. He didn't even budge.

"Come on, let's get you inside, David," Nate said, ignoring me and slipping past. "Where's your bed?"

My dad muttered something incoherent, and Nate frowned at me. I pointed towards the back room, and he led Dad over to it. My dad fell onto the bed face first, but Nate turned him onto his side, making sure to tuck a pillow under his head, then pulled me out of the room before closing the door behind us.

"I can handle it myself," I said, shaking his hand off.

Nate turned as he got to the front door. "I know what it's like. To have an alcoholic dad. And mom." Pain flashed in his eyes, but he shook it off. "It sucks. I wish I had some words of wisdom for you, but my brain is too fuzzy for that." He grinned and I let myself smile briefly. "So, you're going back to LA?"

I inhaled, holding it in my lungs. "I don't know. I don't know anything right now. When James... My dad is falling apart here, and I don't know how to help him. Without my dad, I have nothing." That was way too much to tell a drunk guy I barely knew, but I was so tired of keeping it all inside.

"Nothing? Not even a brown-haired guy with love hearts in his eyes whenever he thinks about you?"

Nate searched my face for an answer I didn't know. He gave me one more long look, then turned and walked out of the house.

I tossed and turned all night, waking up just before noon the next day. I stared up at the ceiling, as any movement hurt too much. The phone rang downstairs, but I ignored it. My dreams weren't exactly nightmares, but they were too confusing to make sense of. What Nate had said about Gray kept rolling through my mind, but I didn't know what to feel. I wanted to be with Gray, but he was here. In Waterbury. Still not having decided if I was staying, I couldn't let Gray be the deciding factor. If I was staying, I had to stay for Dad and me.

My scraped knees and wrists didn't look as bad as they had last night. My skin was rubbed raw in many places and sensitive to the touch—a few bruises appearing on my shins and knees.

Eventually, I made my way downstairs to see if my dad was awake. He was nowhere to be found—his bag and keys gone from the hallway. A sudden hard knock on the door made me jump. My first thought was Gray, my heart fluttering at the thought of seeing him again. A tall, dark shape stood outside the frosted window. I opened the door but it wasn't Gray—outside stood a policeman. He cleared his throat, taking off his cap to rest against his chest. He had short brown hair and light-brown eyes, a tight smile on his face.

"Hi Stella, I'm Officer Maxwell. I'm a friend of your dad's and I've got him in the car. Can I come inside?"

I went numb. I looked up at him before taking a step to the side. My brain couldn't handle what he was going to say.

"Your dad is okay. I want you to know that." He followed me into the kitchen and I leaned up against the counter, tapping my nails against the surface. "I was doing my rounds this morning and found his car off Coal Creek Road, presumably on his way to work. He had driven off the road and into the ditch. No major injuries, but I did a breath test and I'm sorry to say he had been drunk when he was driving. He is sobering up now but is really in no shape to be alone."

I glanced out through the window at the police car parked outside—my dad sitting in the backseat with his head in his hands.

"I know you are both going through a very hard time right now, and because I've known your dad for a long time, I will overlook it." His eyes stared right through me. "But if he had hurt someone, I wouldn't be able to be so lenient. It will be out of my hands if it happens again." The man sighed and his expression relaxed slightly. "He asked me to bring him here after he got checked out by the doctor. I would feel much more comfortable if you stayed with him, at least for today, to make sure he doesn't deteriorate.

I am happy to take him back to the hospital for him to rest, if that is what you would prefer."

How much did he know about my dad's drinking problem? Surely he knew he was drunk more often than not. Most of the town did. I opened my mouth, but no words came out. A tear fell down my cheek, and I wiped it away as I glanced up at the officer.

"I'll keep an eye on him." I wanted to tell him to take my dad away, but I couldn't abandon him like that. It was just another reason we had to get out of this town.

Maxwell tipped his head to me and walked back outside. I was in the hallway when they entered, my dad's eyes landing on me. His wrist was wrapped up in a bandage, and the smell of antiseptic mixed with alcohol burned my nose. I wanted to scream at him. Tell him how selfish he was and what a useless dad he'd always been. But the look of regret on his face stopped me. A whimper rolled from him as Maxwell sat him down on the couch and he cradled his wrist against his chest. I thanked the officer as he left, closing the front door behind him. Dad didn't look up when I came back in, keeping his gaze firmly on the ceiling.

"What were you thinking?" I snarled, my voice hard as steel. We had both tried to run from the pain, but I hadn't driven drunk. He could have caused an accident, or worse, he could have killed himself or someone else. I had to steady myself against the door frame as my knees wobbled. "How could you do that to me? What if you had never come home? Who would I have left?" He jerked with each question I threw at him. "I've had enough of being the responsible one. The one always there to pick up after your mess. I'm done!" I shouted. His outline became blurry. "You have never been here for me when I needed you. James was the only one I could rely on. But we lost him and now all we have is each other, and you're willing to risk that?" My whole body shook, and it was hard to breathe.

I hurried upstairs to my room, leaving my dad a crying mess on the couch. Sobs wracked through my body as I fell on the bed, the salty tears stinging my scraped palms as I wiped them away.

Alone. Again. Again and again and again. I always ended up alone. I glanced at my phone that had fallen onto the covers beside me, wanting to call Gray. Wanting him to make everything okay. But I'd relied on him too much to solve my grief. It was time I faced this head on.

Several hours passed, and I lay on the bed as the anger slowly softened. It was nearly four in the afternoon when there was a gentle knock on my door. I turned my head away. I didn't want to hear Dad's excuses. There was nothing he could say that would make this better.

"Stella?" My dad tried to open my door, but it was locked. He sighed. "I'm sorry. Not only for today, but for everything. I have been selfish and I wish I could do it all over again. I don't want to lose you. You mean so much to me. But you are right, I've never been there for you. And that needs to change. I want to be there for you, so no more drinking." I'd heard that before. A few months after Mom left. When we graduated high school. It was always nothing but a dream.

His footsteps retreated down the hall. I jumped up and ran after him, my fists bunching at my sides as I was ready to argue with him. Dad was staring into James's room when I flung my door open, and all the fight in me vanished.

"I'll go to rehab," he said without looking at me. He straightened and ran a hand over his beard. "I can't say I wouldn't have made all my mistakes if I hadn't been drunk, but it's about time I tried. I want to do this for you."

"When are you going?" I didn't know what else to say. He turned to me.

"Next week. I found a center a few towns over. Will you stay until then? Please?" His breathing became more erratic as he tried not to cry.

I wasn't just too tired to cry; I was also too tired to fight. Walking over, I wrapped my arms around him.

He hugged me back tightly and whispered through my hair, "I promise I will do my best to get back to you." His words echoed in my head. Maybe I was just setting myself up for more disappointment. But it was a risk I had to take.

Chapter Fifteen

- GRAY -

YESTERDAY

The glass of whiskey sat on the coffee table, staring back at me, and I was just drunk enough that my brain was like warm jelly. I'd sat here alone, wallowing in self-pity, since Nate went out with some girl a few hours ago.

The front door opened, then slammed shut. Someone slapped my head. I spun around and Nate stood there, arms crossed over his chest and blond hair all over the place, eyes red.

"What's your problem?" I grunted, going back to running my fingers along the rim of the glass.

He slapped my head again. And again. Each time, a little harder.

"What the fuck?" I jumped up and pushed him away from me.

"What the fuck is right. What the *fuck* did you do to Stella? Did you fuck her?" The previous drunken sheen over his eyes was gone. Now he just looked pissed.

"W-what?" I stuttered, swallowing.

"Did you?"

"No, no. I didn't. Why?"

He glared at me, then sank down on the couch, grabbing the bottle of whiskey. I sat and pushed my glass to him, but he pushed it back, sipping straight from the bottle. "You might need it after what I'm about to tell you. Fuck you and your dick, man."

I tensed. "Tell me what? Is Stella all right?"

He grumbled to himself. "Hell if I know. Walked her home. She wouldn't let me help her clean up the blood. She's safe at least."

"Blood? Safe? Nate, what the fuck are you talking about?" I stood, close to running out the door before he could explain.

"She's fine," he replied, waving his hand dismissively. "And you're too drunk to play the hero, so sit your ass down."

I fell to the couch with a thud because he was right. Nate put his drink down and turned to me.

"She is James's sister. She's still mourning his loss. I don't want to be an asshole, but do you really think you can be what she needs right now? She's been through a lot. She's *going* through a lot." I scoffed—that was an understatement. He held his hands up defensively. "Don't get angry with me. I'm just being the voice of reason."

"That's a first," I snapped. "Sorry, I know you're just trying to help." I punched the couch with a growl.

"Feeling better?" Nate snorted and returned to his drink.

"Not even close."

"So tell me what's going on."

"What do you know?" I peered at him.

"Depends." I shot him another glare. "I know she might be leaving."

My heart dropped. "What? When?" He shrugged. "Where to?" It took him a while to respond.

"I think her dad said LA. He's a real piece of shit too. Getting so drunk he could barely stand up, leaving her to deal with his bullshit so soon after the funeral."

"Wait, slow down." Nate was jumping from one thing to the next before my brain could catch up. "Her dad?"

"Is a drunk." Nate barely missed a beat. "Saw it in his eyes. Just like my old pop." He downed more whiskey before leaning back in his seat. I went silent. Nate rarely spoke of his birth parents. "Though I guess she's luckier than me. Only one of her parents left her." He shrugged, trying to make it sound like he didn't care. That was usually his reaction when asked about it. "Now, tell me what the fuck you did. Cause I was about to call you when I found her, and she freaked out. So there was for sure more than a kiss. You said something stupid, didn't you?"

I was still stuck on the brief sadness I'd seen in his eyes. "I did nothing—

"Bullshit. I saw you with her at the memorial. She was clinging to you like her life depended on it. Then you fought with your dad at work after you said she kissed you. So let's skip the bullshit. Just tell me what happened." He waved the bottle at me, then rested it on his thigh.

"Just tell me she's all right."

He took a deep breath and nodded. "She's fine. Did you fuck her?"

I took the bottle and sipped from it. I scrunched my nose as the liquid rolled down my throat. "No, I didn't sleep with her."

"Cause she's James's sister. That would be fucked up."

"I didn't fuck her!" I said too loudly. "Things just... happened."

"What things?"

"She was sad and hurting and wanted a distraction. So she kissed me."

"Stop lying! Since when the fuck do we lie to each other?" he grunted, slapping the back of my head again.

"We, uh, were on her bed..." I couldn't get the words out. It wasn't that I wanted to lie to him, but it felt too personal for Stella. She wouldn't want Nate to know.

"Fuck," Nate said, shaking his head when I trailed off. "Whatever it was, I'm not drunk enough for whatever kind of stupid you did. It's Stella! James's sister!"

"Yeah, we established that," I growled.

"So you stay the fuck away! You don't..." He waved his hand at my crotch, "Whatever you did. Please tell me you wore a rubber."

"I told you I didn't sleep with her!"

He ran his hand through his hair with a groan. "Shit, I should beat the shit out of you. But I'm too drunk," he muttered. "Just don't fucking do it again. What were you thinking?"

"I think..." I said and rubbed my neck. "Fuck, I don't know what I was thinking. I don't get it. Any of it. All I can think about is her."

"Oh shit. You actually like her, don't you?" He punched my arm. I welcomed the pain, however brief it was. "I'm going to rip your balls off if you keep doing stupid shit like this. Maybe that will finally teach you not to play with things that don't belong to you."

I rubbed my palms over my face. The problem was, I wanted Stella, even though that broke every bro code known to man. Even though I was scared I would end up hurting her, one way or another. After just a few weeks, she had burrowed her way under my skin. Deeper than that. I didn't linger on just how deep.

My phone buzzed in my pocket, and I blinked as I reached for it.

"Shit, it's Kasey." I went to take another sip of my drink, only to find it empty.

"Even though I'd normally tell you to stay away from her, I say go for it. She can handle your bull-shit." He threw me another glare.

I didn't want Kasey, but I couldn't ignore her call. I headed outside on wobbly legs, running a hand through my hair as I answered. "Hi, Kase, what's up?" My words came out slurred.

She snorted on the other side. "Wow, busy night?"

"Something like that."

"Would you mind if I hung out at your place tonight? My mom has this new guy over and I can't

stand him!" Her mom shouted at her and she shouted back before slamming a door.

I thought about what Nate said about distractions
and sighed. Maybe he was right. Maybe hearing
about her issues would take my mind off my own. It
would definitely stop me from going over to Stella's.

"Yeah, sure." I glanced over my shoulder as the
door opened behind me. Nate leaned against it,
glaring at me.

"Thanks, babe. You're the best!" She hung up, and
I turned to Nate.

"Kasey's coming over."

"Fuck." He stood up straighter, his earlier annoy-
ance about Stella seemingly forgotten. "All right, I'm
going to sleep. Tell her to keep it down. Her voice
hurts my ears."

Chapter Sixteen

- STELLA -

ONE WEEK LATER

I walked over to James's desk and sat down in his chair, once again running my fingers over his notes. My eyes drifted over the photos stuck to the wall. One grabbed my attention, and I pulled it off.

It was a picture of James and his friends. They were playing soccer on a beach, dressed in only thin T-shirts and shorts. The sun beamed down on them, sweat glistening on their skin. Nate, Cody, and James played while Damien sat off to the side with a can of beer. Cody stood in their makeshift goal, hunched down low and ready to throw himself at the ball. Nate was kicking the ball to James as he ran across the sand, their motions frozen in time.

I smiled through the ache, and my heart beat a little faster. I turned the photo around to see if there was a date on the back, but the only thing written on it was the quote from his memorial plaque.

Never regret something that once made you smile.

"I'm trying, James," I said to myself, holding the photo to my heart. "I'm trying to learn how to smile again."

"Stella? We should go," my dad called from downstairs.

I shoved the photo into my bag, walking to the hallway where he was waiting.

"Have you got everything?" I asked, nervous jitters running through me.

He nodded, his lips tight and heavy bags under his eyes. The last week had been hard for us both. Since deciding to go into rehab, he'd been trying to cut down on drinking, but he still had a long way to go.

We headed out to the car, the drive to the rehab facility spent mostly in silence. He didn't want me to come in with him, but I sat in the parking lot, watching him disappear into the building. This was good for him, but it was hard knowing I now had no one.

My thoughts drifted to Gray. My feelings for him hadn't changed over the week. If anything, I was craving him more. And it wasn't only the physical side. I wanted the me I felt like when I was with him. The me who wasn't so broken.

Gray occupied my mind as I drove back to Waterbury. With no desire to go back home, I ended up at the beach he had taken me to. I hadn't even known I'd memorized the route, but when I parked, it was where I needed to be right now. My brother loved it here and I needed to feel close to him again. Since it was still the middle of the day, I didn't think anyone would be there, though I guess part of me was hoping I'd run into Gray.

I hadn't called him, nor had I texted. I wasn't sure what he was thinking right now, and I was too scared to find out, in case he wanted nothing to do with me. With Dad going to rehab, I'd called my boss and quit, knowing I wouldn't be able to go back there any time soon. Even when he got out, Dad would need me, and he'd said he didn't want to move. That Waterbury would always be his home. My boss had been pretty amazing about it, saying that if I ever wanted to come back, all I needed to do was call. Knowing I had an out in case this thing with my dad didn't work out was nice, though I was beginning to think that no matter what, I was always going to be tied to this town.

I sat under an enormous Douglas fir by the edge of the sand. It was peaceful, the water lapping against the beach and the birds singing in the tree. The sound of an engine came rolling up the path after about an hour and Gray's Chevy pulled up. Nate sat in the front seat with him, and two girls were in the back. My chest tightened for a moment, thinking he had already moved on to someone else. Nate was the first to spot me, and he slapped Gray's chest. His eyes flew up and he scanned along the sand, finding me in the far corner.

When they stepped out a few seconds later, Josie and Kasey got out from the back. That didn't exactly make me feel better. Had he gone back to her? I shouldn't care. It's not like Gray was ever mine. I had wanted a distraction and he gave it to me.

"Sorry, I didn't think anyone would be here," I said cautiously, giving Gray a small smile when they were close enough.

"It's all right," he said, running his fingers through his hair before placing his cap back on his head. Even that simple movement made my mouth salivate.

Nate waved his hand at the redhead as they both sat down. "This is Josie. Josie, this is Stella. The she-devil over there is Kasey, but you already know her."

Kasey rolled her eyes, her face ashen. "Fuck you too, Keyes." She staggered over to us, sinking down in the sand beside Gray and leaning her forehead on his shoulder. "I feel so sick," she groaned, her hue even greener than before.

Nate scoffed. "You better not fucking puke. You threw up all over the bathroom and that shit stank." He sat down beside me, leaning back on his hands. Kasey narrowed her eyes at him.

"Nate," Gray growled.

"What? She did! And she fucking ate all the bacon this morning." Nate huffed. Gray peered at me, but I couldn't read his face.

"Fuck me, your voice is what's going to make me throw up. I can't stand to be in the same square mile as you for a minute longer," Kasey spat, kicking sand at Nate. He flipped her off, wiping the sand from his leg. She leaned forward and threw more at him, causing Nate to lunge forward to stop her, fury shining like beacons in his eyes.

"Nate, sit down! Jesus Christ, it's like looking after two toddlers," Gray snapped. He took a deep breath, then turned to Kasey. "I don't mind taking you home."

"I do *not* want to go back there. Can I stay with you again tonight? Your bed is a lot more comfortable than mine." My chest constricted. She'd slept in his bed? I was the nauseated one now.

"All right. Want to go now?"

Kasey threw another glare at Nate. "Yes, please."

The two of them stood up and returned to his truck. Gray lingered on my eyes before he shifted the truck into reverse and turned around. I followed the Chevy with my gaze until it disappeared behind the trees.

"I'm going to nap in the boat. You girls try not to get into trouble while I'm gone," Nate smirked, getting up and walking toward the dock.

Josie watched him as he left, then she turned back to me. "I can't stand him sometimes. Can you?" She nodded her head to Nate. Having heard her comment, he laughed at us both.

"You're Damien's cousin, right?" I didn't know much about her, so it was a good place to start. "I saw you at the memorial. Thanks for sitting with my dad."

"Yes, I am, but don't hold it against me!" She giggled. "He's more like a brother to me. All the guys are. I've known them my whole life. Oh wait! I just had the best idea! We're camping here for the weekend. You should totally join us! If you're not busy, of course!"

"Oh, uh. I don't really do camping."

"That's okay. Neither do I. And the guys rarely let me come," she said, looking sad for a moment, but her bright smile quickly reappeared. "But I'm eighteen now, so they can't tell me what to do anymore. There will be swimming, barbecues, and bonfires! It'll be so much fun. We can share stories about James!"

I wanted to say yes, for multiple reasons. First, hearing stories about James was as close to him as I was ever going to get. Second, Gray would be here. We needed to talk. Seeing him again made me realize I didn't want to ignore this thing between us. But if Kasey was back in the picture...

"Are you sure?" I asked.

"Of course! There's always too much testosterone in this group. More girl power will be great!" she replied, smiling widely. Her red hair sparkled in the sun as the breeze blew through it. The freckles on her face told me she spent a lot of time outside and the deep-auburn hair was all natural. "I've got a tent I was going to share with Kasey, but I doubt she'll be back. So you can share with me! At least stay for the evening?" she asked, tilting her head to the side and beaming a smile at me. "If you stick with me, the guys will have to go through me to get to you!" she said, as if her five-foot-two frame was intimidating.

I couldn't help but laugh, and Josie's smile somehow widened even more. "Okay, sure." I'd stay until I got a change to talk to Gray. If he was coming back. Though, sitting here with Josie was nice.

"Would you like a beer?" she asked, getting up to her knees and leaning toward a cooler Nate had brought with him that sat in the sand beside her.

"I don't drink," I replied.

"Oh, that's right! I'm sorry, I forgot about your dad." She sank down into the sand, giving me an apologetic smile.

"No, it's fine. I do, sometimes, but I just dropped him off at rehab, so it doesn't feel right." The words came out before I even knew they were there.

She reached over and squeezed my hand. "I'll get you a Coke." She didn't pry or ask questions. She just smiled at me as she dug through the cooler for a drink. "Truth is, I don't drink either. I know I'm only eighteen and I'm not legally allowed to, but the few times I've tried it, it was disgusting! I don't know how anyone does it." She scrunched up her nose adorably and she shook her head. "Now, tell me ALL about LA!" She wiggled closer, holding her drink against her lips as her eyes beamed at me.

I couldn't help but smile back. Josie's energy was very contagious, and she was like a friend already. Even if nothing happened between Gray and me, maybe I wouldn't be so lonely after all.

Chapter Seventeen

- STELLA -

I sat with Josie on the beach for almost an hour, talking about everything and nothing. It was easy, her joyful soul spilling over into everything she said. When Gray's truck pulled up, followed by two others, she jumped to her feet to greet the guys.

"Yay, you guys are here! Oh, I'm so excited about this weekend!" She gave Damien a kiss on his cheek and flashed a brief smile at Cody. "I can't believe I'm on my first seventy-two-hour bender!"

Damien choked on air, squaring up to her. "You're fucking not. You are camping, and if any of y'all assholes"—he fixed all the guys with a stare—"give her even so much as the taste of a beer, I'll drown you in the lake. Capeesh?" The guys only chuckled at him, his glare intensifying. Josie rolled her eyes and side-stepped him.

They got their stuff from the trucks and began heading down towards the dock. They all spotted me at once and froze, trailing their eyes over to Gray. He pretended like everything was normal. No one said anything, and I could have cut the tension with the back of a wooden spoon.

Josie skipped back over to me, sinking down in the sand. "Stella's joining us for the weekend," she announced, her smile still wide, as if she hadn't noticed the awkwardness.

I flicked my eyes to Gray, hoping what I saw on his face was a pleased smile. It could have just been polite—I was too out of touch with anything flirting related.

"Are we all ready to head out?" Nate called from the boat, his blond hair a sleepy mess on his head. I wasn't sure how he'd managed that in just an hour.

"Yep," Damien replied, shoving Gray's back to get him moving. He turned away but threw me a glance over his shoulder.

My stomach fluttered in response. The rest of the guys followed down to the boat, but Josie stayed with me by the beach. They loaded all the things into the boat, then pulled out of the dock. Gray looked at me one last time before he sat down, flicking his hair out of his face as the wind tugged on it.

"Oh my PICKLES!" Josie squealed when they were far enough away. "Holy smoke machine, that was some look you got from Gray. What's going on there?" I blushed and couldn't hide my smile. "I knew it!" Josie exclaimed too loudly, but luckily the guys were far out on the water now. "Tell me everything!"

"There isn't much to tell," I said, shrugging. "I like him, but things are complicated."

"Because of Kasey? I love her to death, but the girl's a drama queen. She always sucks Gray into it." She rolled her eyes with a smile. My stomach clenched at the thought of Kasey sucking anything that belonged to him. I was being so dramatic.

"No. Well, yes, but mainly because of me. My dad. This town. James."

Josie's smile faded, and she reached for my hand. "If it helps, Gray is one of the kindest guys I've ever known. And I saw the way he looked after you at the memorial. Gray didn't cry when James passed. He didn't cry when he'd break up with Kasey. That meant he was crying for you."

I glanced out over the water, following the boat as the guys drove it up and down, wakeboarding behind it. "I like him," I whispered, allowing myself to say it out loud.

"And he likes you. I can tell." Josie nudged me and I looked back at her. "Want me to talk to him?"

I shook my head. "I've given him the cold shoulder for a week. If anyone should talk to him, it's me. Thanks, though."

"Hey, that's what friends do!" she said, smiling, warming my heart. "Now come on. We've got five tents to put up, and I have no clue what I'm doing. It was the only reason Damien allowed me to come with them." She wrinkled her nose, pulling me up with her.

By the time the guys had finished playing around, Josie and I had barely gotten one tent up. If anything, I think we'd made more of a mess, mixing poles and strings together from different tents.

Damien grumbled at his cousin as he walked up, taking a metal pole from her before she bent it.

"Hey, I almost had it that time!" she whined, glaring at him. He didn't reply, only moved her out of the way and slid the pole into the right place—nowhere near where Josie was trying to get it to fit. "Okay, fine. So maybe not exactly, but I'm trying! Come on, Stella, let's leave these guys to sort the tents out and go swimming."

"Oh, I don't—"

"I thought we had a deal," Damien huffed, undoing most of the poles Josie had incorrectly put together.

"I'm happy to stay and help," she cooed in his ear, but he waved her away. She giggled and bounced over to a truck, pulling a neon-yellow beach bag from the back. "Swimming?" she asked me again, pulling out two towels.

I glanced over at Gray, but he was talking to Nate about something, his brows furrowed. "Uh, I'll come sit with you. I'm not very good at swimming."

Josie gave me another bright smile, taking my hand as we walked down to the docks. She quickly slid out of her jean shorts and tank top, revealing a two-piece underneath. With a graceful dive, she was in the water, her head breaking the surface a few moments later.

"Oh, come on, the water is lovely," Josie called.

I shook my head firmly. "Maybe later," I said, pulling my legs under me.

I watched Josie swim around in the water for a bit before running footsteps came up behind me. Cody and Nate broke me out of my dreams as they trampled past, stripped down to just their underwear, showcasing all their glorious muscles. They ran into the water with laughs and screams as they pushed each other around.

I pictured James running into the water with them, and a small tear fell from my eye. I quickly wiped it away before anyone noticed and adjusted myself on the dock. It wasn't a sad tear, but I still didn't want anyone to see me crying.

A memory of my brother came to mind, and I closed my eyes. It had been a warm summer day, just like this one, and we must have been only thirteen or fourteen. He was chasing me in the shallows, splashing water at me as I screamed and begged for him to stop. He eventually caught up to me and picked me up, spinning me around and then letting me fall down into the water. I could almost taste it now, the slightly vegetative taste of the water mixed with grains of sand as it swirled in my mouth. I lay in the shallows laughing, and James came to lie down with me.

"See, isn't this better than being at home like a boring person?" he mocked, shaking some hair out of his face. *He looked high on life. He had a certain look in his eyes—pupils dilated and spaced out, with a wide grin on his face.*

"The jury is still out," I replied, splashing some water over him.

"Lies. You love it. Just admit it!" He smirked at me, and my body filled with his excitement.

"I'm not admitting anything." He rolled his eyes and dunked my head under the water.

Noises coming from behind me interrupted my thoughts. I looked up to see Liam, Damien, and Gray putting the finishing touches on the tents. They talked between themselves, and Gray chuckled at something Damien said. My insides fluttered, feeling like they were going to completely fly away when Gray's eyes landed on mine, his smile holding steady.

I didn't notice Nate walking out of the water before he sat down on the dock right next to me. Water splashed off his skin and I wiped it from my arm, peering at him. The sneak peek of his stomach that I had before had nothing on seeing him up close. Miles upon miles of tanned and chiseled abs, and a trail of hair leading down with a pronounced V under his wet boxers, which clung to every inch of him. My cheeks flushed, and I snapped my eyes back to his face. He didn't even try to contain a grin at catching me ogling.

"I didn't peg you for the camping type." He leaned back on his hands and his arm muscles flexed against my shoulder. His new position showcased his abs even more, and I was pretty sure he knew that. You didn't look like Nate without knowing you were a supermodel.

"I'm not, really," I answered, trying to keep my voice steady.

"Well, I'm glad you're here. I know one guy who is very happy you're here," Nate drawled, serious for a moment.

"I don't think James would believe it if he knew." I laughed, knowing how excited he would have been.

Nate laughed too. "Yeah, I think you're right. For twins, you sure are nothing alike. But I wasn't talking about James." I flicked my eyes to Nate's, his eyebrow raising slowly.

"Hey guys, food's almost ready," Damien called from the camp, and Nate got up and walked towards them. Josie got out of the water and I handed her a towel, following behind.

The scent of the fire mixed with the appetizing smell of the food filled the air as my stomach growled. Gray stacked some cut-open buns on a tray, next to it was a stack of uncooked hot dogs and sticks. The guys all grabbed one, and Josie grabbed two. She handed one to me, and I gave her a grateful smile.

She had put her top back on, but the guys let the fire dry their underwear first. It really wasn't fair how one group of guys could look so good. I stared back at my hot dog, hovering just above the fire. I wanted to look at Gray, but I refused, knowing gawking at him would send my pulse racing and I might end up drooling. Not cool. I was obviously very attracted to him, but I needed to know if he wanted more before I got my hopes up.

Josie pulled the hot dogs back from the fire and grabbed the buns, handing me one. "Ketchup or mustard?" she asked, wiggling bottles in her hands. I shook my head at both, then I ate my food in silence, listening to the others chatter. They talked about everything under the sun. Girls, trucks, work, music, but mainly soccer. It all seemed very normal and easy.

Eventually, I gave in and glanced over at Gray. He stared into the fire, poking at the embers as they fell to the ground. Our eyes met. He gave me a cautious smile, then got pulled back into conversation with the others. The sexual tension was killing me. I needed to know, but with everyone else around, I couldn't exactly get my answer.

I stared out at the lake. At least out here, I wasn't alone. Yes, I had Josie, and possibly Gray, but there was more. It was like I could feel James in the breeze. Hear his laugh echoing through the trees. This place *was* him. I took a deep breath, then leaned against Josie as she wrapped her arms around me.

Finally, I wasn't alone.

Chapter Eighteen

- GRAY -

Josie had gone off with Cody to collect some more branches for a bonfire, while Stella and Nate had gone the other way. A female laugh rolled through the air, and it wasn't Josie's. Jealousy brewed under the surface. I didn't like the fact that *Nate* was the one who made Stella laugh. Had I heard her laugh before? Like, really laugh? Shaking my hands loose, I continued working on the last tent.

I was still waiting for her to make the first move—to decide what she wanted. It was all I could focus on all week. That and the fact that maybe we weren't a good idea after all. Maybe I would end up screwing up, like I always did with Kasey and work. That was the main reason I hadn't reached out to her either.

Damien waved his hand in front of my face, and I snapped out of my thoughts.

"Sorry," I muttered, taking a metal pole for the tent from him.

"You doing all right? You haven't seemed yourself these last few days. Anything to do with Stella?" Damien stared at me, and I couldn't dodge his question with silence.

"Did Nate say something?"

Damien chuckled and continued to stack logs for a campfire. "Nah, he hasn't needed to. Anyone with a pair of eyes can see how you look at her. So what's up?"

"It's not that simple."

"Well, considering she's James's sister, that's a given."

"Are you guys talking about Stella?" Liam turned around from pushing a stake into the ground.

"Yup. Gray's been eye-fucking her all day, but won't say a word to her. Now that Nate is with her, he looks like he might just run over and punch him."

I rolled my eyes. "I'm not going to hit Nate."

"Wait, you've got a thing for Stella? Since when?" Liam looked at me, confused.

The honest answer to that question was since high school. But I'd been a horny teenager and found lots of girls attractive, so I hadn't known it was more until I got to know her this summer. Though, I sure as shit wouldn't tell Liam and Damien that. "I don't want to talk about it."

"Well, that's too bad, cause we are. That's James's sister!" Damien replied, a little too loud for my liking.

"Keep your voice down. And you think I don't fucking know that? That's part of the problem," I grunted at him and ran my hands through my hair.

"Good. I'm glad you're not completely thinking with your dick."

"Jeez, you sound like Nate."

"Knowing you, you've probably tortured yourself over it enough. Still," he continued, punching my arm with force. I winced and rubbed the spot. "Not cool."

"There is something going on, then?" Liam asked.

"Please, can we just drop it?"

Liam shared a look with Damien, and surprisingly, we continued working in silence. Stella's laugh still ran through my mind, like a soothing balm or a frenzied storm. I didn't understand how it could be both at the same time. Words spilled out of me without control.

"Okay, yes. I like her, but what am I supposed to do with that? She just lost her brother. She's not in a place to be with anyone. And you guys know me. I'd do something stupid as always and fuck it up. James would fucking kick my ass if I ever did anything to hurt Stella. But I like her. Like, really like her."

"You're fucking right, he would. And since he's not here, that responsibility falls to us." The threatening tone in Damien's voice didn't surprise me.

"So, what are you going to do about it?" Liam asked.

I shook my head. "I'm waiting for her. She wanted time. But the more time I have to think about how bad the idea of us together is, the more I freak out—"

"Yeah, it's a fucking bad idea to get with James's sister, but if you feel the way I think you do, then you gotta go for it. I know you. You wouldn't hurt her," Damien said, trying to catch my eye.

"Not on purpose," I whispered sullenly.

"Here." He handed me a small hip flask from his pocket. "If it was me—" he began and held his hands up again when I tried to cut him off. "If it was me, I would take that chance. If she is anything like James, then she is one in a million. How often does a woman like that come around, huh?" I took a long sip of the alcohol and closed my eyes as it burned going down. I didn't want them to be right. It just made it all so much more complicated. "But if you ever fucking hurt her, I swear to god I'll run you over with my truck," Damien growled, his eyes showing he was only half joking.

"I don't want to, but I know I will. How many times did I fuck it up with Kasey in high school?"

"Too many," Liam replied with a shrug. Damien growled and threw a stick at him.

"That girl has issues. I've told you that more times that I can even count, but your dick was doing the talking. That's not what's going on now. Stella is not Kasey."

"No, she's more fragile than that." Despite that, he was right. At first, I had been thinking with my dick, but it was my heart that had the stronger voice now. The rest of me was just along for the ride.

"How do you feel when you're with her?" Damien asked. He got his reply when I glanced at him. Damien grabbed the flask from me. "Then I don't really see the issue, if I'm honest."

Not wanting anything they were saying to make any sense, I closed my eyes. "I don't need you guys to be telling me why it could work, because it won't.

I need you to beat the shit out of me, so I'm not tempted."

"I'll hit you, if that's what you want." Damien smirked.

"I'd rather Liam did it."

"Hey, you saying my punch is weak?" Liam pushed my shoulder. I gave him a small grin.

"She just lost her brother," Damien said. "If she can get through that, she can get through anything. I've known you my whole life. There has never been a woman who has messed you up this way. Not even Kasey had you looking this tormented. And you know for damn sure Josie has already gotten her claws into her and will be there for her no matter what. What you do with your feelings is up to you. Just know we'll all be watching." Damien put some more logs on the fire he was building. It sizzled, cracked, and popped as it grew taller.

Silence filled the air while I contemplated what they'd said. Taking out my fear of hurting her—of her being James's sister—I still didn't know if she wanted anything between us. I guess that was the first thing I needed to find out.

"Just go talk to her," Damien said, as if reading my mind. I looked at him, seeing a much more serious, but not angry, side of him than I was used to.

All the what-ifs still hung heavy on my mind. But maybe the guys were right. Maybe she wasn't as fragile as I thought she was. She seemed to be enjoying herself a lot more than she had at the farm. I'd only caught her wiping tears away once, and it had been followed by a smile. Now she was laughing with my best friend.

I wanted her to laugh with me, and I needed to know if she felt the same. At least if she broke my heart, I wouldn't break hers. I could deal with that. I couldn't deal with hurting her, which meant she had to be my only focus. Fuck work. It wasn't important. She was. She had been since I first saw her in the store. I just hadn't let myself think that deep.

"You sure this is a good idea?" I asked Damien as I stood, looking around the area for any sign of her.

"It's fucking stupid. But you gotta do what you gotta do. And like I said, we'll be watching your every move." He looked too pleased with himself.

I grumbled and turned to find Stella. I suddenly needed her by my side more than ever before. Would she give me a second chance?

My eyes drifted farther down the beach as Nate and Stella came out from behind some trees. They carried branches in their arms, and she giggled at something he said. My chest tightened with a thudding of my heart, but I had to calm myself down. I only had one chance at this. Nate might be a ladies' man, but he wasn't stupid—he wouldn't fuck around with Stella, or Kasey, or Josie, for that matter. He was probably only making sure Stella didn't feel alone, whereas I, like a total jackass, left her to fend for herself all day because I was scared of getting too close.

Nate looked up at me as he dropped the branches on the beach. I nodded for him to come over, and he said something to Stella before crossing the sand.

She sank to the ground, wrapping her arms around her soft legs and staring out over the water, her brown hair waving gently in the wind.

I pulled Nate to the side. "Tell me straight." I took a deep breath, steeling myself for the answer. "Have I been a total idiot?"

Nate looked from me to Stella and back again with a flat look on his face. "Yes." There was a twinge in my heart. I knew it. I'd fucked it up. She wanted nothing to do with me. That's why she hadn't contacted me after the memorial. "Did you finally man up and tell the others? Cause they're both scowling at you," Nate said. I glanced over my shoulder, and sure enough, Liam and Damien had their eyes fixed on me.

"Something like that." I rubbed a hand over the back of my neck. "They told me to go for it."

He scoffed. "Figures. Damien's a fucking romantic. Liam's no better. Lovesick puppies." I ignored his comment. Damien was as uninterested in love as love was with him, and I hadn't ever seen Liam in a relationship. I didn't feel like any of the guys were really that well equipped to be giving me relationship advice, but it was all I had.

"Should I talk to her? Fuck, I don't even know what I'd say. Has she said anything to you?"

Nate fixed his eyes on me. "You're actually doing this? Like, for real?" I nodded, trying to swallow my nerves. "Fuck, if you ask me, it's all a mistake."

I froze, and my heart sank. "Shit. You're right. I can't—"

"Nate, for once in your life, shut up!" Damien growled, stalking over to us.

Nate held his hands up defensively. "Hey, I'm just saying what I think. He's better off with the she-demon."

"Your opinion will be valid when you stop using girls for something other than sex," Damien grunted. He turned to me, punching my shoulder. "Man up, or leave Stella alone. There's no in between. You got me?"

"Are you sure?" I ducked when he lifted his hand to hit me again.

"Just go to her!" He shook his head with a grunt, then turned around to grab the cooler full of beers. Nate gave me a look, then followed.

I turned around to see Stella still sitting in the sand. The sun was just dipping below the distant mountains, and the earlier heat was releasing its grip, but it was still warm enough to not huddle up near the fire. The aura surrounding her seemed to have multiplied, and I couldn't tear my eyes away.

Taking a deep breath and shaking my hands loose, I made my way over to her. She sat up straighter and pulled her legs even closer to her body when she saw me in the corner of her eye. I hated that I'd caused her to feel this way. I never wanted to add more stress to her life—it was part of the reason I pulled away. But like Damien said, it was all or nothing.

"Hey." I exhaled, flicking my shoes off to dig my feet into the sand.

"Hi," she squeaked. She rested her chin on her knees, only giving me a quick glimpse of her face, a cautious smile lining her soft lips.

Well, that was a start. I didn't know what to say next. Peering behind me, I found the other guys watching us while chuckling quietly to each other. I glared at them before turning back around.

Great. We had an audience.

"I'm sorry I didn't call you," she mumbled. "My dad was in a car accident and now he's in rehab. I quit my job and I don't really know what to do next." Her words tumbled out of her, followed by a long silence, her eyes glued on the sand between her feet.

"You okay?" I asked, moving closer.

She looked up at me, the corners of her eyes red. "No. And yes. I meant to bring Dad back to LA with me for a fresh start. I needed to get away from all the memories of James. But now? I don't think I can leave. I need the memories. They are all I have left of him." She reached for something in her pocket. "I found this picture in his room this morning." She held it out to me.

My eyes drifted up the smooth skin on her arms before focusing on the picture. It was a snapshot of us playing soccer on the beach. I smiled, remembering when I took that photo. I had tried to get Liam to play too, but he had been a sullen dick that summer. It was after his accident, but before everything else went down. Despite that, we had a good time. We'd just graduated from high school, and the world was our oyster. I flipped the photo over, reading the quote on the back.

Never regret something that once made you smile.

I looked at her, my heart jolting when she smiled at me. When I opened my mouth to say something, the other guys strolled down to the fire. That was all the privacy we were going to get. Nate dumped the cooler right behind us, causing her to jump in the sand.

"Who's ready for something to drink?" He winked at me, knowing he'd interrupted us. Not that I'd said much. I was so tongue-tied and nervous.

"Have you got anything nonalcoholic?" Stella asked, peering at the cooler. I pulled out a Coke and handed it to her. My fingers grazed hers and she sucked in a breath, flicking her eyes up to mine.

I would make it work. I had to.

Chapter Nineteen

- STELLA -

J osie ended her story about my brother, and a tear fell down her cheek. She wiped it away and lifted her soda to the sky. My cheeks were anything but dry. I wasn't bawling or sobbing, but the tears flowed freely; some of them sad, some of them happy—all of them filled with more love than I thought I could hold.

"To James," she said. Everyone else joined in.

As the sun set, everyone took turns telling their favorite story of James, and every single one made it feel like he was back here with us. I closed my eyes and pretended he was sitting in the sand on my left, and though the ground was empty as I turned my head, he was here in his own way.

Nate had grabbed his guitar from the truck and was strumming away to some song I'd never heard. Josie joined in, and her clear, ethereal voice carried over the water.

"How are you feeling?" Gray asked.

I sighed and shrugged. Remembering James as the pure light he was made the loneliness feel less intense, as did having all his friends here to share the memories with. It was more cathartic than I could have ever imagined. But everything was still very raw, and I was only just learning how to come to terms with that. Gray smiled at me, his eyes trailing slowly over my face before he shook his head and looked away. His smile widened into a grin as he took another sip of his beer.

"What?" I asked, my voice a higher pitch than I would have liked.

"Nothing," he replied, and lay down flat on the sand.

I bit my lip, dug the Coke into the sand next to me, and joined him. The stars twinkled against the darkening background, reminding me of the night , and the flickering heat coming off the bonfire made some of them look like they were dancing. Gray turned his head to look at me when I sighed again; a relaxed, contented sigh this time. He stared at me for a while, and under his gaze, I was like a school-girl. It was ridiculous.

He turned his gaze back up above us. "They're really pretty, aren't they?"

"They are."

"Not as pretty as you, though," he whispered. I turned to see him looking at me again. There was something different in his eyes. Something deeper, but slightly uncertain. My cheeks burned. Wasn't he with Kasey? She'd spent the night with him, and to say they had history was an understatement.

Before I could question what I heard, he brushed my hand with his fingers. I held my breath as he laced them through mine, trying to slow down my racing thoughts, but that was easier said than done.

He gently ran his thumb up and down the sensitive skin between my fingers. Delicious goosebumps trailing up my arm. The hairs on the back of my neck stood up, followed by the hairs covering the rest of my body. I could feel every little movement he made, and it made me dizzy. Like he wasn't just touching my hand, but caressing all of me.

I looked up at the sky, trying to compose myself before my body overheated. "Josie said you've had a hard time at work. Is everything okay?"

He grumbled something incoherent. "It's fine, I guess. My mind's been somewhere else lately."

"Yeah, Kasey seems to be a handful." While I hoped that wasn't the only reason, I had to know if there was anything between them, but I didn't know how to ask him without sounding jealous.

"What?" he drawled, leaning on his elbows to look at me. I bit the inside of my cheek, keeping my eyes glued to the stars. He took my hand back in his and looked out over the water. "Yes, I've had a bit of a shit time with work. And Kasey drives me up the wall most of the time, but that's got nothing to do with it. It's all you."

I glanced up at him. He swallowed and then parted his lips slightly. "You have me wound up so tight and you don't even know it." He nodded at my face. "That look in your eyes almost breaks me. I just need to know if you want more. I tried giving you time to think it through, but it's killing me waiting for the answer when I just want to be with you."

I swallowed hard, my heart beating faster. "But you're with Kasey."

He pulled me up, shaking his head. "No. There is no Kasey. There's only you."

My breathing became shallower the more I thought about it. Did he really feel that way? He was breathing faster too, and scanning my eyes. I had to look away. If I didn't, I might kiss him again, and that really had not ended well last time. Despite the emotion in his eyes, I was scared.

Damien yawned loudly, snapping both Gray and me out of the moment we were having. "All right, well, I'm heading off to sleep. I'm exhausted." Damien stood up, his legs looking unsteady. "You kids behave." He fixed his eyes on Gray, then stumbled half drunkenly over to his tent. I was pretty sure he was snoring before he even hit the ground.

Liam, Nate, and Cody went to sleep too. Josie followed soon after, but not before throwing me a knowing look over her shoulder. Nate had barely closed his tent behind him when Gray pulled me up to standing.

"Let's sit on the dock," he said, tucking some hair over my shoulder. His fingertips grazing my skin made me shiver. He looked at me and it was clear there was something on his mind, but no words came out. His brows drew together, and then he let out a sharp exhale. "Do you trust me?" he asked, watching me for an answer as we walked out to the dock.

I didn't have to think for long. When I nodded, Gray's entire body relaxed, and a smile tugged at his lips.

"So, if I asked you to go swimming with me, would you? I heard you talking to Josie." Red crept up his cheeks as he looked over the moonlit water.

It was like it was taken straight out of a rom-com. The super hot guy asks the girl if she trusts him. She says yes, and they live happily ever after. Tears burned in the back of my eyes and I dropped my gaze down. How could I live happily ever after when my brother wouldn't have that chance? The pain appeared out of nowhere, slicing me open as the dam broke.

Gray pulled me into his arms without hesitation. Tears soaked his shirt as I moved closer, wanting more than anything for the pain to go away. Little by little, it slipped away. But James didn't. His love warmed my chest more than it ever had. Gray said nothing, only holding me close and gently stroking the back of my head like he had many times before. When the tears slowed down, I pulled back. Gray wiped them away from my cheek with his thumbs.

"I wish I could take it all away. You deserve so much more than this."

I let out a shuddering exhale. James would have said the same thing. He wouldn't have wanted this for me. He always did everything he could to make sure I was happy. Was that why I'd started crying? Because I felt happy for the first time in a long time?

I wiped the last tear away from my cheek and looked up at Gray. He had once again made me feel less alone. That was what James would have wanted. Or he would have been an overprotective brother and started a fight with Gray. That thought almost made me smile. Gray's eyes softened when he dropped them to my mouth.

"Swimming sounds good," I whispered, nodding.

This was part of moving on. Being happy, being... me? I wasn't sure who that person was yet, but I would find her one day. I stood up and removed my shirt and my jeans, trying to remain unaffected by the way Gray's eyes were eating me up. Once I had only my bra and underwear on, I sat down on the edge of the dock, dipping one foot into the water. My body slid over the edge and I let my head sink under the surface. The water spread through my hair, and I savored the weightlessness allowing my body to sink. My feet hadn't even touched the bottom before a hand wrapped around my waist, pulling me back up.

My head broke the surface next to Gray's, and I blinked the water from my vision. His eyes came into focus, stealing my ability to breathe with a burning look that pierced right through me. His naked torso peeked out from the water, and I itched to run my fingers along it but I was frozen. We kicked our feet for a moment before he pulled me back to the ladder on the side of the dock. He held himself up with one hand, the other still wrapped around my waist like he was worried I would sink. I wasn't. I trusted him.

Every inch of my body came alive when he pressed his lips to mine. It was soft and slow, like he was savoring each moment as much as I was, committing it to memory. I wrapped my hands around his neck and held on as his tongue grazed my lips, and I opened without hesitation. I was falling and floating. I wouldn't be surprised if I opened my eyes and found myself up amongst the stars or at the bottom of the lake.

His torso pressed against my breasts as he tried to find a spot for his feet, hard muscle caging me in. A hand slid from my waist and up to my hair, tilting me to the perfect angle as he deepened the kiss, taking control. My back arched towards him, silently begging him to touch me.

Just as I felt like I might faint from the slow pace he was moving at, he pulled his lips away from mine and traced gentle pecks all the way along my jaw and down my neck. I struggled to think. A whimper rolled from me when he sucked below my ear, and he chuckled, breathy and hot against my skin. Glazed eyes looked up at me. If we hadn't been in a lake, I would have combusted by now.

"James would kill me if he knew I kissed you like this," he chuckled, but his lust-filled eyes didn't hold any playfulness.

I leaned back in, sucking his lip into my mouth. I didn't want to talk or think about my brother right now. Gray moaned and deepened the kiss instantly. There was nothing soft about this one. Our tongues danced and fought in the darkness of the night. He gripped my hips firmly and shifting them towards him, making me gasp when he dipped his thumb below my underwear and his hardness pressed against my hip.

"I can't do it anymore. *You* will end up killing me," he winced and swam backwards a few strokes.

I held on to the ladder behind me with a trembling grip, my mind and body not understanding why he'd left me so alone and cold. He was panting, his neck and cheeks flushed, and his eyes drifted from my lips and fixated on my gaze. For a moment, I thought he could see right through me. That he could see the me I was underneath all this pain and hurt. The me I had never become.

"Come here." He held his hand out to me, water dripping from his fingers. I gripped them tightly, suddenly remembering my lack of swimming skills. "Take a deep breath and hold it." He tilted his head back, his body floating to the surface.

I copied him. The weightlessness returned, but instead of sinking this time, I floated beside him. He kept one hand under my back, and my body hummed at the touch. I smiled up at the stars as the water tickled the inside of my ear. I hadn't felt this free in a long time. Maybe ever. Gray's hand didn't leave my back. A falling star flew across the night sky, but instead of crying, I smiled. That must be James's way of saying he was watching me.

"Do you want to head back?" Gray asked me after a few minutes. I let out a big exhale as my body sunk back into the water. He wrapped his hand around me, pulling me flush against him. His heart was thumping almost in time with mine, and he traced a few more kisses along my jaw before ending at my lips.

"Damn, you taste so good," he mumbled. I smiled, thinking the same thing as I sucked his bottom lip into my mouth. I just wasn't able to use my voice right then, worried I would moan or gasp.

After he broke the kiss, we swam back to the beach. Watching Gray walk out of the water with droplets running down muscular skin, I had to fan myself as another wave of heat surged through me, pooling in my belly. Luckily, his back was turned, but as soon as he looked over his shoulder, I dropped my hand. We didn't get much further before our lips found each other again, still ankle deep in the water. The kiss was more demanding this time, his tongue moving with purpose. The skin under his touch tingled with pleasure, but I eventually had to come up for air, sinking back down on my heels as I batted my lashes up at him.

"Stay in my tent? Please? We don't have to do anything else, I just... Please?" Gray pleaded, my face still held tenderly between his hands.

I nodded, wanting nothing more than to spend more time alone with Gray. Now that I had this, I wasn't ready to let it go. Gray wrapped his arm around my shoulder, and we walked back towards the camp after retrieving our clothes.

Chapter Twenty

- STELLA -

It was still dark when I woke up. Wrapped up in Gray's T-shirt, arms, and blanket, I was more than content. But something was still bugging me. Kasey. While Gray and I hadn't been a thing when they slept together, I needed to make sure it wouldn't happen again.

"Gray?" I whispered, almost not loud enough for even myself to hear. There was no movement beside me—his gentle breathing rolling through his chest. "Are you awake?" I asked, slightly louder.

"Stella?" His voice was a deep rumble, and my heart pulsed violently. "You all right?" He sat up in the dark.

"I'm okay," I whispered. He rested his hand on my thigh as he turned to face me, sending delightful shivers to my core at the strength of his fingers wrapping around me. When I didn't say anything or move, he shifted closer.

"What's wrong? Tell me. I'll fix it—"

"Kasey." It caused his words to stick in his throat.

"What about her?"

I shrugged. God, I was feeling so stupid. "I can't let myself... If there is something between you two, I can't—"

"Stella, no." He shifted even closer and took my face in his hands. "Kasey is my friend and nothing else."

"But you slept with her last night." My voice sounded so defeated. I hated it. The glimpse of the happy girl I could be was slipping through my fingers.

"What? No. Shit, no," he groaned between clenched teeth. "She had a fight with her mom and needed somewhere to crash, so she slept in my bed. That's all. I slept on the couch. You can ask Nate. I always sleep on the couch when she stays over."

I lifted my gaze to study him. Despite it being dark, he was close enough that I could see his eyes, worried and tense. "I want to believe you. I'm just scared of being hurt." Of more pain. I looked away again.

"Fuck, Stella. I'm scared too. I've never felt this way before. Since that day in the store, I haven't been able to think straight. You just walked into my life and took over." His lips were on mine in an instant, the desperation mimicked in the kiss. "But I promise, I won't hurt you." His voice hitched, and he rested his forehead on mine as he stole gentle pecks.

I believed him. My heart had decided to as soon as the words came out of his mouth. It was just taking my brain longer to catch up. I wrapped my arms around him and kissed him, tilting his head back as I slid my tongue between his lips. When his chest brushed against my nipples, I moaned. The fire he'd stoked in me earlier hadn't released, and I needed it. He slid his hand down my hip, tugging at my underwear. He froze with a groan and slowly retreated up my body. I could have cried.

"What's wrong?" I whispered breathlessly, close to begging him to continue. Being with Gray like this was too good.

He covered my face with more kisses, then slumped down to the ground beside me. "I don't have a condom." He pulled me down to rest on his chest. "But it's all right, we've got time," he whispered against my forehead, tangling his hand in my hair.

Damn, why was he so perfect? I tilted my head up. He smiled down at me, gently stroking my cheek. Despite the lack of protection, my body ached for release. Ached for him. I ran my hand down his chest and cupped his erection through his underwear. He groaned and twitched under my touch, tightening his grip on my hair.

"Stella," he hissed through his teeth.

I wasn't sure if it was a plea to stop or keep going. I did the latter. I slipped my hand under the fabric, moving rhythmically up and down his hard, silky length, mouth watering at the feel of it. He pulled my face back to his and claimed my mouth, swirling his tongue at the same speed as my hand.

But I wanted more. I shimmied down, kissing and licking his chest as his hand found its way to my hair, tugging it back and out of the way. I gripped the base of his length and licked one straight line up to the tip. Gray's entire body tensed, his erection growing even thicker as I wrapped my lips around it.

"Stella," he hissed again, followed by a string of curses as he looked down to see himself disappear inside of me.

I moved slowly, enjoying the feel of the silk in my mouth. When his breathing became more erratic, I sped up. He bucked with a dampened groan, spilling himself into me as I swallowed it all. Every muscle in his body relaxed, apart from his hand that still held my hair back.

His touch was delicate, almost reverent, as he let his fingers run through my strands, then in a second he pinned me on my back, my body still humming for the taste of him. He darted his tongue out to lick down my neck, and I squirmed in pleasure, eyes rolling to the back of my head. His hand moved under my top and massaged my breasts, lips soon meeting them as he lavished me. He squeezed and sucked, over and over, until I was ready to beg him for more.

"There is no one else I want but you. You don't know how hard it was to not fuck you on your bed that day," he whispered against my neck. "And now. Fuck, Stella, I want you so bad. I want to make you feel fucking amazing."

I shivered in response. Dirty talk had never sounded so sexy. I wanted that too. He moved his head down my chest, leaving a line of heat then cold behind. I fisted my hands in his messy hair as he tugged on my shorts. They slid down my legs and were discarded somewhere in the corner. He sucked in a breath after he'd removed them, his eyes fixated on the part of me that was screaming for his attention.

"So beautiful." He grazed my wetness with a finger, and I twitched, whimpering. He covered my mouth with his hand. "You have to be quiet, baby. Can you do that?"

I nodded. I wasn't sure I could keep that promise, but I would say whatever he wanted me to right now. His hand stayed on my mouth as he ran circles around my sensitive flesh, giving me the pleasure I needed. Another moan left me when his tongue joined in—dampened by his hand and his fingers pressing between my lips.

I was so close to the edge. Watching him find his release only made me crave my own even more. My body spasmed and squirmed as he pushed a finger inside, tightening his grip on my mouth. Whatever he did sent me over the edge in seconds, and I clenched around his fingers, exploding into a supernova in his tent. Nothing else mattered but his touch on me, his fingers slipping between my lips.

His pace slowed when my muscles relaxed, and he kissed a trail back up to my mouth. I floated back to reality when his lips landed on mine, the taste of me still lingering on his tongue.

"That was the sexiest thing I've ever seen." If his voice didn't wobble, I probably wouldn't have believed him. I had acted like a crazy person. "But I think you might have woken someone up. I heard a tent open." My eyes shot open, and I slapped my hand over my mouth. He grinned, shamelessly licking his fingers as I watched, tugging a warmth in my core again, then he rolled out from between my hips. He tucked me against him, covering us up with a blanket.

My cheeks flushed, knowing someone might have heard, but it didn't last long when he trailed his fingers over me. They rounded the curve of my hips, down the valley to my waist, and circled back to run up my shoulder blades. I closed my eyes and enjoyed it all. His soothing touch, his heartbeat thudding against my temple, and the sound of his warm breath as it tickled my ear. He ducked his head down to kiss me.

"This is all I want," he whispered against my lips.

The birds were singing in the trees when I opened my eyes, though it was probably the loud snoring from one of the other tents that actually woke me. The arms I had fallen asleep in were still wrapped around me, along with a leg tucked between mine.

"Good morning," Gray mumbled. His voice was deeper than normal and slightly raspy, sending a wave of pleasure through me. He ducked down and pressed a sweet kiss to my lips, messy brown hair all over the place. Damn it, if he didn't look even sexier today. I didn't know that was possible, but his bedhead and hooded eyes were something else. "Are you hungry?"

"A little." I grabbed my underwear and shorts from the corner of the tent, trying to hide a grin.

He put a fresh T-shirt on, adjusting himself in his boxers shamelessly while smirking back at me. I bit my lip when naughty thoughts rushed through my mind, causing a groan to roll from his chest, and he quickly exited the tent before either of us could give into temptation. By the time I made it outside, he was over by the firepit on the other side of camp. Damien sat across from him, staring at some pots while he waited for the water to boil. He turned to me as I sat down. His eyes were barely open, but they held a playful glint.

"Did you lovebirds sleep well?"

I turned into a beetroot, wanting nothing more than to sink into the ground. He grinned at me, picking up a bag of coffee.

Gray flipped his friend off and rested his arm over my shoulder. "Very." He nestled his nose against my burning-hot cheek, but his nearness really wasn't helping with my embarrassment.

"Coffee?" Damien grabbed two mugs for us when we nodded. Gray continued running his nose up and down my cheek, sprinkling kisses as he went. Damien rolled his eyes at us. "You look exhausted, G."

"Yeah, I didn't get much sleep."

Damien snorted, filling up his mug with more caffeine. Gray pulled me closer to him and inhaled into my hair, while my cheeks somehow burned even hotter. Maybe this was the time I'd actually set myself on fire. I would turn into one of those phoenixes soon, burning into a pile of ash.

"I heard," Damien snickered a few moments later.

My heart sank, and I wanted to be swallowed into a hole.

"Shut up," Gray grunted, trying to hide a smirk. He tilted my face up and gave me a long, slow kiss. I soon forgot why I had felt humiliated. I could do this forever, be perfectly content to kiss and hold onto Gray until I died.

We ate the breakfast Damien made in silence, the only sound coming from the birds.

I smiled. It was good. It was right. I was happy.

Chapter Twenty-One

- GRAY -

The day went by in a blur. I caught myself staring at Stella more than I probably should have, but her laugh and smile were too mesmerizing. I hadn't seen her this happy before and I hoped that at least to a small degree I'd helped in that.

We spent most of the time out on the boat that day, Stella sitting between my legs with her back pressed against my chest. She hadn't stopped smiling since Josie began telling her something—I wasn't paying attention to what. The summer sun glared down on us, causing the back of her neck to be damp underneath all her thick, wavy hair that I couldn't help but wrap my fingers in.

Nate rolled his eyes at me and made gagging faces, but I ignored him. He'd been doing it the entire day. I wasn't sure why he was so against me being with Stella, but I wasn't about to hash it out with him here. That could wait until we were alone. I frowned at him and wrapped my arm tighter around Stella's stomach, inhaling her scent that I couldn't seem to get enough of. It calmed any anger in an instant.

She nestled into me and sighed, clutching her necklace in her fingers. "It doesn't feel so bad out here, you know?" she whispered, just loud enough for me to hear. "It's almost like I can feel James." She turned to me, blushing. "That must sound so stupid."

"No." I kissed her shoulder. "Not at all."

She turned her head to study me, scanning for any sign I was lying. I moved my hand up and took the necklace from her fingers—the once shiny gold plate was now scratched and dinged, but the *J & S* was still visible. I smiled and kissed her ear.

"He would want you to be happy, and because he can't give you that happiness, I will," I whispered. I wasn't sure if saying that would make her pain worse, but it was true.

She looked out over the water. A shiver rolled through her body, the hairs on her arms standing up and it pebbled her skin. It made me excited in ways that were not appropriate with our friends around, and I eased my hips away from her before I could get *too* excited. All my stupid dick could think about was having her naked and alone, buried deep inside of her where it knew it would find heaven.

Thankfully, Damien kept his promise of keeping a close eye on me. Along with not wanting to move too fast too soon, his gaze kept my hands from straying.

Damien pulled out his flask from his pocket and took a sip, then handed it to Liam. Liam did the same. We passed it around until the flask ended up in my hand. I took a long sip, then held it out for Stella to take. She looked at it for a moment before having a quick taste, her face contorting as if it was the most disgusting thing she'd ever tasted, head wiggling from side to side as she laughed. I smiled, kissing the space between her neck and shoulder. She made a pleased sound, and I had to force myself to stop again. I caught Damien's eye and he raised his eyebrow. I swallowed and gave him a small nod, leaning away from my own private paradise. He held the flask to the sky, then poured a splash over the edge. Stella tensed as she watched, fingers digging into my arm.

"Is that for James?" Her voice trembled, as did her body.

I pressed her against me for support. I didn't need to answer. She gave a tender smile as she looked from Damien and over to all my friends. Her friends. They all knew she was here to stay. Whether I could get my act together or not, she would always have them.

We headed back to pack up camp a while later. Stella and Josie packed their bags as I walked over to my tent to take it all down. Damien looked over his shoulder as I came closer, his tent right beside mine.

"You're so whipped." He grinned.

I slapped his arm. "Shut up." I was.

We drove back to town together. I wanted Stella as close to me as possible, so she was in the front seat beside me. I hadn't managed to talk her into sitting on my lap, which for everyone's safety was probably a good thing. Nate sat behind me, and Josie beside him, her constant chatter the only sound filling the truck.

I dropped Stella off first and walked her into the house. The door closed behind me, giving us a few moments of privacy from watchful eyes. What I really wanted to do was take Stella up to her room—specific parts of my body and I were more than ready, but they would have to be patient. Again.

"Thanks for letting me join you guys," she mumbled, chewing on the inside of her cheek with a smile. "Your friends are great."

"Our friends."

She moved her gaze to me and bit her lip to stop from beaming. Fuck, she was gorgeous. Instead of throwing her over my shoulder, I grabbed her hand and kissed the back of it, then bowed my head as I left. I needed to get out of this house. Right now.

"Miss," I said playfully. She giggled as I walked away, and it was the most amazing sound ever. It rang through me like a bell, my heart soaring and pounding behind my ribs. I jumped into the driver's seat, feeling like I was high, not sure if it was even safe for me to drive in this state.

Nate quickly brought me back to reality by flicking my shoulder. "Wipe that grin off your face and let's go. I've got a date tonight!"

"Date? You mean booty call?" I started the engine up, peering towards the kitchen window in hopes I'd see Stella.

"Same thing," he grunted, slapping my leg in brief succession. I rolled my eyes at him, reluctantly driving away. I headed straight to the bathroom when we got back, locking the door behind me. After last night and today, I needed a long, cold shower.

My phone rang on the desk next to me. It was Kasey. Dad was busy on a call, so I walked out of the office. The outside of the house was almost done, the last few days having gone by quickly. I got to work in the morning and as soon as I finished, I drove over to Stella's place to keep her company.

Well, that's what I was telling myself. I think I did it more for my sanity than anything else. Being near her was intoxicating, and she knew she had me under her spell. The guys also knew, and they took every chance they could to tease me.

"Gray, you have to come and get me right now. I can't do this anymore. I swear to God I will kill her!" Kasey sobbed on the other end of the line as soon as I answered. My heart sunk in my chest so fast it was like I was on a roller coaster. Fuck, she had never sounded this desperate.

"What happened?" I rushed back into the office, trying to get my dad's attention. He looked up at me from the papers in front of him with an irritated look. "Can I cut today short?"

He waved me off without question, returning to his call. He'd not been himself today. Something major had gone wrong, and he'd been scrambling to fix it. He didn't want to tell me what.

I grabbed my keys and jumped into my truck, gravel flying into the air as the tires spun. "Where are you?"

"One of my mom's boyfriends hurt Dion. I'm heading out the door with him now. I'll meet you at the end of the road." She hung up while shouting at her mom, her voice echoing in my ears.

Dion had to be okay. He had to. I kept chanting that in my head as I drove.

I found Kasey standing by the entrance to the trailer park, rocking her brother in her arms. Her eyes were bloodshot and her shirt wet from tears. As soon as I got out, she threw her arm around me, almost crushing Dion between us.

"Are you okay?" I asked when I saw a cut and bruise on her cheek, but she moved my hand away when I tried to touch it. Her wrist was also bruised. My blood boiled, but I didn't want to freak either of them out more. "Hey, Dion, how are you doing, little man?" I said with a faked ease that didn't give away my thundering heart or boiling blood.

The little boy peered up with the saddest look ever. His bottom lip was cut open and still bleeding, shivering as tears pooled in his eyes. I swore silently a few times as I grabbed my hoodie from the seat behind me and handed it to Kasey.

"Put some pressure on it. We'll get him to the hospital." She slid in beside him after I fitted in the car seat. I barely waited for her to do up her seatbelt. I needed to get away before I ran into the trailer and beat the guy up, but getting Dion to a hospital was the priority. My knuckles turned white on the steering wheel as I listened to Kasey sobbing quietly while she tried to soothe Dion with kisses and cuddles.

She told me to stay in the truck while she went into the hospital. I paced up and down, kicking the tire several times until my phone buzzed in my pocket.

Nate

Where did you fly off to?

Gray

Just had to go handle something. I'll tell you later.

Dots appeared at the bottom of the screen but quickly disappeared again. I flicked over to my texts with Stella.

Gray

Hey, babe. I might be a bit late tonight.

I couldn't leave Kasey and Dion like this, but I wasn't sure having Kasey and Stella in the same room yet was a good idea. When Kasey came back out with Dion, Stella still hadn't replied. I slipped the phone back in my pocket, letting out a sigh when Dion giggled at me and the noose eased from my neck.

"Gray!" He held his hands out, wrapping his arms around me before pointing to his lip. "Look!" He had a single stitch and a small piece of white tape over the cut. The excitement on his face eased my anger some more.

"Wow, look at that! You are so brave." I forced a smile.

"Let's get out of here," Kasey muttered, the wound on her cheek cleaned but still angry-looking. I opened my mouth to ask what happened, but she cut me off with a death glare that made me shut it just as fast. Now was clearly not the time. She took Dion from me and buckled him in.

"Where are we going?" I looked back at Kasey after I'd sat down.

"Anywhere but here. Just drive." She turned and stroked Dion's curly hair, leaning as close to him as she could.

I drove her out of town, out onto the highway with no destination in mind. We stopped for gas and some food a while later, and as I paid the cashier, Kasey leaned against the counter beside me.

"I think we'll go stay with my grandma. There is no way I'm letting him go back to that whore." Her words came out sharp as daggers, and the lady behind the register gasped. Kasey didn't exactly look tough with her blonde hair and sweet blue eyes, but right now, she was a fire-breathing dragon who would show no mercy to those who stood in her way.

I handed the lady some money with an apologetic look, then led Kasey back to the truck. Dion was playing with a baseball in the backseat, bouncing it against the inside of the window.

"How are you going to get there? You haven't got your stuff or money." She peered at me. I ran my hand over my face. "Kase!"

"I'm sorry, but it's not like I have any other choice! Please, it will only take us a few more hours to drive there." I kept rubbing my face, then nodded, bracing myself for the long drive down I-5.

"All right, let me just text—" I didn't finish the sentence. Kasey didn't know about Stella yet, and this wasn't how I wanted her to find out. I wasn't sure what her reaction would be, and she had enough on her mind right now. As I pulled my phone out of my pocket, the battery flashed in the top corner. Five percent. I rummaged through the side pocket where I usually kept my charger, but it was nowhere to be found. Nate must have borrowed it. I fired off a message to Stella, then turned the phone off, hoping to conserve the battery. I could turn it back on when we got to Kasey's grandma's.

Kasey peered over my shoulder at my phone. "Were you having dinner with your mom tonight? I'm sorry."

"Hey, it's not your fault," I said, avoiding answering the question. "Let's just get to your grandma's and get Dion settled in. He looks like he could use a good sleep."

The little boy only finished half of his sandwich before he fell asleep. Kasey took the food from him and gingerly wiped some crumbs from his face, a hardness forming over her eyes that I'd never seen more.

Mile after mile passed, and I glanced at the phone next to my leg, hoping my battery would last long enough for me to see if Stella had replied.

Chapter Twenty-Two

- GRAY -

K asey snuck out of the room where she had just put Dion to sleep and tiptoed over to me. It was almost eleven p.m., way past his bedtime, but he'd been napping on and off in the truck.

"He's finally asleep." She smiled weakly. The cut on her cheek had turned a darker shade of red, almost black, and the bruise that had formed looked bright purple and angry.

I hadn't asked her what had happened yet because she wouldn't tell me. She forced her emotions down to look after her brother. Dion was her priority, and until he was okay, she wouldn't focus on herself.

We walked to the kitchen where her grandma, Brenda, was waiting. She'd been getting into bed when we knocked on the door. At first, her face had been confused, then happy, and then worried as she took in the state of her two grandchildren, quickly ushering us all inside.

"I'm sorry to do this. I didn't have anywhere else to turn." Kasey kissed her grandma's cheek. The gray-haired lady who shared a lot of Kasey's facial features, including bright-blue eyes, turned to her with a tight smile.

"Oh nonsense, I haven't seen my two favorite grandchildren in forever! I just wish it was under better circumstances." Her smile turned upside down, and she reached for her cup of tea. "Don't you worry. We will get it all sorted out in the morning. Dion will not be going back there and neither will you. Over my dead body." The determination in her words made me feel more at ease, and some of the weight on my shoulders eased.

"I should probably head out," I said, stretching my arms over my head. Leaving Kasey here was hard, but she wasn't on her own. Brenda would look after her, and hopefully she could get Kasey to open up to her. The last thing I wanted to do right now was drive for another six hours, but I needed to get back to Stella.

"What? No, you can't drive all the way back already. You won't get back before the sun comes up," Kasey replied, shaking her head.

After giving her a firm look, I stood. "I can't stay, Kase. I have to get back home."

She followed me outside, desperate to say anything to get me to stay, but only muffled sighs came out. I yanked the door to the truck open, running a hand over my face as I slid into the seat. Kasey held it open while I started the truck, her eyes boring a hole in my head.

"You sure you can't stay?" she eventually said, her voice weak. It tugged at my resolve and I turned to her as I pressed the engine button.

"Kasey, I can't. I've got work and... I can't stay. But I'm just a phone call away."

She nodded slowly. "It's okay. I get it. Drive safe." I turned in my seat and pulled her into a hug, and she melted into my arms, a quiet sob shaking her body.

"You've got this," I said, stroking her back. "Dion needs you more than you need me." I kissed the side of her head and she stepped from my embrace, closing the door between us. I pressed on the gas, rolling out of the drive. The truck was reluctant to get moving, a strange clunk sounding from the back.

"Gray!" Kasey called, waving at me to stop. "The tire." She pointed at the back when I peered out of the window, and I grunted at the flat tire. Jumping out, I walked over to see how bad it was, quickly spotting a huge-ass nail stuck in the side.

"Fuck," I grumbled, kicking at it. Too fucking tired for this shit, I lowered myself onto the drive to get the spare tire out from under the truck. Since it was almost pitch black and there were no streetlights, I fumbled around for a while, not feeling the tire where it should be. My stomach sank more and more as I waved my hand around in nothingness and another grunt rolled from me. Where the fuck was it? I bet you this was Nate too. Could he not leave my things alone? I was going to kill him.

"Everything all right?" Kasey asked, standing right beside me.

I crawled out from under the truck, leaning my back against the flat tire. "No spare tire. Nate must have fucking—" I took a deep breath, closing my eyes tightly as I pinched the bridge of my nose. "No chance your grandma has a spare somewhere?" Kasey didn't need to reply. I got up, wiping some dust from my jeans before rubbing my hands over my face, one last groan coming out.

"I can ask her if she knows someone who can fix it?" Kasey wrapped a gentle hand around my wrist, pulling my hands from my face.

I nodded, though the likelihood of someone being able to fix it this late at night in a small town was damn near zero. "All right, worth a try." We headed back inside. Brenda still sat at the kitchen table, and she looked up when we came in.

"Gray's got a flat tire. Do you know anyone who can fix it?" Kasey asked, waving her hand toward the front door.

Brenda took a painfully slow sip from her mug, then shook her head, confirming my fears. "Not at this time of night. Tomorrow, maybe."

"Shit," I mumbled. Brenda gave me a displeased look. "Sorry."

"You can stay here tonight and go back tomorrow," Kasey said, hugging her arms around herself and gently massaging her wrist.

"I guess I have no choice." I pulled my phone out of my pocket and turned it on. The battery symbol showed I only had one percent left, and I quickly opened a text message that had come through from Stella.

Stella:

> That's okay. See you tomorrow? <3

The phone died before I could reply, the screen fading to black. "Fu—" I peered at Brenda again, but she pretended not to hear. "My phone is dead. Kasey, have you got a charger?"

She shook her head. I didn't even bother looking at her grandma—by the state of her old TV and the handset hanging on the wall, a phone charger had probably never seen the inside of this house.

"All right, I'll stay. Just for the night. I'm going as soon as they fix the tire tomorrow, okay?" I ran my hands over my face, letting out a sigh. It would be fine. Stella knew I wouldn't see her tonight, and I could explain everything when I got back. It was definitely a conversation I needed to have face-to-face, or she might freak out.

Kasey smiled at me, but it was tense and tight. "I could use a drink."

"There is no alcohol in this house," Brenda said, fixing her with a firm stare.

Kasey rolled her eyes, turning to head to the door. "Good thing I saw a bar down on the corner, then. Don't wait up for me!" She was out the door before she'd even finished the sentence.

Brenda opened her mouth to call after her, but I shook my head. "I've got it. Thanks for letting me stay." I gave her an apologetic smile, then jogged outside. "Kase, slow down."

"Please, I don't want to talk," she said, closing her eyes tightly for a moment.

We walked the short distance down the road to a small bar with an old neon sign. I held the door open for Kasey, and she walked straight to the bartender to order shots.

Despite it being almost midnight, the place was busy. Big, burly men with long beards and dressed in leather jackets turned when Kasey wiggled her way through the crowd, scanning her up and down. I jumped forward, placing a protective hand on her back as she continued to the bar.

"Kasey, I don't think we should be here."

She replied with a wave over her shoulder, dismissing my comment. "I've had a shit day. Please let me drink and forget about it all." She ordered several shots, her face twisting as the strong liquor slid down her throat. "Your turn." She pushed a glass over to me.

I looked around once more, relaxing some when I noticed everyone had gone back to ignoring us. I slumped to the barstool next to her, allowing myself just one shot. One of us should stay sober, and it wouldn't be Kasey. I didn't push her to talk, although the bruise on her wrist and cut on her cheek made me furious every time I looked at it.

When it looked like she was nearing her limit of shots and I was about to tell her we should head home, she hopped off her stool and stumbled over to an antique jukebox in the corner. I stayed in my seat, watching her drunkenly try to figure out how it worked. To my horror and everyone else's in the bar, it was an old Britney Spears song that poured through the speakers. Kasey snapped her head around with a pleased and intoxicated grin.

"Dance with me!" she squealed, wiggling her fingers at me.

I laughed at her, shaking my head. "*Baby One More Time*" flowed through the bar as Kasey shimmied closer. "No way. You're on your own," I chuckled, holding my hands up between us. She might be drunk enough for this, but I was not.

"Oh, come on. You used to be fun!" She wrapped her arms around my wrist. I groaned, letting her pull me to my feet.

"One song, then we're going home," I muttered, mainly because it looked like someone else was going to take her up on her offer to dance if I didn't. She squealed again. I spun her round and round on the floor, and I don't think she even noticed I was barely moving—she was moving enough for the two of us.

She pulled out her phone and took some pictures of herself, pulling some amusing faces. The screen turned to me and she snapped a few more.

"All right, I think that's enough dancing." I chuckled and eased her away from me. I was worried if I pushed too hard, she would end up on the floor.

"What?" She pouted. "You used to enjoy dancing with me," she cooed with a wink and bit her lip seductively. I shook my head with a laugh. She skipped past me to pick up another shot, and though I tried to stop her, I got there too late.

"You've had enough," I said, placing myself between the bar and her once she'd put the glass down. I really didn't want to have to carry her home.

She slapped my chest. "Not even close," she muttered. There was still a lot of pain in her eyes, but drinking until she passed out wouldn't help that. I didn't move from my spot and she stumbled onto a stool, having to catch herself on my arm. It caught the eye of the bartender, and he gave me a displeased look.

"Come on, Kasey. I think we've outstayed our welcome," I whispered in her ear, wrapping my arm around her waist as I was pretty confident she couldn't stand up herself.

"Where are you taking me, handsome?" she purred. She hopped off her stool and stayed upright, much to my surprise.

"We should head home."

"Oh yes, take me home." She giggled, pressing her body against me.

Yeah, she'd definitely had too much to drink. The only time she got this flirty with me was when she was absolutely wasted. I hadn't counted the shots, but by the look of the empty glasses on the bar, it was a lot. I grabbed some money out of my wallet with one hand, the other one fighting to keep Kasey upright. With an apologetic smile to the bartender, I led Kasey outside. She was pretty unstable in my arms, but at least she was walking.

She suddenly gasped, letting go of me. Before I could stop her, she freed herself from my grip and ran to a children's park across the street, not even looking around for cars in her drunken state.

"Kasey, stop!" I called out. She continued to giggle as she jumped the small fence to the playground, climbing up the slide onto a wooden pirate ship.

"Come get me," she called from the top, dancing in the moonlight. Her golden hair flung around her head like a crown as she spun, but it wasn't long before she lost her balance and tumbled to the ground.

"You okay?" I grumbled, more annoyed than worried.

She shook her head, tears forming in her eyes. "How could she do that to Dion? He's just a child."

A wave of sadness washed over me. I jumped up to sit next to her and she rested her head in my lap. I moved some hair out of her face, but I wasn't sure she even noticed. Her eyes looked empty as she stared out into nothing.

"I hate her so much," she hissed.

"You're out of there now, though." I stroked her hair hanging over my thigh. I wasn't sure what else to say.

"And I've got you." She reached for my hand and gave it a kiss. "You're too good to me."

"I've met someone," I blurted out, then waited for the explosion.

She turned her head to look up at me through red, tear-filled eyes. "Who?"

"Stella." The word barely came out of my mouth.

"Stella, as in James's sister?" I peered down at her, surprised she wasn't screaming and slapping me. I nodded, and she smiled through her tears. "When did this happen?" She punched my shoulder.

I chuckled, relieved she wasn't mad. "This is so not how I thought you would react."

"Oh, is that so? And how was I meant to react? Should I turn into the jealous ex-girlfriend and be a bitch? Surely you didn't think that? That was high school. You're my friend, Gray. I want you to be happy." She sat up. "We both know we're not meant to be, and I'd never stand in the way if you found someone."

I shrugged with a nod. "Yeah, but I don't know. I thought it might get confusing."

She snorted at me as she rolled her eyes. "It's only confusing if you make it confusing!" She yawned. "I'm happy for you. I really am."

I gave her a smile, softly running my thumb over her bruised cheek. "Want to tell me what happened?"

She blinked hard, tears forming in her eyes. With her jaw clenched, she shook her head. We sat quietly, but with another yawn, she said, "Let's go get some sleep. Dion will have me up early in the morning."

She rolled off the pirate ship and stumbled her way over to the fence. There was a gate just off to the left, but I guess she didn't notice. We walked back to her grandma's house, and she pushed me with a smile as we entered.

"Honestly, babe. I'm happy for you. You deserve to have someone special," she said a bit too loudly, considering her grandma and little brother were probably both asleep.

I wrapped my hand around my dead phone in the back pocket of my jeans as I followed her through the small house. All I wanted right now was to hear Stella's voice. But even if I could call her, what would I say? She had already expressed her concerns about Kasey, and this wasn't exactly going to look good.

I was happy that the little boy wasn't in bed when I opened the door to the guest room. He must have woken up and went to find his grandma, and by the lack of screaming and crying, fallen back asleep. Kasey was staring at herself in the mirror, trailing her fingertips over her wrist and then grazing the cut on her cheek as the tears started flowing again.

"Let's get you to sleep," I whispered, nudging her towards the twin-sized bed.

She slid in under the covers but clasped my hand. "Please don't go," she sniveled. The sadness in her eyes stopped me from pulling away. "Could you just sit with me? I don't want to be alone."

I nodded and sat down on the floor next to her, feeling déjà vu from when I did this same thing with Stella. Kasey scrolled through Instagram on her phone, probably to keep her mind busy, while I rested my head against the side table and closed my eyes.

It had been a long day and all I could think about was having Stella wrapped up in my arms again. Her lips on mine, our bodies fitting together like two pieces of a puzzle.

Chapter Twenty-Three

- STELLA -

EARLIER THAT DAY

A knock on the door woke me from my slumber on the couch, the bright moon hanging high in the sky outside. I sat up, dazed and sleepy, but with a smile on my lips. I had been sad and angry for so long that smiling and laughing were foreign. But with Gray, I was learning to enjoy life.

I opened the door, expecting to see him there even though his text had said he couldn't make it, but it was Officer Maxwell who stood there with his hat over his chest and his lips pressed tightly together. "Stella," he said, clearing his throat. "Your father has been taken to the hospital."

My head started spinning. No, no, no. This couldn't be happening again. My dad couldn't be gone. He just couldn't. He was all I had left. I saw Maxwell speak, but I couldn't hear any of his words. He caught me as my knees gave way, pulling me back up to standing. His hands were on my face, but my ears were ringing and the corners of my vision fading as I spiraled.

"Stella." He sounded like he was a million miles away. "He's alive. I'll take you to see him."

I looked at him with only one thing running through my mind. "He's not—" I couldn't say the word. I gagged, but luckily nothing came up. Maxwell didn't even shift out of the way.

"He's alive, but he is in surgery. Do you have anyone I can call to meet us there?" He looked over at the side table, grabbing my purse. "Get some stuff and I'll drive you there."

I didn't know what to do. Maxwell gently but firmly pushed the bag to me again, so I turned to grab my wallet and keys from the bowl behind me, then checked for my phone in my back pocket. Should I call Gray now or in the car?

"Let's go. We've got no time to lose." Maxwell ushered me out the door. He opened the passenger side of his police car for me and I slid into the worn leather seat with my bag on my lap. He dashed around the front of the car and gave me a quick glance before turning the keys in the ignition. "I'm going to turn on the lights and sirens when we get out of town, okay? It's going to be loud, but we'll get there faster."

I only nodded in reply, tears constricting my throat. With trembling hands, I called Gray. The phone rang for a while until I reached his voicemail. I hung up, calling it again. The time on my phone said it was after midnight, but even if he was asleep, he would hear the ringtone, right? He had to answer. I needed him. After trying several more times, he still hadn't picked up. I called Josie instead, and she picked up after a few rings.

"Stella? Everything okay?" Her voice was thick with sleep.

"My dad's in the hospital," I stuttered.

She gasped. "Oh, is he okay? Where are you? I'll come get you."

"A police officer is driving me there." A few more tears fell from my eyes, and I let them roll over my jaw and drip onto my shirt.

"Did you just leave?"

"Mm-hmm."

"Tell him to go past Pastor Andrews's house. He'll know where it is. I'm not letting you go there alone."

I turned to tell Maxwell, but he just nodded, having overheard our conversation. When we turned down a residential road, Josie waved us down. She was still wearing her pajama shorts, a thick hoodie almost swallowing her up. I jumped out of the car to crash into her, red hair wrapping me up as if I was in a cocoon.

"Oh, darling," she whispered, stroking my hair to calm me down.

"We need to go," Maxwell called, unlocking the back doors.

"Come here." Josie guided me back to the car, and we slid in together.

I couldn't let go of her. If I did, I worried I might spiral down—deep, deep down. She buckled my seatbelt and nodded at Maxwell to go. I didn't know how long it took us to drive there, but it was like an eternity and an instant all at once. He guided us through the quiet hospital, stopping to ask for directions a few times from lonely night workers.

We finally ended up in a waiting room where Josie sat me down on a chair. Maxwell kneeled in front of me.

"Stella, honey. Your dad is still in surgery. I'll see if I can find out what happened and when he'll be out. You wait here with your friend and I will be back." He squeezed my knee. I nodded at him through my tears.

My dad was going to be fine. He had to be. I continued to chant that in my head, rocking back and forth with my arms wrapped around my legs.

He had to be, he had to be.

The wait felt like forever. All I could hear was the slow ticking of the clock on the wall as the arm crawled around.

Over an hour later, Maxwell returned with a doctor dressed in scrubs. I jumped to my feet so fast it made me dizzy, but thankfully Josie steadied me. "Hi, I'm Doctor Ortiz. You must be the daughter," he said, looking at me. The calm in his eyes did nothing for my nerves. "From what I gathered, your father was lacerated with a shard of glass, causing internal bleeding in his abdomen."

My heart beat quicker, and I squeezed Josie's hand harder. "Is he okay?"

"Your dad will be fine. He had to undergo surgery to make sure he didn't rupture any organs and that the bleeding was under control. He is recovering in his room now. Let me take you there."

I impatiently followed behind him while Josie didn't let go of my hand until we reached the room. My dad lay on the bed with his mouth open and eyes closed, a few wires attached to his chest and a machine beeping gently in time with his heart.

"Dad?" I stuttered, taking his hand in mine. His warmth confirmed he was alive and I let out a trembling exhale.

"He will be unconscious for a while until the sedative wears off. You are welcome to stay here or in the waiting room."

"I'm not leaving," I said, not taking my eyes off my dad.

It had been over a week since I'd dropped him off at the rehab, and that seemed like too long of a time already. I hadn't realized how much I had missed him until I thought he was gone. But he was here. He wasn't gone, and he was going to be fine. I let out another heavy exhale.

He was fine, he was fine.

Maxwell said something to Josie, then left the room. She wrapped her arms around my shoulders and rubbed the side of her face against mine.

"He'll be fine," she repeated without having heard my thoughts. She gave me a peck on the temple before sitting down on a chair right next to me. "Officer Maxwell had to go, but I won't, okay? I'll stay here for as long as you want me to."

I gave her a grateful smile before turning back to my dad. Those few seconds, or minutes—I wasn't sure how long it was when I'd thought he might have left me just like James had—were almost too much to handle. My phone buzzed in my pocket and I picked it up, thinking it might be Gray, but it was just some stupid email. I swiped the notification away with a groan.

"Have you called him?" Josie asked when she saw me staring at my phone.

"I tried, but he didn't pick up."

She frowned. "Let me try," she muttered and walked out of the room. Several minutes later, she came back in with her lip between her teeth.

"Did you talk to him?" I asked, wanting him here so badly. I couldn't do this without him.

"No, I spoke with some of the guys. They haven't heard from or seen him since he left work early today. Nate said he'll try to track him down, though. I'm sure his phone is just dead." She was trying to sound more confident than she looked.

She sat back down next to me and started scrolling through her phone to pass the time. I turned back to my dad, watching his chest move up and down to remind myself that he was still here. His eyes twitched slightly, and I leaned over.

"Dad?" I reached for his hand. He slowly opened one eye, then the other.

"Darling?" he croaked, with a bewildered look on his face.

A few happy tears fell from my face, and I smiled at him. "I'm here," I whispered, squeezing his hand.

He took a deep breath as he fell back to sleep. I gave him a gentle kiss before sitting back down. Josie suddenly gasped behind me and I turned to see her quickly put her phone away.

"What is it?"

"Oh, it's nothing. Unwanted dick pic," she said, waving her hand dismissively. "Are you thirsty?" I was, but I shook my head. Despite knowing Dad was going to be okay, I didn't want to leave his side. "I'll bring you something." She squeezed my hand before walking out the door. I went to stare out the window.

It was calm outside the hospital, except for the odd ambulance siren going off. The moon was lower in the sky now, playing peekaboo behind some clouds. I climbed up on the windowsill and rested my head against the cold glass. Exhausted, every single cell in my body screamed for me to close my eyes and go to sleep, but I didn't want my dad to wake up alone.

"Stella?" a familiar voice called from behind, a silhouette of a man in the doorway. A bright light behind him obscured everything but his shape. I tried to open my mouth to say something, but it was like my vocal chords had stopped working. "It's okay. I can hear you."

I realized who the shape was, and an overpowering warmth spread across my chest. "James," I whispered, almost no sound coming out. The light pulsed behind him, a glowing halo of stars and white smoke. When the shape faded into the background, I wanted to scream. Another gentle whisper came out, echoing over the walls. "Don't go."

The light brightened, and James walked over to our dad on the bed, the surrounding glow exuding warmth and peace. I tried to move, but my body wouldn't listen. James leaned over the bed and whispered something in Dad's ear, then turned his head back to me. When his eyes found mine, my heart was about to explode. Not from sadness, fear, or anger. But from love. My breath caught in my throat, and a single tear rolled down my cheek. There was a change in the air as he looked at the door.

"I have to go." His voice sailed across the room.

"Please don't leave us. I can't do this alone," I whimpered. James took a few steps around the bed towards me, floating along the ground. When he reached for my hand, and his glow wrapped around me, I was falling and flying at the same time, struggling to take a full breath.

"You are never alone, Stella," he said, softly kissing my hand. "Never. I will always be with you, no matter what."

My body was weightless, almost like I was hovering just above the ground with him. I closed my eyes as his hand left mine.

"James!" I exclaimed with a jerk.

Josie made her way towards me from the doorway James had just exited through. "You're okay," she called and grabbed my hands, her brows drawn tightly together. "You fell asleep. Oh, you're so pale, honey. Do you want me to get the doctor?" She ran her hand over my cheek.

I shook my head. I was fine. Exhausted and probably dehydrated, but I'd recover. Outside, the sun was rising and birds sang to each other in the trees. How long had I been asleep? My tongue stuck to the roof of my mouth and my head throbbed with pain.

"Look who's awake," my dad groaned. I jumped up and wrapped my arms around him. "Hey, now," he shushed while stroking my hair.

I crawled onto the bed to lie next to him, holding onto him tightly. He continued to stroke my head until I finally looked up at him, and even though he looked rough, his eyes were clearer than they had been for a long time.

"Hey, darling," he said with a sad but warm smile.

"James." I suddenly remembered him and looked around the room.

"Shhh." My dad pressed my head back against his chest. I lay there, listening to his heartbeat. Dad gently ran his fingers over my back like he would when I was really little and had trouble sleeping. We lay there for hours before Doctor Ortiz walked in through the door.

"Ah, you're awake. Good!" He grabbed the clipboard from the end of the bed. "How are you feeling?"

"Okay," my dad mumbled uncomfortably. I sat up, worried I was hurting him. He smiled reassuringly at me.

"Good, that's what I want to hear. I will be back in a couple of hours and if you are still progressing well and there is no sign of bleeding or infection, we can talk about sending you home soon! No use in lying in an uncomfortable hospital bed when you've got your own." He winked at us both and disappeared out the door.

The hustle and bustle of the hospital faded away when the door closed. I stared at it for a moment, remembering so clearly seeing James standing there. The peace still filled my heart, warming me up from the inside. He'd come back. One last time.

My dad shifted in the bed with a moan, breaking me from my thoughts. I helped him rearrange his pillows behind his back before slumping down on the chair behind me.

"You scared me." I slapped his thigh.

He chuckled, holding his hand against his stomach before looking back at me. "I'm sorry, darling. I never want to cause you more pain."

"What happened? If you don't mind me asking," Josie piped from behind me. She was sipping on a smoothie, and the sight of it caused my stomach to growl. I don't remember the last time I ate.

He sighed. "I was walking down the corridor at the rehab, and there was this other man that came out of nowhere. He must have lost his marbles. He threw a chair through a window, and when I tried to stop him from jumping out, he stabbed me with a piece of glass." He tensed his brows as he thought back to the moment, but he soon shook his head. "I don't remember much." He slid his hand over my cheek when he saw the worried look on my face. "But I'm okay. Now you," he said to Josie, "take this girl and get her some food. She looks exhausted." He tapped my face and reached for his phone on the side table.

I shook my head, but he waved me away. Josie pulled on my arm, and I followed her out of the room without a fight. A few minutes away from him wouldn't kill me.

It was a quick walk down to the cafeteria. Josie got me a smoothie, and we headed outside to find somewhere quiet to sit. The morning sun hit my face, warm rays peeking through a layer of clouds against a pink and orange background. I took a deep breath of fresh air before strolling after her, heading to a bench over by a tree.

I reached for my phone in my back pocket to see if Gray had replied to any of my texts or calls. A knot formed in my stomach when there was nothing. Where was he? Why wasn't he replying?

"Josie," I said, swallowing, "has anyone tracked down Gray yet?"

A frown appeared between her brows. She shook her head and handed me the smoothie before taking a sip out of her own. "No, Nate called me just before you woke up and said he can't find him anywhere. Drink your smoothie." She faked a smile, taking several long sips of her drink.

Her normally bright and spirited state was dulled by whatever she was hiding from me, but I was too tired to force her to tell me. I stared up towards the windows of the hospital and decided I didn't care. I thought I needed Gray here, but I'd been fine without him—I'd gotten through it. Maybe I was stronger than I gave myself credit for.

James was here with me. That was all that mattered. I peered up at the cloud-covered sky, smiling. I'd always have him.

"Oh, it's Nate," Josie said when her phone rang. "Have you found him?"

There was silence on the other end. "Eh, yes. Sort of. Is Stella with you?"

Josie glanced at me. I shook my head, wanting to hear what he had to say. "No," Josie said, gripping the phone tighter. I could barely hear him, so I moved closer.

Nate groaned heavily before speaking. "He is with Kasey like I thought. I don't know where the fuck he would be, though. Damn near spent all night looking for him. I don't recognize the dive bar they are at in the photos."

My heart dropped, tears burning my nose. He was with her. I was so stupid. It made sense. I'd seen them break up and get back together more than once in high school, but I'd assumed that was just a teenage thing. That we were more grown up than that now. Had he lied about sleeping on the sofa that day? What else had he lied about? The thought made me feel sick, the smoothie doing a U-turn in my stomach.

Josie looked at me, and the horrified look on her face said it all. "Okay. Thanks, Nate," she mumbled, dropping the phone to the bench and wrapping her arms around me.

"What pictures, Josie?" I wasn't angry or sad. I was just empty. Maybe I should have seen it coming. There was too much water under their bridge it was no surprise I ended up a shipwreck in their storm.

"Forget about him. All that matters is that your dad is going to be all right," she reminded me and took my hand.

"I want to see them."

She blinked, then looked down at her phone, tapped a few buttons, and handed it to me. It was Kasey in a bar, looking more than slightly intoxicated. Gray stood just behind her, his hand wrapped around her waist, with a smile on his face. I handed the phone back. If I had to look at another one, I would throw up.

"Let's go back inside," Josie said, and I let her drag me back into the hospital.

As we entered the doors, I tried to shed the part of me that still wanted Gray, leaving it outside on the ground. If he was done with me, there was no use in hanging on to it any more. If I thought about it for too long, the pain would return and I didn't want that. I had other things to worry about, and he wouldn't be one of them.

Chapter Twenty-Four

- GRAY -

Kasey got smaller in the rearview mirror until she eventually disappeared. A part of me wanted to stay and make sure she'd be okay, but I wanted to get back to Stella more. The thought of wrapping her up in my arms sent a warmth through me, lodging itself firmly in my heart.

I'd fallen fast. So fast I'd barely had time to breathe. But I wasn't complaining. Every second spent with her was a gift. Since coming back from the trip, she'd shown a strength unlike any I'd seen before. I'd helped her go through James's room, boxing things up and cleaning the surfaces. She shed tears, but it was with a smile.

I looked to the open road, the sun rising with its lilac and golden hues. I'd bought a charging cable for my phone from a nearby gas station while the tire on my truck got fixed, and the phone was just starting up. It dinged once, then continued many more times. I frowned, picking it up to see several missed calls from Stella, all the guys, and my dad, including a few texts from them asking where I was. As I scrolled through them, another call from Nate came through.

"What the fuck?" He sounded more irritated than usual.

I sighed. "It's a long story. I'm heading back now."

"Dude, you better get here right now. I don't know where to start. I'm going to fucking kill you. If the others don't get to you first."

The rage in his voice scared me. "Why? What's wrong?"

"Stella's dad was in some sort of accident and ended up in the hospital. Josie's been with her the whole time. But dude, you should have been there. I think he's going to pull through, but he was in bad shape for a while. Stella called Josie when she found out. She called Damien, and he called me. I couldn't get a fucking hold of you. Where the fuck were you?" There was a darkness in his tone I'd never heard before.

I broke out into a cold sweat at the thought of Stella in the hospital. She must have been so scared. And where was I? In another fucking state with my ex. I knew this would happen. The first opportunity I had to show her I could be there for her, and I wasn't.

"I, eh... Which hospital?" The sign by the side of the road told me I was still several hours away.

"He's a few towns over. I'll text you the details. What the fuck are you thinking, hanging out with Kasey? We both know how that story goes."

"How do you know where I was?" I growled even though it wasn't important. I stared at the road ahead, wishing the truck would go faster. I didn't want to get into it right now with Nate, not when Stella was sitting in some hospital room.

"The pictures."

"Pictures? What pictures?" I tensed. The moment of hesitation was very unlike him. "Nate!" I roared at the speaker.

He sighed. "There are a few photos on Instagram of Kasey looking very drunk at a bar, with you in the background looking like you are having the time of your life." He inhaled before continuing. "If I saw them, you know Josie will too."

I suddenly remembered the pictures Kasey had taken while dancing. Had she uploaded those? Shit, that would not make explaining to Stella where I'd been any easier.

"Dude, you still there?" Nate asked after a long pause.

"I'll be back in a few hours." I hung up, slamming my fist into the steering wheel over and over.

Fuck, this just got complicated. The odds of Josie not having seen the picture by now were extremely low. All I could do was pray to god she hadn't shown it to Stella. I needed to call Kasey and make her take them down, and somehow I needed to make this six-hour drive go faster.

I hastily parked my truck in the hospital parking lot at just past one in the afternoon. I dashed and weaved around obstacles; patients being rolled out in wheelchairs and children playing in the hallway while their parents waited to be called. When I got to the front desk, I was panting and close to blowing a fuse. Could everyone just get out of the fucking way?

"Hey, my girlfriend's dad was brought in recently. Can you tell me where to go?" I asked the lady behind the counter. She looked up at me from behind her glasses and took a sip of her coffee.

"Are you a relative?"

"No, but—"

"Then no," she stated, looking back at her computer.

Anger raged in me. I wanted to slam my fist on the desk, but knew it wouldn't help. I tried to reel it in. "Please," I pleaded. "My girlfriend is up there all alone." She shook her head without taking her eyes off the screen. I would have gotten down on my knees and begged if I thought it would have made a difference.

I reached for my phone and dialed Stella's number, though it wasn't like I hadn't already tried calling and texting her several times. She wouldn't pick up. Why the fuck wouldn't she pick up? The phone rang for a while, then went to her voicemail like all the times before. I called Josie, but she didn't respond either. I called my friends one by one, but was only greeted with the same situation.

Shit, this was bad. I slid it back into my pocket, unsure of what to do. If they weren't responding, they must be beyond pissed. I suddenly feared for my life. Visions of them lining up at Damien's farm with rifles and lassos should have probably made me chuckle, but all it did was send an ice-cold shiver through my core and caused a sweat to form all over my body.

I walked outside to stare up at the windows of the hospital. Which room was Stella in?

Wait. She might have gone back home. If I went to her house and she was there, she'd have to talk to me. I raced back to my truck and slammed it in reverse, the gears and tires screaming.

"FUCK!" I punched the wheel, turning out onto the highway.

This couldn't be happening. How could it be less than one week, and I had already fucked it up? I just needed her to hear me out, and she would understand. She had to believe me when I told her what had happened. My hands ached when I let go of the steering wheel, and I left the door open as I ran up the stairs to her house, knocking hard on the door several times and hoping she would hear me.

"Stella?" I called, listening for any noises. The other side was silent. "Stella, if you're there, please open the door," I begged as I continued to knock with more and more desperation. I suddenly remembered the key hidden under the plant pot. Moving it out of the way, the floorboards were empty. "Shit!"

"Excuse me," a voice said, and I spun around. The old lady who lived across the street stood in her front yard, watering the plants. "There is no one home. They are out for the day. Maybe you should come back later."

I stifled a groan. "Okay, thanks." I stalked back over to the truck, the tires spinning as I pulled away.

My phone rang in my pocket, and I grabbed it immediately, thinking it must be Stella. I didn't even check who was calling before I answered.

"Hello?" I answered desperately and waited to hear her voice.

"Grayson, it's about time you picked up!" My mom's voice rang through the line. "Your dad has been trying to reach you."

"Uh, yeah, sorry. My phone died."

"He said you ran out of work yesterday and never came back. Is everything all right?"

I didn't want to get into it now because, no, everything was not all right. It was very much the opposite. "Hey, Mom, can I call you back later? I'm busy."

"Sure, honey. But swing by the office. Your dad had something he wanted to discuss with you today and he said it couldn't wait. Love you."

"Love you too, Mom." I hung up, then rolled to a stop by the side of the road.

Shit, I hadn't even thought about how my dad would react when I didn't show up to work this morning. All my focus had been on Kasey, then on Stella. I glanced at the clock. He would be in the office, and I really had no clue where else to look for Stella. I could swing back here later tonight. Maybe she would be home then. If not, I'd plant my ass in the waiting room until she came out. But I had to face my dad first. If I lost my job, whatever. I just wanted to explain. I needed someone to believe me.

The drive to work went quicker than I would have liked. Nate poked his head out of the site, staring blankly at me. His eyes were cold as he shook his head, the anger clear in his body, and he turned and disappeared back inside the building without a word. Even when we were fighting, he would always talk to me, though usually he'd yell and shout at me. He was never silent.

I took a deep breath before opening the door to the office. My dad sat at his desk and didn't even lift his head when I sat down opposite him. I opened my mouth to say something, but he just held his finger up to stop me. He continued reading from the document in his hand—the vein on his forehead telling me exactly what I was in for. A few minutes of silence later, probably just to torture me, my dad finally moved the documents to one side and slowly looked up at me.

"I don't want to hear the excuse you've come up with." He clenched his jaw as he spoke. "This was your last chance. Your last chance to prove to me you've changed. I don't even know why I'm disappointed. Should have seen it coming. I did see it coming, yet here we are." The chuckle that followed was hard and loaded with emotions.

"Dad, I—"

"Be quiet!" he shouted, flinging the paperwork to the floor with his hand and slamming his fist down. "I thought this time would be different. That maybe, just maybe, you were finally growing up and would actually do something with your life. I have only ever given you the best. You have never wanted for anything. WHY DO YOU KEEP DOING THIS TO ME?" he thundered, veins popping out all over the place.

I kept my head down. I deserved all of it. None of this mattered, anyway, and it was stupid to think he would have listened. The feeling of disappointing him I'd had when I was younger was nothing compared to this. He was right in thinking I had changed. I thought I had. Now, I didn't care what he thought. Stella was what I cared about, and I needed to find her.

"I'm sorry," I growled. He roared at me to speak up. "I'm sorry, sir." My jaw ached and I fisted my hands at my sides as I held back my anger.

He stood up and pointed to the door. "You are not welcome here. When you pulled your act together, I thought I saw myself in you. But you are nothing like me. I know what you've been up to. I saw the picture with you and your girlfriend in the bar, so don't give me some crap excuse." He spat the words out. The rage in his voice lit a spark in my chest. I stood up quickly, the chair falling to the ground behind me.

"I'm not you!" I snarled, the anger erupting inside of me. "I've never wanted to be like you. This"—I threw my arms around—"is not me. It's all you. And I was willing to give myself up for that. Nate and I have come up with a business plan to make a difference in life instead of all this bullshit, and I hoped one day you would actually take me seriously. And Kasey isn't my fucking girlfriend, Dad. You would have known that if you ever paid attention to what is going on in my life. She needed my help, so I helped her. I fucked up, okay? But stop trying to make me into something I'm not. I'm just me, flaws and all." I stared back at him, my breathing erratic and labored.

He slumped down in his chair. My entire body trembled, and I slumped down too. I was so tired, so fucking tired of it all. I had done what I'd thought was right when I helped Kasey, but now everything was falling apart around me and the only person I wanted by my side wouldn't even answer my fucking call. What if she left for LA and I never saw her again? Tears burned my eyes as my heart tore in two. No, I wouldn't let that happen.

"Then tell me," my dad said from the other side of the empty desk, looking exhausted. "I never wanted you to be me. I was only doing what I thought was best for you. Tell me about this business plan and explain to me where you have been, and I will listen and try to understand. Because I can't go on like this." He wrapped his hands together and rested them on his desk.

I blinked at him. This was new. We'd fought many times before, but this was definitely the worst one yet. From the tone in his voice, I had thought for sure this would be it for us. That there was no salvaging this. His offer to hear me out was foreign, and I wasn't sure how to react.

"It's all so screwed up." I ran my hands over my face. "You really want to know?" I asked, not convinced.

He still had his shields up, but he nodded. "You're a smart man. I never doubted that. I didn't think you had the ambition to do anything. Prove me wrong." His voice was hollow and throaty from shouting.

So I talked. I told him about the business idea, Dion and his cut lip, James's memorial, Stella's dad being in the hospital, and everything that had happened since James passed away. It took me almost an hour get it all out, but he listened without interruption. He was a whole different man when I looked up. Dad stood up and walked over to a cabinet, pulling out a bottle of rum and two glasses.

"I was saving this for the day we signed off on the project, but I think we could both use some right now." He walked back over to his desk to pour the drinks. He slid one across the desk, and I took it happily, downing it in one gulp. Refilling it, he said, "I never wanted you to be like me. I didn't know how to get through to you. But instead of focusing on all the things you got wrong, I should have been asking why. I didn't know you had so much going on. I thought you were just going out and getting drunk every weekend. And your idea is interesting. I'd have to crunch the numbers, but if that's what you want to do, do it. I'll help you if I can." He held his glass up to me. "So from now on, let's communicate better. I will try to be more understanding of what you are going through if you let me."

I frowned, my brain aching with the events of the day. I held my rum up to him and we clinked glasses. "Better communication. I can deal with that."

We sat in silence as we finished our drinks. "So this Stella, is she the one?"

His question took me by surprise. It probably didn't matter anymore. I could never take back the pain I had caused her.

"I think she could have been. I've never felt the way I feel about her."

"Not even with Kasey? You were together for a long time. I thought you were still—"

"We're not," I interrupted, tightening my fingers on the glass. "Kasey is my friend, nothing more. Hasn't been anything else since high school. She's part of the reason everything is so messed up. I went to her and wasn't there when Stella needed me. I promised her I'd be there. Now she wants nothing to do with me. My friends aren't answering my calls and are probably planning how to best torture me for messing with James's sister. Everything is ruined because of one stupid mistake." I dropped my face into my hands. Everything hurt, like I was being ripped apart from the inside.

"Then you have to fight for her. If she means as much to you as you make it sound, then you don't want to let it slip through your fingers, trust me. I almost made that mistake with your mother when I went overseas. We were close to calling it all off, but we patched things up."

I frowned. "I didn't realize you and Mom almost got divorced."

"This was long before we got married. We had only just finished high school when I enlisted. She said she couldn't sit around and wait to be told I had passed away. But somehow, we made it work. I'm thankful for that every day." He exhaled. His voice was raspy but had a softness to it that matched the look in his eyes. The anger we both threw around earlier seemed to have dissipated.

I looked down at my phone and wanted so desperately to hear Stella's voice again.

"Go on. Get the girl. Take the rest of the day. Your job will be here when you come back. But I expect to see you here, bright and early tomorrow, with that business plan of yours."

I chuckled, knowing he was only half joking. With a deep breath, I stood, trying to come up with a game plan, but everything I came up with was so inadequate. Before I walked out of the office, I turned to my dad. He was back to focusing on work, but gave me a tiny, tight smile. We still had a long way to go to get back on track. If Mom found out, she'd wring both our necks.

When I opened the door, I didn't have much peace before I found Nate leaning against my truck. I took another deep breath in before walking over to him. He squared up to me as I approached, clenching his fists tightly by his sides.

"Let me explain," I began. He just shook his head and threw his fist into my face. It connected with my jaw, sending me tumbling backwards until I hit the ground. Dust settled around me as I stroked my aching jaw and coughed, stars swirling in my vision. "I deserved that." Turning to sit on the ground, I peered up in anticipation of more hits.

"Yeah, you fucking did." Nate sighed, then held his hand out to me. "Get up." He pulled me up to standing, then stared me down, disappointment heavy in his eyes. "How could you do that, man? She needed you."

I took a step back and wiped the dirt off my hands. "I swear, I didn't know. If I had known..." I stopped as the anger built inside me again. Anger wouldn't help this. I needed my emotions in check if I was going to figure out a way to get Stella back.

Nate pushed me back and walked over to the truck to lean his hands on it. "Just explain to me what the fuck went through your mind when you went out with Kasey."

I leaned against the truck next to him. Kasey wouldn't want anyone to find out about her situation, but right now, it was the least of my worries. I'd already lost Stella. I couldn't lose my best friend too.

"I didn't go out with her. Kasey has a complicated home life. She called me up that afternoon and begged me to come get her. One of her mom's many male visitors had hit her and Dion. I took them to the hospital."

"Is she all right? And her brother?" The protective gleam in his eyes surprised me, though he still looked like he wanted to punch me. I was grateful he was hearing me out. This situation was completely my fault. If I had just explained it to Nate from the start, none of this confusion would have happened. He could have explained it to Stella when I couldn't.

"Dion's okay. Kasey... I don't know. One day, maybe. She didn't want to talk about it, but she looked different. Something deep inside of her broke, I think. They needed somewhere safe to stay, so I drove her to her grandma's out of state, and I would have driven back that evening, but I had a flat tire and no fucking spare under the truck and the mobile charging cable was missing. So thanks for that." Nate tilted his head down when I threw him a glare. "I thought I was doing what was right. Kasey needed me."

"Stella needed you too, dude."

"I know, and it's too late now. She won't return any of my calls."

We stood there, quiet for a moment. "Fucking right, she isn't taking your calls. You've been an ass. But I'm driving them back from the hospital tonight so they can shower and get some proper sleep, so I can see if I can get a feeling of what she's thinking. No promises, though."

I blinked. A small smile curled on his lips. "Really? You'd do that for me? I thought you didn't want me with her."

He sighed and looked at me with a glint in his eyes. "Even though it made me want to be physically sick seeing you follow her around like a lost puppy, it was also kind of entertaining. And I kind of feel responsible. But only a tiny bit." He smirked. "And I can tell she means a lot to you. I still think all of this is a fucking stupid idea—case in point," he said, waving his hand at my face. "But yeah, I'll talk to her."

I was so relieved I could kiss him. He quickly took a step back when I tried to hug him and held his hands out between us with a laugh. He glanced at his phone, then looked over my shoulder towards the office.

"How about we get out of here? I'm sure your old man won't notice if I take off." He winked at me and climbed into the passenger seat. I quickly jumped in the truck with him and we drove away from the site with the radio blasting.

Nate rested his feet on the dashboard like he always did and drummed away on his lap. Somehow, I'd patched up two relationships today when I hadn't deserved either of their forgiveness. I stared out onto the road in front of me and grabbed the wheel tighter. With the most important one still left to fix, I didn't know where to start or if it was even possible, but I'd make her see. She had to understand.

Chapter Twenty-Five

- STELLA -

I was sitting next to my dad in the hospital bed when Josie walked back into the room.

"Nate's outside," she said, and put her phone back in her pocket.

"Go, darling," he ordered. "If I miss you too much, I will call you, okay? Get out before I call security." He laughed, holding his stomach from the pain it caused.

I turned to look at him one last time before Josie dragged me down the hallway, and we took the elevator down to the ground floor. When we walked outside, Nate was leaning up against an old Ford that had definitely seen better days. He stood up straight, sliding his hands into his pockets and darting his eyes between me and Josie. He looked at me as if he wanted to say something, then looked at Josie, a softness forming in his eyes.

"You girls ready to go?"

I looked behind me again before Josie literally had to push me into the car. She shook her head at me.

"God help me. He is fine. Let's go home and get some sleep. I don't know about you, but I'm exhausted and could really use a change of clothes."

I slid into the seat next to her, leaning my head against her shoulder and catching Nate glancing at me with a tight look on his face.

"Did you find him?" I asked.

He peered at the road ahead, then back at me as he answered, "Eh, yeah, I saw him earlier."

"That jerk. I never thought Gray would be such a knucklehead," Josie muttered.

I dropped my eyes. I wanted to ask Nate more, but I wasn't sure I wanted to know. And I needed to focus on myself and my dad. My heart and brain didn't have the capacity for anything else.

"He said he's been calling you," Nate added, readjusting his grip on the wheel and shifting in his seat while flicking his eyes across the road.

Every time Gray's name had appeared on my phone screen today, my heart jolted. After a while, I turned the phone off, tired of feeling the hurt over and over. He'd picked her over me, and now I picked me over him.

"I know he was with Kasey. I saw the picture." I looked out the window. "Did he sleep with her? The other day, before the beach."

"No." Nate shook his head firmly. "No, he slept on the couch the entire night." He looked truthful, but trusting him was hard.

"And last night?"

"I don't know. I don't think he'd do that. If you'd talk to him—"

"Whatever he has to say... He chose her and..." I trailed off. I wasn't sure what to say, my brain still too muddled to make coherent thoughts.

Nate glanced at me with a torn look on his face. "Are you sure about that?"

I wasn't sure what the answer was. Gray hadn't been there for me when I needed him, like he had promised. Knowing he ran straight back into Kasey's bed broke a whole new part of me I didn't even know existed, and I was so done with feeling pain. I took a breath and looked Nate straight in his eyes.

"I'm sure." I pushed the pain back into the endless pit inside of me, adding it to the list of things not to think about. When my dad had recovered, maybe we would go to LA after all.

As we pulled up to my house, Nate offered to stay with us for a while. I said yes. It was nice to fill the house with people and life, and even after everything, I considered Nate a friend. It wasn't his fault his best friend broke my heart. Josie grabbed my stuff from the back, and we walked into the cold and dark house. I turned some lights on, but it still felt dead, like no one had lived here in a long time. I guess, in a way, no one had. Josie's humming filled the space and sent a tingle up my spine, reminding me of James walking around singing.

"Let's order some pizza and watch a show. You have a shower. I'll wait down here." Josie ran her hand along my arm.

I didn't spend a long time in the bathroom. My whole body was tired, and all I wanted to do was curl up on the couch and turn off. Josie was only gone a few minutes as well before skipping back down the stairs, sliding under the blanket beside me in some spare clothes I had left out for her. We watched the first season of *Gilmore Girls* while I ate more slices of pizza than I think I ever had. Nate fell asleep in the armchair across the room after getting his fill and snored his way through most of the episodes. Josie ran her fingers through my hair as my head rested in her lap until she also fell asleep.

I woke up a few hours later—three slices of cold pizza left on the coffee table. I sat up slowly and looked at the time on the wall. It was almost midnight.

A noise from upstairs caught my attention, and the hairs on my arms stood up. There was a slow scraping of wood, followed by a few quiet footsteps. I panicked when I realized someone was breaking into the house and threw the remote at Nate, needing to have someone awake to help me. He woke with a jolt. I pointed upstairs, holding my finger over my mouth. He sat there for a moment and listened until he also heard the sound, then he got up, grabbing a metal candleholder from the cabinet and sneaking over to the stairs.

My heart raced and I curled up tighter under my blanket. I waited for the sound of a struggle, but all I heard were some mumbled words and sounds from the top of the stairs. I tried to hear what they said, but it was too quiet. Had someone grabbed Nate and hurt him? Was that why it was so quiet?

With my heart thumping in my chest, I slowly got up and left Josie still asleep on the couch. I tiptoed to the stairs, but there were still only hushed voices. I took a deep breath to calm myself before calling out.

"Nate?" My voice was hoarse, and I tried to swallow the lump in my throat.

The voices stopped. I crept up the stairs to find Nate just about to close the door to James's room behind him. Relieved to see he hadn't been hurt, that feeling soon left as he turned to me. His face was tense and his jaw clenched. He blinked at me several times.

"What's going on?" I asked, stopping before I reached the top step. My heart beat even faster, and he didn't need to answer. That look could only mean one thing, and the scraping wood now made sense. Gray was in that room. My hands trembled as I gripped onto the rail, shifting my weight backwards.

"Tell me what to do," Nate pleaded. My feet moved of their own accord, and I walked to stand next to him. "You don't have to go in there." He rested his hand on my stomach.

I did. I hadn't been able to say goodbye to James, so for my sanity, I needed that with Gray. "It's okay. I need to end this. I need closure." That was all the explanation I could give. A single tear fell from my cheek as I looked up at Nate, but he dropped his hand when I nodded, his eyes still glued to mine. With a sigh, he walked toward the stairs.

"We're just downstairs if you need us. Call and I will be right back." He glanced at the door before disappearing.

I slowly turned the handle and pushed the door open. Gray stood by the window with his hands in his pockets, staring out onto the road. When he saw me, he moved closer, but I took a step back.

I couldn't have him too close. He jerked, looking down at the floor and slumped on the bed.

"Fuck, Stella. I'm so sorry," he groaned. His voice tugged at my heart.

I steeled myself as I walked in and closed the door behind me. Standing with my back against it, my hand was still on the handle and I was ready to run out if I needed to.

"I know I fucked up, and I can't take that back. I should have been there and I—" He kept his gaze down on the floor and scratched the back of his hand nervously as he spoke. "I know you saw the photos, and I wish with everything that I could erase them. But I promise you, they're not what they look like. I said I would be here when you needed me—"

"You weren't. That's the thing. I trusted you to be here for me, but you weren't. You were with *her*. I opened myself up to you at my most vulnerable." A jagged breath came out of my mouth. A tear fell, but I couldn't let go of the handle to wipe it away. I hated that I was crying. I wanted to be stronger than this. After all the pain I'd felt over the last year, I was reduced to tears over a guy I'd known for all but a few weeks.

Gray turned, and when he met my eyes, a tear fell down his cheek as well. Shit, I hadn't been expecting him to cry.

"Yes, I was with Kasey. But not like you think. I should have been there for you. I never should have left," he ranted. "If I could take it all back, I would. Even if you don't want me"—his voice broke—"I'll never regret what we had because you mean so much to me, Stella."

I didn't regret any of it, either. It hurt to admit, but being near Gray had made me excited for the future, something I had never felt before. But I tried to block out his words. I couldn't afford to believe them. "Kasey is everything I wish I could be. Of course you would want to be with her. She's popular, she's pretty... she's happy," I mumbled, closing my eyes. We may not have a future, but they did. Letting him go was all I could do. I had enough self-respect not to beg him to stay when he clearly wanted someone else.

He stood up, hesitantly taking one step closer, but stopped when I jerked back.

"Is that what you think? That she's... more than you?" he asked and took another tentative step towards me.

I pressed my body tighter against the door, my knuckles turning white on the handle, screaming in pain. He continued to take small steps until he stood in front of me. His chest moved up and down, but I forced myself to look away.

"Stella," he pleaded, reaching for my hand. My body ignored my attempts to pull away. "You are you. You are fucking amazing the way you are. Kasey was once what I thought I wanted, but she doesn't even come close to comparing to you. No one ever could." He laced his fingers with mine, and I sucked in a breath at his gentle touch. I allowed myself to glance up at him.

He was so close I could see the tears that had yet to fall, even with the glow of the moon behind him. His hair was all over the place, like he'd been running his hands through it over and over, and he had more than a five o'clock shadow on his jaw. I drifted my eyes over his beautiful face, then dropped my gaze back down to the floor.

"Stella, I don't want her."

My heart thumped in my chest. I closed my eyes, not wanting to hear what he was going to say. Whatever it was, it would only end up hurting me more. But his voice was raw and honest, and that he was here, trying to explain, had to mean something, right? His fingers left mine and he traced them up my arm. A traitorous shiver ran along my spine and spread out over my scalp. I turned away as he reached my shoulder, pressing myself against the door again. Why did his touch do this to me? I couldn't breathe. My head was spinning so fast it was hard to keep my balance.

"I know I don't deserve it, but if you would let me, I will spend every single moment trying to make it up to you. Prove to you that you can trust me. Nothing happened between me and Kasey, I promise you. I haven't kissed or touched her that way since high school. She called me, and I had to take her and her brother to the hospital. Then she made me drive her to her grandma's. It's a fucking seven-hour drive." He was ranting again, darting his eyes all over the place. "My phone died after I saw your text, so I thought everything was fine. As I was about to leave, the tire on my truck was flat, so I couldn't.

"Kasey got fucking wasted, dancing to Britney Spears in a bar we really shouldn't have been in. I had some shots. One, maybe two. She blindsided me with the pictures, but I didn't do anything with her." He fixed his eyes on me, wide and desperate. "I slept on the couch. The most uncomfortable thing I have ever felt. All I could think about was getting back to you. Every single second I couldn't hear your voice was killing me. Please, believe me." His voice was scratchy, filled with torment and misery, and he sucked in a breath when he finished, filling his lungs like he had forgotten to breathe.

I dropped my hand from the handle and rested it by my side, a smile forming at his frantic rant. He tensed his brow as he studied my face.

I should say no. I should push him away and run back downstairs, but something stopped me. His words ate at my resolve not to want him, like tiny little hammers chipping at the wall.

A tear fell from his eye, and I reached over and wiped it away. He pushed his cheek against my hand with a groan, rough under my fingers. The anguish in his eyes caused the hammers to hit harder, and I grabbed the end of his T-shirt with my other hand and pulled him to me. His eyes burned with regret and desire, and my body responded the only way it knew how.

Maybe this would only bring more heartbreak, like I had with my dad, but at least I was alive to feel it. James never shied away from life just because it was hard, and the need to be more like him had been stronger lately. Maybe that was who I was, under all the pain. Maybe this was the first leap I needed to take.

Never regret something that once made you smile.

I didn't regret being with Gray. Now I had to trust him.

I pushed my back off the door and moved closer to him, our chests colliding and his hot breath spilling over my face. I smiled, and he looked at me, dumbfounded.

"Why are you smiling? Does that mean you believe me?" He moved his hand from my shoulder and nestled it into the hair at the back of my neck. I watched him for a moment, feeling the magnetic force between us. My smile grew wider.

"It was a good speech." He still looked undecided about my reaction. "I believe you." He froze for a moment, then pushed me against the door, wrapping both his hands around my head as if he was worried I'd slip through his fingers. He flicked his eyes between mine so quickly I thought he might get dizzy. The kiss he enveloped me in a second later deepened quickly, nipping and sucking on my lips and tongue like he couldn't get enough. My stomach did backflips and somersaults as I tasted him and slid my leg onto his hip, gripping onto him even though it felt like he would never let me go.

Maybe he would only break my heart again. But standing here, I knew I would survive it. James's death had almost broken me. Then my dad's accident. But I was still here. I was still standing, though bruised and battered. If I could survive that, I could survive anything. Moving forward, I wanted to do more than survive. I wanted to live. I wanted to laugh, smile, and experience life in all its ups and downs. I wanted to love. And maybe I could have that with Gray.

The kisses moved down my neck. I tugged on his head and he tilted to look at me. The burning in his eyes was stronger than ever before, making me feel things I shouldn't. It was too soon for love.

I opened the door behind us and pulled him to my room, not wanting to wait another second. He stumbled after me, never letting his eyes leave mine. I let go of his hand and crawled onto my bed, sliding my shirt over my head and discarding it onto the floor.

Gray quickly closed the door and the distance between us. He held his weight on his forearms, stroking the hair out of my face with a gentle caress. Then he crashed his desperate lips down with fiery urgency. Our teeth clashes, lips sliding, tongues warring. I pulled at his top, needing to feel more of him—all of him. He quickly flung it off, trailing his hot tongue down my neck and causing me to moan. His hand slid into mine and lifted it above my head, holding it down on the bed as he continued to explore every part of my body like a starving man.

I was about to explode from his touch. I wasn't sure how much more I could take. As another moan came out, I threw my head back, and it only made him move with more vigor. His chest pushed up against mine as we breathed, and he slid his hand behind my back to undo my bra. Kisses trailed back up my neck until he reached the corner of my lips.

I waited for the touch, but he pulled back ever so slightly.

"Are you sure about this?" he asked, frozen like a statue. Through the depths of his eyes, he wasn't talking about the physical side.

I blinked, giving him a quick nod as I slipped out from under him to reach for my bedside table, grabbing a condom. He took it from me, keeping eye contact the entire time in case I changed my mind. He stood up and relieved himself of all his clothes, his erection springing free and standing proudly in front of him. I swallowed hard and pushed my shorts down, but he swatted my hands away. Kissing a trail down my thigh as he pulled my shorts off, I threw my head back on the bed.

"Look at me," he ordered. I shot my head back up as my core tightened. "There is no one but you." His voice was nothing more than a deep groan.

My heart soared at his words. Everything in his eyes told me it was true. He rolled the condom over himself, then settled between my legs. He tangled his hand with mine, holding it as he guided himself inside.

We moaned in unison as he stretched and filled me. The burning in me built as he moved, slowly at first. He traced his tongue and perfect lips over every part of my neck, gently nipping at the delicate skin behind my ear. My hips shifted to meet his, and a louder moan rolled from me when he hit a spot deep inside. I slapped my hand over my mouth, suddenly aware of Nate and Josie downstairs.

"Don't." Gray pulled my hand from my mouth. "I want to hear you."

"But—"

He stopped my words with a kiss. He gripped my waist and turned until I was sitting on him. Flashbacks of us on my bed after the memorial tried to break through my mind, but the feeling of him in me was too strong. He moved faster, meeting me halfway as I pressed down. I moaned with each thrust, but the sounds only traveled into his mouth as he devoured every sound, every move I made. I clung onto his face, never wanting this moment to end.

"Stella." He panted into my mouth, pulling back to stare into my soul. His cognac eyes were a swirl of emotions, hooded and glossy. "Only you. Only ever you."

His words finished me. I bucked, my body wrapping itself around him like a glove. His lips crashed back to mine—I wasn't sure what sort of noises I was making now. I wasn't even sure I cared. He jerked, grunting, and then eventually stilled. I could still feel him in me, twitching as he released the last drop.

I slowly returned to the world, wrapped up in sweaty muscle.

He peeled away from me to look into my eyes. "Stella, I—" I cut him off with a kiss this time. Words would ruin this perfect moment. He lifted me off him, rolling onto his side to hold me tight against his chest. We lay there in silence for a long time, my heart taking some time to return to a normal rhythm. He shifted in my arms, and I grabbed onto his waist, digging my fingers into solid muscle.

"Please stay," I whispered. It rolled from my mouth before I knew it was there.

He blinked open his eyes, heavy with satisfaction. I drank in all of it, my love for him almost spilling over at his words. "I'm never leaving you."

Chapter Twenty-Six

- GRAY -

When I woke up in the morning, it took me a second to remember where I was. Stella was fast asleep on the pillow next to me, wrapped up in the covers, her silky body a treasure only I would have. Her lips moved gently as she breathed, a tiny bit of dribble hanging from her lip and soaking into the pillow.

She was perfect. If I had to spend every day making it up to her, it would all be worth it. I'd never give her a reason to doubt me again. Fucking never.

Even though I wanted to stay here and stare at her, Nate would still be downstairs. He wouldn't have left after seeing the sad look on her face. Dang, he'd been close to pushing me out of the window when he saw me in James's room.

He would definitely still be downstairs.

I slowly slid out of bed, sliding my jeans back on. Stella turned to her side, pulling the covers tighter against her naked body. I tiptoed out of her room before I decided to climb back beside her and show her just how much I wanted to worship her body. The TV was on downstairs—maybe Josie was still here too. I walked down and found Nate sitting in the kitchen, drinking a cup of coffee. He was frowning, but it turned into a grin when he saw me topless.

He snorted. "So I take it things went well?"

I held up my middle finger and poured myself a coffee. "Honestly, I don't know why she forgave me. I don't feel like I deserve it."

"She's special, just like James was. So don't go and fucking throw it away again," he growled, then leaned back in his chair with a smirk.

"Trust me, I have no intention of doing that."

"You guys want us to take off? Josie wanted to stay last night in case things didn't go well."

I looked over at the living room. Josie was curled up on the couch, as fast asleep as Stella had been when I left her. "Nah, that's all right. Let her sleep. She's had a long few days too. I'm so grateful she was there for Stella when I wasn't."

"She's something, isn't she?" Nate muttered, his tone more serious than before. I looked from him to the sleeping redhead, wondering how deep that comment really ran. Before I could ask, Nate flicked his eyes towards the stairs, widening his grin. "Good morning, gorgeous." He snickered over my shoulder. I turned, Stella standing there in her pajama shorts and my T-shirt.

I grabbed her hand and pulled her over to me, planting a big kiss on her lips because she looked too good not to get a taste. She gasped quietly, but soon melted into my arms, wrapping hers around my neck to deepen the kiss. Before it could get out of hand, I let her face go, but continued to stare at her, soaking in every perfection I could see. That sleepy look from our midnight drive was there again, and seeing her in my shirt also did something wonderful to my insides. It was the sexiest thing I had ever seen, apart from seeing her hair spread out around her naked body last night. There was definitely no topping that. Maybe we could we combine the two.

"Hi, Nate." She gave him a shy smile and bit her bottom lip. How did that make me jealous? I had to dip down for another taste myself, but she pushed we away with a giggle.

He winked at her, still grinning, and then nodded to Josie in the other room. "Josie's still here, if you want to talk to her." Stella left us in the kitchen, and I stared at her until Nate pulled me out of my dirty thoughts of ripping her shorts off and taking her right there against the stairs. "Well, I guess I'd better be off," he said, putting his empty cup in the sink. "I'm guessing you're staying?"

I nodded. "There is no way I am leaving," I said, laughing when Nate faked a gag. I slapped him on the back of the head. Work and my dad popped into my head, and I winced. "Shit, I gotta call Dad."

Nate winced with me. "All right, Casanova. Don't get fired, all right? I quite like bossing you around." He grinned at his own joke.

"One day, man, you're going to fall too, and I will be there to see it!"

"Dream on. Ain't no girl ever going to tie down all this," Nate called over his shoulder, doing a twirl in the hallway with his hands out next to him. I laughed. Jerk.

I waved goodbye as he headed out the door, then went to the dining room to call my dad. He answered on the second ring. A sweat had broken out over my neck after the first one.

"Uh, Dad. Hi."

"Grayson." I couldn't read his tone.

"I know you said I had to be in today. Well, I... uh... Stella..."

He scoffed. "Stay. Just treat her right, you hear me? And bring her over for dinner. You know your mom would love to spoil her rotten."

His words shocked me, but I wasn't exactly going to argue. "Yes, sir." I nodded, despite the fact he couldn't see me. "I'll be in tomorrow, I promise."

I tried to swallow past the lump in my throat. I was under no misconceptions that Dad and I were fine yet, and we still had work to do to get there.

I walked back to the girls. They were whispering to each other, both smiling widely, and Josie bit her lip when our eyes met, yet the grin was ridiculously wide. I was pretty sure I knew what the topic of conversation was, not that I minded at all.

"Well, I guess I should go home too," she said, giving Stella a look as she squeezed her hand.

"Oh, you're going?" Stella asked, disappointment on her face. On the other hand, I couldn't wait for Josie to leave. The quicker, the better. I had hoped to tell Nate to go home, then make it back to Stella's bed before she woke up so we could have had some time alone. Naked time alone, preferably. Although I wasn't against the T-shirt staying on.

"Yes, I need to get back to church and help my dad. He's got this big thing planned for tomorrow's service." She sighed, shrugging. "But I will see you soon, okay? I'll call you tonight!" Josie gave Stella a quick kiss on the cheek before bouncing out the door, leaving us on the couch.

I glanced over at Stella, waiting for the front door to close. As soon as it did, I climbed on top of her. I wanted more of what we'd had last night, and I didn't want to wait any longer. She giggled and playfully struggled against me until I pressed my lips to hers, my erection pressing against her crotch. She went still, enjoying it just as much as I was by the sounds of the ungodly moan that slipped into my mouth. How did it make her taste even sweeter?

"Gray, I..." she breathed against my lips, but I slid my hand down the inside of her thigh towards the warmth I craved. She gasped, her eyes striking in the morning sun peeking through the curtains.

"You were saying?" I pulled away from her to see the desire sparkling in her eyes.

"Nothing. Most definitely nothing." She wrapped her fingers around my neck and pulled me back down to her.

I laughed and dove back down, wasting no time to remove her underwear. She went to pull her shirt off, but I stopped her. "That's staying on," I said.

She frowned at me, then rolled her eyes. "Really? You don't think that's a little bit cave-man?"

I growled and claimed her mouth. "So? I can still fuck you with it on."

A shiver rolled through her body and when my blunt tip pressed against her delicious heat, we both froze.

"Condom," we said in unison, and my head tipped forward to rest on her chest. "I'll get it," I muttered and peeled myself from her. I took the staircase in three steps, sliding into her room and digging through the drawer she had pulled one from last night. "Where the fuck it is?" I groaned when I couldn't find one.

"You looking for this?" Stella asked from behind me. I spun around and almost fell to my knees.

She had her underwear in one hand, a condom stuck between her teeth as she leaned against the doorway. Her brown hair flowed around her like a halo, and all my mind could think was *angel*. My angel.

I stalked over and dove into her, needing her taste all at once. Her hand wrapped around me, pulling at my trousers until they pooled on the floor. I tried to stay still while she rolled the condom on, but my hips were to desperate for any movement. Once it was on, I lifted her up and wrapped her legs around me, sheathing myself into her in one long thrust.

My angel. My fucking angel.

It was around midday when Stella finally forced me to get off the couch with her. After round two right here, we'd fallen asleep wrapped up in each other and I never, ever wanted to leave this heaven.

"I want to see my dad," she said.

"Just a bit more?" I winked at her when she let go of my hand and walked out of the room with my T-shirt just about covering her bare ass. That was a sight I could get used to.

"You said that several hours ago. Now, come on."

I got up and ran after her, tucking her against my chest and spinning her in the hallway.

"Put me down!" She laughed, smacking my shoulder. The sound was incredible, sending my heart into overdrive. Spinning her around once more before setting her down, she ran up the stairs, but stopped halfway. "I'll be a minute. I just need to get changed." She threw my T-shirt at me from the top of the stairs, and I was close to running up after her, knowing she was now fully naked. Somehow, I stopped myself. If she wanted to see her dad, I wouldn't stop her. Anything to make her happy. We'd have time for more fun stuff later because she was it. As far as I was concerned, I would either die alone or as a lucky man beside her.

The thought might have scared most men, but I didn't even hesitate.

The shirt smelled of that sweet, almost vanilla scent she seemed to produce naturally. After sniffing my shirt for a moment and making myself light-headed, I pulled it on and headed out to the front. It was even hotter than normal today and just standing in the shade was making me sweat.

"Let's go," Stella called as she hopped past me down the wooden steps a few minutes later. Dressed in cutoff shorts and a white razorback top that revealed a lot of that silky skin I was already addicted to, my jaw fell open. Her brown hair swung against her back as she moved, and it absolutely mesmerized me. Yup. Pure angel.

The closer we got to the hospital, the bigger Stella's smile got. She almost bounced into her dad's room while I followed behind her quietly, trying to figure out how to introduce myself.

She gave her dad a big hug, and they shared a few quiet words between them. Then he saw me standing in the doorway.

"And who's this?" David asked, continuing to stare at me.

"Dad, you know Gray," Stella said, standing next to him by the bed. "He was James's friend. And he's my boyfriend," she added quickly, biting her lip to stop herself from smiling. I wanted to punch my fist into the air and jump around. My heart burst as I stared at the perfect woman in front of me. She gave me a look and flicked her eyes to her dad, still watching me.

"Uh. Hello, David, sir," I greeted, shaking his outstretched hand.

"Yes, sorry. My memory is foggy on all these painkillers." He smiled, then looked between us. "Boyfriend, huh? When did that happen?" His tone was firm, and it made me straighten. Stella slapped his hand.

"Oh, Dad, since when did you become so protective? And anyway, he's good to me." She held her hand out to me and I took it, surprised by her answer. I didn't want to be. But considering my big fuckup, there were many other words I would have used to describe myself. A loser, for starters. And that was being kind.

"Well then," David grumbled, still staring me down. "Did you see the doctor on the way in? I can't wait to get out of here."

On cue, a doctor walked in through the doors and broke the staring contest between us. "So let's see what we've got here, shall we?" He picked up a clipboard at the end of the bed and looked through the notes with a smile. "Very good. And how are you feeling? No new bruising or pain anywhere?"

David finally stopped staring at me and looked over at the doctor. "No, I'm feeling fantastic. Good enough to go home." He sounded hopeful and smiled at the doctor.

"Ah, well, I would like to keep you for a few more days, just to be sure the antibiotics are working." David sank deeper into the bed.

"I'll help look after him," I blurted, surprising everyone in the room, including myself.

"Oh, are you his son?"

Pain flashed across both Stella's and her dad's face. I shook my head. "No, but I live just around the corner and I'll be over every day." Then I glanced at her dad and he was looking at me with an expression I couldn't quite read. If I had to beg the doctor to let David go home, I probably would. I just wanted to make Stella happy. It was like an all-consuming need and I was done pulling away from it.

"Well, I would feel better knowing there were a few people around to help take care of you, David," the doctor mumbled, considering saying yes. "Hmm, okay... I will let you go home on the condition that you see your local doctor for a check-up daily, starting tomorrow, to make sure things are still progressing the way they should. And you should get in contact with your rehab team. There will be temptations when you get home you might not be ready for. They will help you prepare."

"So I can go home?" he asked, moving the blanket from his legs.

The doctor shook his head with a laugh. "Are we really so horrible here that you can't wait to get away? But yes, you are free to go. Just promise me you will get checked tomorrow?" The doctor fixed his eyes on David, and both he and Stella nodded. "I'll have a nurse help you out."

We got him out of the bed, taking slow and careful movements. He winced from the pain, and I wasn't too sure if he really should be leaving. I kept that thought to myself—the doctor wouldn't have let him go if he wasn't ready. A nurse rolling a wheelchair appeared at the door, and as David was about to complain, Stella turned to him with a firm look on her face that almost floored me. She bunched her fists on her hips, her eyebrows drawing together. Damn, she looked cute when she tried to look stern. Why was she so perfect in every single way?

"Dad, don't argue. You can barely get out of the bed. How are you meant to walk to the truck?"

David sighed and slowly allowed us to lower him into the wheelchair, all the while grumbling. She grabbed the handles and started pushing him towards the exit. Her petite frame struggled to get him going, and I thought about reaching out and helping her, but I think she needed to do this. I also didn't think David would be too pleased if I were the one pushing him. So I stayed in front of them, leading the way to the truck, his stare burning a hole in the back of my head, though I pretended not to notice. I could tell him I would take care of his daughter, but I'd rather show him. And her.

When we got home, Stella helped her dad get into bed. I went to the kitchen to get him a glass of water for his painkillers, then walked back into the room. She was tucking him in and giving him a soft peck on the cheek.

"Now, you stay here. I don't want to drag you back to the hospital just because you couldn't follow some simple instructions. Resting is all you need to do." She poked his chest.

"All right, darling."

She grabbed the glass of water from me and handed it along with the painkillers to him. He swallowed them obediently. "Get some sleep. Gray and I will be outside if you need anything."

She closed the door behind us and walked out to the back porch. Rain clouds obscured the sun from earlier, rolling down from the mountains, and there was a deep rumble of thunder in the distance, making the hairs on my arms stand up.

Stella stopped by the railing and crossed her arms over her chest. I walked up behind her, snuggling my face into the crook of her neck. She giggled and turned to kiss my forehead.

"Thanks for convincing the doctor," she mumbled, looking out over the yard. "My dad doesn't do well with hospitals." She trailed off towards the end and sighed.

"I'm glad I could help." I squeezed her tighter against me, hating that her smile turned upside down so quickly.

We stood there in silence, her head resting up against mine. We breathed in the smell of fresh-cut grass from a neighboring backyard mixed with that specific smell you only get during summer thunderstorms. I nestled my face even closer to her and her scent mixed with the rain in my lungs. I felt like I was high.

"Gray?" she whispered. I blinked my eyes open. She turned around in my arms, resting her palms on my chest while nervously raking her teeth over her bottom lip. "Thank you for coming back." She dropped her gaze. I lifted her chin so she could look at me when I replied.

"I had to. I love you." Shit. I hadn't meant to say it. *Shit.* I wanted it to be more special than this.

Her lashes fluttered as she sucked in a breath. "Gray. You can't just... just..." she stammered.

I swallowed, then decided to just go with it. "Just what? Love you? Because I do. I know I don't deserve to, but you're my world, Stella. When I thought I'd lost you, I couldn't think straight. If that's not love, I don't know what is."

"Gray," she whispered, her eyes filling with tears.

"And if I have to spend the rest of my life proving that to you, I will. Fuck, if you want me to cut Kasey out of my life, I'll try." I chuckled nervously. "She might not take it well and try to dig her claws into me, but I will. If you want me to. Your happiness is more important than anything else."

She smiled up at me, nibbling on her lip. "I don't want that," she said. "If you say nothing happened—"

"Nothing happened." I took her face in my hands, scanning her eyes for any sign she didn't believe me.

"But she's your friend. I would never come between that. And who knows, maybe one day she will be my friend too. We might not have much in common—"

"You're more alike than you think," I interrupted, smirking. She rolled her eyes. I couldn't help but lean in and kiss her. Soon I was ready to devour her right here on the porch. Didn't even care if the whole neighborhood heard us. She pulled away when I slid my hands down to hike her legs up around my waist.

"I love you too."

My heart stopped in my chest. Or was it racing? I blinked my eyes open and stared at her, her beautiful doe-like eyes peering up at me as her cheeks flushed.

"What?" I swallowed. Had I heard that right?

"You make me feel whole. When I didn't have you at the hospital, I was okay." Her words stung in my chest. "But I wasn't whole. I don't think I knew that then. But being with you last night, and now, I know I wasn't. I didn't have this." She held her hand over her heart, then rested it on mine. "So, even though I'm scared... I love you, Gray."

I grabbed her face and kissed her. With everything in me, I tried to convey my love for her. But it wasn't enough. Nothing I could ever do would be enough to explain what I felt for her. Deciding that kissing wasn't enough, I leaned my forehead against hers.

"I love you, Stella." Even that wasn't enough. How could I ever get through to her what I felt?

She giggled and wrapped herself back up in my arms. Standing with her like this, I was the one who was whole.

Epilogue

- GRAY -

After a long week at work, it was finally Saturday, and the guys and I had planned a chill day at the beach. Between getting up early for work, helping Stella look after her dad in the evenings, and spending the nights utterly enchanted by her, I could use a break. Not from her, though. Stella had wound her way deep into my soul and if I had a say, I'd never let her leave.

I wiggled my fingers into hers on the console between us as I parked the truck. Memories of holding her hand in the sand that first week she'd been back came flooding back, and I peered over at her, wanting to punch the air and cheer when her smile stayed firmly on her face.

Things were still tense between my friends and me. They had accepted Stella and I were together, but it was like they watched my every move under a microscope. I was pretty sure anything Stella told Josie was relayed to Damien, his way of hearing her side of the story. So far, he must have been happy with what he was hearing because I hadn't been beaten up.

Work was... work. I was still working three days a week in the office and two on-site, but my dad was giving me more responsibilities. And for the first time, it was all right. I had a reason to succeed. Stella was my reason. I wanted to give her the world, and I could only do that if I worked hard. I had also discussed the business idea with Dad, and we were trying to work out the best way to move forward. Despite him struggling to release control, he was working on it, and I was earning his trust, little by little.

"Oh yay, you're here!" Josie ran up and hugged Stella, who had slid out of the truck, returning the hug just as lovingly. The two of them had become inseparable, and it warmed my heart. I waved at the guys and grabbed the cooler of beers from the bed of the truck before walking over to them.

"It's about time. What took you so long?" Damien asked as he finished his beer.

I chuckled, trying hard not to smirk. "It took us longer to leave the house than we'd planned," I said. Nate rolled his eyes at the other end of the beach. The only time I saw him now was when I was at work, as I spent every single moment I could with Stella.

"You guys are ridiculous." Damien laughed, punching my shoulder as I tried to drink, spilling beer over my shorts. It wasn't as friendly as it once had been, but by the smirk on his face, he'd done it on purpose. I gave him a nervous smile.

"You're going to have to be without her for a moment. We need some girl time," Josie called, skipping down the beach towards the boat. She hopped up and dangled her feet over the side. Stella slipped off her sandals and followed behind the redhead, dragging her feet through the sand with a smile. This was the happiest I had ever seen her. The glow around her was as bright as the sun when she smiled. I couldn't look away. Or maybe that was just because I now knew what she looked like naked, and it was hard not to think about it.

"So, how's life as newlyweds?" Nate mocked. I flipped him off.

"Fuck off. I'm telling you, one day you will find that girl and you won't even know what hit you." The guys all laughed, nodding in agreement. Nate just glared at me.

"Whoever that is, they are going to have to wait a while. I ain't done having my fun yet," he retorted, jumping sideways when Liam threw his empty can of beer at him.

I leaned back in the sun chair and took a deep breath. This was exactly what life should be like. While it hadn't exactly been smooth sailing to get here, it was worth every moment if I got forever with Stella.

The girls giggled with each other on the boat, and my heart could have burst with happiness. What did I ever do to deserve her? And what did I ever do to deserve such amazing friends? My gaze moved over to the guys. We would be okay. I'd prove to them I had nothing but good intentions with my brunette angel.

There was a chuckle from my side, and I turned, almost expecting to see James there. The sand was empty, but he was here. He always would be. I doubted he would let us have all the fun without him.

"You okay?" Damien drew me out of my thoughts, clinking his beer against mine. He furrowed his brows as he looked from me to the sand I'd been staring at.

Over his shoulder, Stella caught my eye and beamed. I turned to Damien with a smile that grew into a grin to match hers. "I'm in heaven."

Want More of Stella and Gray?

Don't miss out on their exclusive extended epilogue! Sign up for my newsletter, and I'll send you this special bonus for free.

Scan this code

Teaser: Weak for You

NATE KNOWS HE SHOULDN'T WANT HER. SHE'S HIS BEST FRIEND'S LITTLE COUSIN, BUT ONE KISS MIGHT BE ALL IT TAKES TO UNRAVEL HIM...

ELIN KIND

The night buzzed with the steady chirping of crickets in the tall grass that stretched out to the woods. I took a sip of whiskey, letting the quiet sink in.

The door behind me creaked open, disrupting the serenity almost offensively. Josie appeared, dressed in a blue plaid nightshirt that barely concealed her legs.

"Having trouble sleeping?" I asked, looking away and trying to shake off the distracting image and the warmth it brought with it.

She settled beside me, her bare legs curling up under the blanket I extended over her. "Yeah. I just have a lot on my mind. What does it taste like?"

I turned to her with a questioning grin, seeing her eyeing the bottle that only had a few sips left. "What, the whiskey?" She nodded and reached for it. "Damien would kill me if he knew I let you drink," I said, holding it away from her.

Her emerald eyes locked onto mine, a penetrating gaze that seemed to freeze me in place. "It's my eighteenth birthday," she declared, her voice carrying a hint of defiance. "I want to try it."

I didn't know it was her birthday. Feeling a pang of guilt, I handed her the bottle and watched her take a sip. "Happy birthday."

She grimaced as she tasted the liquid, her red hair falling around her face, a few strands brushing her neck. My gaze lingered before I forced myself to look away.

"Why would you drink this?" She placed the bottle on her thigh and clicked her tongue in mild distaste.

"I don't do it for the taste, Sunshine." *Damien's cousin. Damien's cousin.* Repeating the mantra mentally, I turned back to her, finding that she had nearly finished the bottle. With a lighthearted laugh, I reached out to stop her. "Hey, it's not soda. Slow down."

"Ugh, my week has been so bad," she grunted and ran a hand over her mouth to get rid of a drop clinging to her lips. I took the bottle from her, and she slouched further into her seat, her notebook now the target of her irritated glare.

"What's wrong? Can't find the right words for a song?" I asked. Talking to my friend's cousin about her emotions wasn't exactly my idea of a riveting conversation. Yet, seeing this somber side of Josie was unsettling. She was meant to exude happiness, to be carefree and ever-smiling. I realized how much I missed her infectious smile whenever it faded.

"It's not just about the song," she confessed, her voice carrying the weight of unresolved conflicts before she set off on a rant. "My mom and I are butting heads. She's dead-set on me going to college, while I only want to attend one that's already rejected me. I'm feeling lost, unsure about what to do next. I want my future to be in music. Just how, I'm not sure. Can't I just have some time to figure it all out?" She turned to me, her frown deepening, but she didn't pause for my response. "Is that too much to ask for? Do I have to conform and be like everyone else? Does she even realize I'm eighteen now? It doesn't feel like it."

Frustration dripped from her words as she crossed her arms over her chest, her flannel shifting with her movement. Her skin peeked out, and my gaze shot up to her face, my eyes widening.

She threw a glance my way, her fingers fidgeting in her lap. "I just... I don't know. It's stupid."

"It's not stupid," I responded, though even to my own ears, it sounded more like a question. She let out a snort.

"Do you think I'm hot?" she asked in a whisper.

I coughed, a spray of whiskey erupting from my mouth. I turned to look at her, finding curiosity gleaming in her eyes. *Ah, fuck this. I was not having this conversation with her.*

"I, uh—"

"I'm not ugly, right?" she cut in abruptly.

"What are you talking about, Josie?" I asked, blaming it on the alcohol—not that she'd had that much, right?

"I know I'm not your type," she said with some disgust that I couldn't help but snicker at. "But am I ugly?"

Was she serious? She was far from ugly. Most girls would envy her looks—especially those freckles that adorned her face and her plump, naturally red lips.

"No, you're not ugly," I said, my voice soft.

She let out a dismissive "pffsschtt" sound and rolled her eyes.

"Guys could find me sexy, right?"

Setting the empty bottle on the floor, I turned to her, rubbing the back of my neck. "Where's all this coming from? You're Damien's cousin—"

"Oh, no, I don't mean I want you to think I'm sexy," she stammered, her face flushing crimson, lips pursed. "I mean, other guys. I know I'm not your type, but am I just undateable? I get it, my hair is kinda meh, my boobs are… well, tiny, and my ass…" She rolled her eyes in frustration. "I'm just tired of everyone seeing me as the pastor's daughter. I can be more than that—I want to be more than that. I just don't know what that 'more' is."

I didn't know how to respond. She'd grown up quickly, and ignoring that fact had become increasingly difficult. Even though I wasn't supposed to, I had noticed her. I'd watched her curves fill out year by year, and she definitely lacked nothing.

But she was Damien's cousin, strictly off-limits. That didn't mean, however, that I hadn't sometimes wondered what it would be like. What would her hair feel like if I ran my fingers through it? Would her kisses be gentle or wild?

Okay, definitely too much alcohol or something for both of us.

"You're, um... I mean, you?" I stumbled over my words. Her face fell, a tear tracing a path down her cheek, and she abruptly got up, hurrying back into the house. I couldn't let her continue down whatever path her thoughts were taking her. It was her birthday, and now she wasn't just frowning; she was crying. Because of me.

Without thinking, I reached out and took hold of her arm, standing up and gently pulling her back toward me. She collided with my chest, our faces mere inches apart. Her eyes were so big as they stared up at me, round and doe-like. Her gasp was the prelude to her mouth pressing against mine. The kiss was fleeting, almost over before it had begun, and I scrambled back, my foot colliding with the bottle on the floor. *SHIT. What the fuck had just happened?*

"Josie, go back inside," I growled, still convinced this had to be some bizarre dream. Sweet Josie was here, half-naked, wanting me to kiss her. Uh-uh, no way. That was not happening. This was not "good girls gone wild."

"I-I don't want to," she stuttered. I kept my eyes tightly shut, afraid of what I might see, afraid of what I wanted to see.

I jerked and reluctantly opened my eyes to meet her gaze. She looked up at me with eyes wide and innocent, so glossy I could see the moon reflecting through them. If I'd been a good guy, I would have stopped myself. I should have stopped myself from leaning down and claiming her mouth. But I didn't. I was selfish, and I needed a taste.

From the Author

If this story touched you, leaving a comment on your favorite review website would mean so much—it helps others find this book and supports me in writing more.

I hope you'll join me for the next journey in the *You* Series*!*

Want more romance, behind-the-scenes looks at my books, and exclusive updates?

Visit my website to explore everything I've got in store for you! You can find it here: https://elinkind.com/

Books by Elin

FREE: Staying for You – Prequel Novella

Tropes: Fake relationship, Cop, Self-discovery, Slow burn

Teaser: As Ki and Waylon's pretend romance slowly ignites into something undeniably real, will either of them be brave enough to risk everything and take the leap?

Memories of You

Tropes: Brother's Best Friend, Small-Town Romance, Family Drama, Love After Loss, Slow Burn

Teaser: This town is a graveyard of everything I loved and lost. He wasn't supposed to make it feel like home again.

Weak for You

Tropes: Brother's Best Friend, Good Girl/Bad Boy, Forbidden Romance, Self-discovery

Teaser: He never looked at me. I certainly shouldn't look at him. So why is he a melody I can't stop playing?

Trusting You

Tropes: Love After Heart-break, Forced Proximity, College Romance, Second Chances, Learning to trust after a broken heart.
Teaser: Love was always a subplot I never wanted. He turned it into the only story that mattered.

More with You

Tropes: Friends with Benefits, Road Trip Romance, Family Secrets, Slow Burn
Teaser: For one summer, we could be anyone. But even the perfect escape can't erase the past.

Glimpses of You

Tropes: Second Chance, Sport, Forced Proximity, Best friends to Strangers to Lovers, Slow Burn

Teaser: He wasn't that boy anymore. And I'd fought too hard to still be that girl. Yet one look, and we're back where it all fell apart.

About the Author

B orn and raised in Sweden, Elin moved to the UK in 2013. Writing wasn't on her radar then, but that all changed in 2021, and now it's her life—sometimes *too much*, if you ask her husband. As a classic introvert, spending her days immersed in stories is a dream come true, and she loves that she gets to share them with readers like you. She writes for fans of character-driven, slow-burn romance, with stubborn, complex characters who stay with you long after the last page.

When she's not writing, Elin loves to get hands-on with DIY projects, crafting, or painting—anything that lets her creativity run wild. She's also the proud mom of two adorable little dogs, Alfie and Tilly, who keep her company while she writes. Alfie loves to snuggle up beside her, while Tilly prefers to keep her feet warm.

Stay Connected!

Want more behind-the-scenes moments, sneak peeks, and all the romance vibes? Follow me on social media! I love connecting with my readers and sharing all the bookish fun.

Instagram: @elinkindbooks

TikTok: @elinkind.author
Facebook: Elin Kind Author
Let's keep the love stories going!

Acknowledgements

I can't believe what a journey it's been to get this book written and published. There have been many hurdles along the way, but if you're reading this, it meant I conquered them all, and I'm pretty damn proud of that!

It would not have been possible without my loving husband. You always stand by my side to cheer me on, even when you have no idea what I'm talking about. I would say I'm sorry about my craziness, but we both know I'm not! But you never complain, you let me talk and get it all off my chest, then help in any way you can. You are my best friend and I couldn't imagine spending my time with anyone else.

Mamma, Pappa... You have been so supportive of me no matter what I've done. I have jumped back and forth in all sorts of endeavors since becoming an adult but you have always been there. I am so deeply thankful for everything you have done for me. I may not say it enough, but I love you both!

My lovely women in RWC, you bring so much joy to an otherwise stressful time. So many times I've been worrying about something, and I know exactly where to turn. As with my husband, I can't promise

I won't freak out over something small again, but know that I will always be slightly uncomfortable.

And lastly I want to thank all the incredible writers I have met along this crazy journey. Each and every-one that has helped me with this book has taught me something important and I wish I could name you all. Just know that without you, this book would never have seen the light of day. Thank you!

Made in the USA
Monee, IL
16 February 2025